My Hard Heart

Helen Garner was born in Geelong, Victoria, and was educated there and at Melbourne University. She has worked as a high school teacher and freelance journalist, and has won numerous literary awards (including the 1978 National Book Council Award for *Monkey Grip*; the 1986 South Australian Premier's Festival Award for *The Children's Bach*; the 1986 New South Wales Premier's Award for *Postcards from Surfers*, a collection of short stories) and a Walkley Award for journalism in 1993. She has also published *Cosmo Cosmolino* (1992), *The Last Days of Chez Nous & Two Friends* (screenplays, 1992), *The First Stone* (1995) and *True Stories* (1996). She now lives in Sydney.

Other books by Helen Garner

Monkey Grip

Honour & Other People's Children

Postcards from Surfers

The Children's Bach

Cosmo Cosmolino

*The Last Days of Chez Nous
& Two Friends* (screenplays)

The First Stone

True Stories

HELEN GARNER

My hard heart

SELECTED FICTION

VIKING

Viking
Penguin Books Australia Ltd
487 Maroondah Highway, PO Box 257
Ringwood, Victoria 3134, Australia
Penguin Books Ltd
Harmondsworth, Middlesex, England
Viking Penguin, A Division of Penguin Books USA Inc.
375 Hudson Street, New York, New York 10014, USA
Penguin Books Canada Limited
10 Alcorn Avenue, Toronto, Ontario, Canada M4V 3B2
Penguin Books (NZ) Ltd
Cnr Rosedale and Airborne Roads, Albany, Auckland, New Zealand

This collection first published by Penguin Books Australia Ltd 1998

1 3 5 7 9 10 8 6 4 2

Text design by Tony Palmer, Penguin Design Studio
Cover design by Ellie Exarchos, Penguin Design Studio
Cover photography by Sonya Pletes
Author photograph by Cathryn Tremain/*The Age*. Reproduced by permission.
Typeset in 13/17½ pt Perpetua by Post Pre-press Group, Brisbane
Made and printed in Australia by Australian Print Group, Maryborough, Victoria

National Library of Australia
Cataloguing-in-Publication data:

Garner, Helen, 1942– .
My hard heart: selected fiction.

ISBN 0 670 87874 X.

I. Title.

A823.3

Contents

My hard heart

'DO YOU CALL THAT SOUL, THAT THING
THAT CHIRPS IN YOU SO TIMOROUSLY?'
Rainer Maria Rilke

I met my husband at the air-
port, and there he told me some things that wiped the smile off
my face. He put his suitcase down outside the Intercontinental
Bar and leant his face and arms on the fire hose: he wept, I did
not. We drove home. He lay on the bed and sobbed. I went
downstairs and sat beside my daughter on the couch. She was
watching a Fred Astaire movie and did not notice how I gazed at
the side of her smiling face, as if in that glossy skin I might find
meaning.

I lay beside him in the hard bed and listened to him talking,
explaining, crying. I said nothing. My limbs and torso swelled.
Slowly I ballooned. I became tremendous. I was colossal, a thing
that weighed a ton, a bulky immovable slab of clay set cold,
baked hard and heartless. Somewhere in the centre of this inert
mass was a tiny spark, hardly a spark at all, only barely alight.

In a day he was gone. The smell of the house changed immediately. I got up in the morning and stepped out of my bedroom. The door of his old room, the upstairs one with the balcony, stood open, and across its empty air fell a slice of sunlight.

The front of the house was festooned with great twining loops of wisteria. People walked slowly past, gazing up. A delicate, warm scent puffed out of the dangling flowers, and when I sat on a cushion on the doorstep and played my ukulele I saw that the flower clumps were full of bees.

I knew it was a passing euphoria, but all my senses were working. Crowds parted as I approached, old men and boys and babies smiled at me in the street, waitresses spoke to me with a tender address. When I tried to play, notes placed themselves under my fingers. Milky clouds covered the sky, a warm dry wind blew all day, shocks of perfume came from behind fences. I remembered being a student, the delicious agony of exams in spring.

'You wait,' said Suzie in the wine bar. 'In six weeks you'll be walking on rocks. You'll have a brick wall six inches in front of your face.'

I bought a Petpak at Ansett and took our cat with me to visit Vanessa in the country. I set him free at the door and he bolted away into what would one day be a garden. Vanessa was wearing sagging purple socks. I sat with her at the kitchen table. She showed me a book by C. G. Jung which contained a series of mandalas painted by one of his patients. The first pictures were grim prisons of rocks and stones, but as the series progressed, oceans appeared and the air inside the circular frames flushed, thinned and became breathable.

'What *is* a mandala, exactly?'

'I don't know,' she said. 'Is it a picture of the soul, at a given moment?'

I pulled a chair over to the big window and sat watching the movements of the long grasses in the wind.

'Will I be walking on rocks?'

Vanessa shrugged. She lives alone in a house which from the outside looks small and square but which encloses, with a light touch, one enormous room on several levels, a space of unusual flexibility. The kitchen is right in the centre: everything else radiates from there.

The cat returned at five in the morning and began to complain and cry. At home I would have thrown him into the kitchen and shut the door, but here, because I was a visitor in the huge room where Vanessa also slept, I had to feed him and bring him on to my bed. When at last he settled down with my hand on his side, I remembered the nights with a new baby: the alarm, the broken sleep, the silently turned doorknob, the plodding from task to task; the despair of fatigue, but the weary patience, and the acceptance of the fact that it is absolutely required of one to do these things: the bearing of duty.

I approached our house in the evening. It was 'lit up from door to top'. I knew there was no one inside it now but my daughter: I felt her tough little spirit burning away inside its many rooms. I cooked a meal and we tried to eat it elegantly, facing each other across the white tablecloth. She put on an old Aretha Franklin record: I had brought her up not to be like the girl in the song, the one who 'don't remember the Queen of Soul'. At those feathery cries we rolled our eyes and gave each other shy smiles. We washed the dishes together. I put my forehead on the windowsill and cried with my hands still in the hot water, and she said, 'I know this is much worse for you than it is for me.'

In the café Elizabeth told me her husband was dying of a tumour.

'I used to think there was justice,' she said, 'and fairness. That there was a contract, that things meant something. Now I know your foot can go straight through the floor.'

'And what's on the other side?'

'Nothing.'

'Nothing?'

'Nothing.'

Tears, black with mascara, poured off her face. She cried in silence, without sobs.

'I think what I'm trying to do,' she said, 'is to die. Because I can't *bear* him to have to go out there on his own.'

I was ashamed of my story when she asked for it, a simple tale of marriage betrayed, but she listened with respect.

'We were bright girls, weren't we,' she said. 'What bright girls we were!'

We kissed goodbye, and sat quietly. I put my hand on her stockinged leg. 'Aren't those boots beautiful,' I said.

We looked at the boots without speaking. In perfect unison we heaved two great sighs.

I saw my husband sitting in the café with a woman we both knew. I went without thinking to the same table: the three of us said good morning and they went on reading the papers. When my husband got up to go to work he nodded to me and said to the other woman, 'I'll pay yours.'

At home I answered the phone. A young woman asked for my husband.

'He's not here,' I said, 'at the moment. This is his wife speaking.' I told her my name.

'Oh yes!' said the young woman. 'He told me he was involved with you.'

'Involved!' I said. 'He's *married* to me.'

'Oh well,' she said with an airy laugh. 'Married . . . involved . . .'

I filled the bucket and got the mop out of the yard and began to wash the kitchen floor. The tiles were filthy and I had to scrub; their edges chipped and crumbled in the foam. My daughter came into the room behind me and opened the fridge. She uttered a dramatic cry of pain. I was used to this.

'What happened?' I said, without turning round.

'I hit myself in the *eye*. With the freezer *door*.'

'How'd you manage to do that?' I said, and continued to mop.

She said nothing, and did not move. When I looked around, she was still standing at the closed fridge door with her palms over her eyes. I stripped off the rubber gloves and went to put my arms round her. She was as stiff as a rail.

'Are you all right?'

'Obviously not,' she snapped from behind her hands.

I flinched. 'Oh – don't talk to me like that.'

'You never know!' she burst out. 'You never know how to comfort someone who's hurt themselves! And now I'm the same – I can't either. I've picked it up from *you*.'

I met Steve in the bank. He had driven down from Sydney in a panel van so heavy with carpentry equipment that he parked it under a tree outside my house and went everywhere by tram. He had a very small black bible which he carried in his shirt pocket. I knew his brother, but I didn't know him.

He put his budgie's cage on the highest kitchen cupboard and we watched the cat licking its lips. The budgie perched on my daughter's shoulder while she played the piano, and accompanied her with thrilling inventions.

'Have you ever been married?' I said.

'No,' said Steve. 'But I'm familiar with the pain.'

After dinner we watched an American gospel show on TV: the pastor stood waist-deep in a brown river and dunked the people one by one: up they came, spouting and fighting and babbling in strange tongues. Their faces were distorted, their eyes were closed, their bodies bloated or emaciated. Somebody somewhere was picking at a banjo: that tricky, tough, humble music.

Between the gospel show and *Six Centuries of British Verse* we took the dog out and walked a figure of eight around the enormous park. The night was starry, the air was cool, the big avenues of elms looked low and humped from where we were, in the middle of the football ovals.

'Did you get baptised in a river?' I said. It was a kind of flirtation, but he never bit. He looked at me with his face open, ready to laugh.

'No,' he said. 'At a beach. In the ocean.'

'What happened, exactly?'

'Oh — I don't know if all that detail would be useful to you.'

'Are you trying to be "useful" to me?' I said sharply.

He turned and looked at me. 'You asked me,' he said, 'and I'm trying to answer.'

We walked. The dog heard possums in the trees and sprang

helplessly into the air at the base of the thick, ridged trunks. Half a mile away, along the western boundary of the huge park, silent headlights moved in a formal line, as if in convoy to a funeral, or a wedding.

'I haven't slept with anyone for a really long time,' he said. 'For years.'

'You must be absolutely radiant with it,' I said.

He laughed. 'I'm celibate, but I'm not asexual. It's not so bad. It's not bad at all. I was like you. I had a heart of stone. I was all black inside. I was grieving over everything. I'd feel an impending relationship, and I'd know I had nothing to give. So I stopped. In Ezekiel, I think it is, he says, "I will take away your heart of stone, and I will give you a heart of flesh".'

That night the poet on *Six Centuries of British Verse* was Milton. Across the screen stumbled painted Adams and Eves from every era but ours: in various postures denoting shame, humiliation and grief, they staggered into exile.

When the program was finished he stood up and leaned over me, and kissed me on the cheek.

'Good night!' we said. 'Sleep well!'

Upstairs in my room I pulled the curtain open and lay down in a current of night air. The curtain brushed and brushed against the windowsill. I heard a tram go chattering through the intersection, then the street outside was quiet.

The little flame stirred in its cage of clay: I felt it shiver, and begin to move.

The psychological effect of wearing stripes

Here is my photo of Philip. I took it at the check-in counter. See that bag? His linen jacket's in there, rolled up. That's how he gets it crushed in exactly the right way. He travels a lot, so much that I never know where he is or when he's going to turn up. He likes this photo, or so he said when he rang. 'Thanks,' he said. 'Usually I pose, but this one's really nice. You caught me.' It wasn't hard. I've seen people pose. Cameras are bad enough, but have you ever watched someone you know front their own reflection in a mirror? (I exclude actors, who examine themselves coldly and without vanity, like workers checking their tools.) You see a stiffening, a closing, a dimming; you see them pull on their idea of themselves, the caricature that will soften and melt away the minute they think of something other than the enemy before them. When I raised the camera, though, and it's a stolen camera, not even morally mine, when I pointed it at Philip and dropped the frame around his head and shoulders, he did something I'd never seen: he looked straight into the lens, straight in, as if into the eyes of a lover from whom forgiveness was not yet required or judgement to be feared, and his features *performed*. They swam, the way a dancer loosens his limbs, they composed themselves, and then they waited. It was a quiet flourish, a slow-motion blossoming of skin and muscle. Instead of closing he became porous. See? One elbow rests on the high counter. The strap of the bag pulls his collar askew. His skin is tanned. The day we went out on the river he took his camera (an Instamatic: 'I got it for $3.99 in a junk shop in New York') and lined me up across the table. The beam of his eye passed through the lens, hit me, and bounced off unwelcomed. I felt the skin droop on my skull and the light go out of my face; I felt myself pursing. He lowered the camera without taking a shot and said with a cross laugh, 'You're the worst subject!' 'I know,' I said, and I am. This is no accident. *I* want to be the one doing the looking. I have developed a whole social demeanour with the aim of deflecting attention from my appearance. I actively dislike being looked at. I don't know how so-called *beautiful women* can stand it. 'Looks shouldn't matter,' says Philip without conviction. On another day, in another mood, he says with a vehemence that sounds like anger, 'All this seventies bullshit about there being no such thing as beauty. There's nothing democratic about beauty. Some people are beautiful and that's all there is to it.' You should see the way he speaks to waitresses, and the size of the serves they bring him. I want to say, 'It's all right for *you*,' except that last year I resolved never to become the kind of person who says, 'It's all right for *you*.'

'I understand women,' says Philip. 'I love being looked at.' Maybe that's what beauty is: loving being looked at. The beautiful are greedy. They suck other people's eye-beams into their blood cells and feast on them, growing lovelier and more opulent, while puritans like me who starve themselves for the sake of power diminish daily, wither and shrink till all that's left of them is a hard rail of will. For example. Philip sat down opposite me in the café. 'Look at that,' I whispered. He had already noticed, but was gracious enough to glance up as if surprised. A young woman, a girl, was established alone at a central table. She was dark and smooth, with glossy shins and arms, and dressed in scarlet, white and black – socks, lipstick, ponytail, you know the style, but with that wonderful skin and startling whiteness of eye. Her cup was empty, her chair stood at an angle from the table, her gaze was lost in ether. She sat like a goddess, blind-eyed and motion-less, presenting to the world a face innocent of anything that would normally be categorised as expression, but at the same time so outrageously voracious of eye-beams that the café was full of a psychological commotion. I had a terrific urge to laugh, to shout out something – I don't know what; but for the first time in my life I understood why soldiers desecrate shrines. 'Now that,' said Philip with respect, 'is what you would have to call pure.' 'Pure what?' I said. 'Pure being,' he said, then laughed and looked around for the waiter. Is *that* pure being? I thought pure being was when you were alone, when there were no mir-rors or shop windows or hubcaps or still pools. Even as I write my story I am aware that I am nowhere near the point of this, that the point recedes from me as I write, that I should be writ-ing about something else. About a man 'half mad with hospitality and thoughts of alcohol'. A club that has no rituals: 'all clubs are sadness clubs,' says its one remaining member, departing. 'The sea that we've all heard so much about.' A dream of death: 'tief und tausendfach zu leben'. Music, whose 'manifestation is the displacement of air'. It should even be about 'the working class', or a dress 'the colour of hyacinths', or about the battle against sentimentalism: look at the gum tree, see 'the usual mess on the ground'. Once upon a time two women met in a bar. 'I will not talk about the past,' said the furious one. 'But we must,' said the one who burst into tears. Each was afraid that the death of friendship, its murder, would be discovered to be her fault. *I do not give you permission to write about me.* Is there anything cleaner than a clean white shirt? 'This is the hour of lead.' The dirty teeth and lips of red-wine drinkers. The psychological effect of wearing stripes. The punishment of the sick. The punishment for not being beautiful. This is a lifelong thing and begins early. 'No, dear, but you have a face full of character.' And yet perhaps the punishment is for something more serious and obscure than a simple failure to be beautiful. Otherwise why would my lovely, dainty, light-footed . . . contemporary, my shadow figure Louise, when we were twenty-three, feel the need to press on me the gift of her least flattering hat? Why examine with ostentatious attention the promises on my jar of face cream, then turn on me a blast of her heart-stopping smile and say, '*Poor old thing*'? There was no question in anyone's mind that she was beautiful, I was not. If only I could have been allowed to contemplate her, with frank looks and happy pleasure, as men do – but someone laughs and says, 'I bet you wish you looked like *her*' – so I have to stand beside her, where I can cast only crooked glances, bent ones out of the corner of my eye. *Elle est plus belle que toi*. I know. You are right. She is. But years later, minding her house, I forced the lock on the cupboard under the stairs and found a shoe-box stuffed with photos of her taken (you could tell) by besotted men. She lay sated in lacy disarray, or pouted against a puffing, translucent curtain. I looked, and then I put them back in order, and now I am writing this. Still, we hear of brutal strokes: 'you must remember,' says the famous Greek composer to Charmian Clift on her island, 'that you are no longer young, no longer beautiful'; of clear statements of hierarchy: a man, speechless at the question 'And what does Mrs Calvino do?', replies at last in a reverential tone, 'Mrs Calvino . . . is a very beautiful woman'; of whipflicks in moving cars: 'And what does your daughter look like? Does she wear ugly ankle socks, like you?' The heart, always eager to be of service, trips over with its tray of china and lies down disconsolate among the pieces. But bow the head, kiss the rod. In humble acceptance stirs the seed of power. Philip read a story I published about him. He made no comment, though he told me later that a woman we both knew had asked him what he was *going to do about it* (I will be obliged to take action, says the woman in the bar) but at one o'clock in the morning (high sum-mer, I'll stick in a moon, some elms on an avenue half a mile away, a hot wind streaming in off the stony rises, sleep not possible) I saw him moving towards me across the bare park, walking slowly in his flapping trousers, trying like me to breathe the hot wind, and I saw immediately that there was no point in greeting him. The grass made a small stiff sound where I put my feet, I did not call out but kept on walking, we passed in silence with our eyes on the ground, and the next time I saw him, in daylight in a street, he said, 'At that moment I would have liked to sink into the ground. I did not want to be part of what you were looking at.' I am writing this in a hotel room. I like the room, I pay for it, for the moment it is mine, but its mirror, some kind of false antique in a heavy frame, is hung on a wall that's at right angles to the table where I work, and whenever I look up from this exercise book I have to see myself getting older, my doubtful expressions and downward lines; so every morning after I have read the paper with scissors in my hand and stuck its manageable stories ('manslaughter, or jealousy, or business, or motor-car racing') into my notebook, I heave the mirror down and stand it on the carpet with its face to the wall. Once I brought my camera here and took some pictures of myself in the mirror. They came out crooked. One side of my head looked higher than the other, and slightly flatter. I couldn't tell whether this was due to the way I had slept on my hair, or whether the lens – or perhaps the mirror itself – contained some distorting property which in waking life, I mean life without camera, was not apparent. Anyway I showed the photos to my friend, a painter, who glanced at them and said with a laugh, handing them back, 'The artist's obligatory self-portrait.' She was only teasing but I was abashed, as if caught out in a naivety. In the afternoons I go out walking (gardens, the bank, shops displaying racks of the ill-made shoes our country produces) and when I return the maids have done the room and hung the mirror back on its hook. I let it be. I even look at myself. Outside my hotel window a tremendous excavation is under way. Early on I thought of taking a series of photos of the progress of the hole, and I did begin it, but now I find it's more fun just to stand at the window with the camera up to my eye and not press the shutter at all, even when the men in hard hats spot me and caper about, rolling their bare shoulders and mugging to make me laugh. I'm just practising looking. The racket from the site is indescribable, and according to law they are not permitted to turn on the gouging machines till seven a.m., but sometimes at night or very early in the morning, before light, someone comes on to the site and shifts things, as if to make a point. Once, at four a.m., I half woke and heard some metal pipes being slung about, but because they were big and hollow, or because I was happy in this room and because nobody knows where I am, I experienced the sound as music: they clashed and chimed with a foreign melody, in a rhythm that was syncopated and full of long pauses, and when the morning came and I woke properly I remembered my dream: that Philip had found me, that he had come to the room and brought me a bunch of grapes which was a work of art. A woman had written a story on the grapes. Each grape bore a single word. I ate each one as I read it, and was so absorbed that I got three-quarters of the way through the bunch before I realised that it had been meant as a present for somebody else, and that perhaps the woman who had written the story on the grapes was me. The people at the hotel are not able to tell me what kind of building is to be erected on the site when the excavation is completed. One day trucks will pour the concrete; the next, workers will walk across it in boots. I'd like to show my photos of the hole to someone. Look — you can see its squared-out sandy bottom scarred by backhoe treads, its yellow and opal walls dripping rust stains, a wooden ladder (feeble as a thought) reaching only halfway out, the floor's six cuboid indentations like escape routes that lead deeper into the rock — but most people prefer photos of other human beings, or of themselves. 'I was a beautiful baby,' says Philip. 'I had all this curly hair, and always a wicked look, turning away.' The photo, when he shows it to me, is of a puddingy baby with oiled locks and a smug expression. There is a story to be written about that photo, but this is not it.

What we say

I was kneeling at the open fridge door, with the cloth in my right hand and the glass shelf balanced on the palm of my left. She came past at a fast clip, wearing my black shoes and pretending I wasn't there. I spoke sharply to her, from my supplicant's posture.

'Death to mother. Death,' she replied, and clapped the gate to behind her.

It had once been a kind of family joke, but I lost the knack of the shelf for a moment and though it didn't break there was quite a bit of blood. After I had cleaned up and put the apron in a bucket to soak, I went to the phone and began to make arrangements.

In Sydney my friend, the old-fashioned sort of friend who works on your visit and wants you to be happy, gave me two tickets to the morning dress rehearsal of *Rigoletto*. I went with Natalie.

She knew how to get there and which door to go in. 'At your age, you've never been inside the *Opera* House?' Great things and small forged through the blinding Harbour water. We hurried, we ran.

At the first interval we went outside. A man I knew said, 'I like your shirt. What would you call that colour – hyacinth?' At the second interval we stayed in our seats so we could keep up our conversation which is no more I suppose than exalted gossip but which seems, because of Natalie's oblique perceptions, a most delicate, hilarious and ephemeral tissue of mind.

At lunchtime we dashed, puffy-eyed and red-nosed, into the kitchen of my thoughtful friend. He was standing at the stove, looking up at us over his shoulder and smiling: he likes to teach me things, he likes to see me learning.

'How was it?'

'Fabulous! We cried *buckets*!'

Another man was leaning against the window frame with his arms crossed and his hair standing on end. His skin was pale, as if he had crept out from some burrow where he had lain for a long time in a cramped and twisted position.

'You cried?' he said. 'You mean you actually shed tears?'

Look out, I thought; one of these. I was still having to blow my nose, and was ready to ride rough-shod. My friend put the spaghetti on the table and we all sat down.

'I'm starving,' said Natalie.

'What a plot,' I raved. 'So tight you couldn't stick a pin in it.'

'What was your worst moment?' said Natalie.

'Oh, when he bends over the sack to gloat, and then from off-stage comes the Duke's voice, singing his song. The way he freezes, in that bent-over posture, over the sack.'

The sack, in a sack. I had a best friend once, my intellectual companion of ten years, on paper from land to land and then in person: she was the one who first told me the story of *Rigoletto* and I will never forget the way her voice sank to a thread of horror: 'And the murderer gives him his daughter's body on the river-bank, *in a sack*.' A river flows: that is its nature. Its sluggish water can work any discarded object loose from the bank and carry it further, lump it lengthwise, nudge it and roll it and shift it, bear it away and along and out of sight.

'Yes, that was bad all right,' said Natalie, 'but mine was when he realised that his daughter was in the bed-chamber with the Duke.'

We picked up our forks and began to eat. The back door opened on to a narrow concrete yard, but light was bouncing down the grey walls and the air was warm, and as I ate I thought, Why don't I live here? In the sun?

'Also,' I said, 'I *love* what it's about. About the impossibility of shielding your children from the evil of the world.'

There was a pause.

'Well, yes, it is about that,' said my tactful friend, 'but it's also about the greatest fear men have. Which is the fear of losing their daughters. Of losing them to younger men. Into the world of sex.'

We sat at the table quietly eating. Words which people use and pretend to understand floated in silence and bumped among our heads. Virgin. Treasure. Perfect. Clean. My darling. Anima. Soul.

Natalie spoke in her light, courteous voice. 'If that's what it's about,' she said, 'what do you think the women in the audience were responding to?' — for in our bags were two sodden handkerchiefs.

The salad went round.

'I don't know,' said my friend. 'You tell me.'

We said nothing. We looked into our plates.

'That fear men have,' said my friend. 'Literature and art are full of it.'

My skin gave a mutinous prickle.

'*Do* women have a fundamental fear?' said my friend.

Natalie and I glanced at each other and back to the tabletop.

'A fear of violation, maybe?' he said. He got up and filled the kettle. The silence was not a silence but a quietness of thinking. I knew what Natalie was thinking. She was wishing the conversation had not taken this particular turn. I was wishing the same thing. Stumped, struck dumb: failed again, failed to think and talk in that pattern they use. I had nothing to say. Nothing came to my mind that had any bearing on the matter.

Should I say 'But violation is our destiny'? Or should I say '*Nothing can be sole or whole / That has not been rent*'? But before I could open my mouth, a worst moment came to me: the letter arrives from my best friend on the road in another country: 'He was wearing mirror sunglasses which he did not take off, I tried to plead but I could not speak his language, he tore out handfuls of my hair, he kicked me and pushed me out of the car, I crawled to the river, I could smell the water, it was dirty but I washed myself, a farm girl found me, her family is looking after me, I think I will be all right, please answer, above all, don't tell my father, love.' I got down on my elbows in the yard and put my face into the dirt, I wept, I groaned. That night I went as usual to the lesson. *All I can do is try to make something perfect for you, for your poor body, with my clumsy and ignorant one*: I breathed and moved as the teacher showed us, and she came past me in the class and

19

touched me on the head and said, 'This must mean a lot to you — you are doing it so beautifully.'

'Violation,' said Natalie, as if to gain time.

'It would be necessary,' I said, 'to examine all of women's writing, to see if the fear of violation is the major theme of it.'

'Some feminist theoretician somewhere has probably already done it,' said the stranger who had been surprised that *Rigoletto* could draw tears.

'Barbara Baynton, for instance,' said my friend. 'Have you read that story of hers called *The Chosen Vessel*? The woman knows the man is outside waiting for dark. She puts the brooch on the table. It's the only valuable thing she owns. She puts it there as an offering — to appease him. She wants to buy him off.'

The brooch. The mirror sunglasses. The feeble lock. The weakened wall that gives. What stops these conversations is shame, and grief.

'We don't have a tradition in the way you blokes do,' I said.

Everybody moved and laughed, with relief.

'There must be a line of women's writing,' said Natalie, 'running from the beginning till now.'

'It's a shadow tradition,' I said. 'It's there, but nobody knows what it is.'

'We've been trained in *your* tradition,' said Natalie. 'We're honorary men.'

She was not looking at me, nor I at her.

The coffee was ready, and we drank it. Natalie went to pick up her children from school. My friend put in the plug and began to wash the dishes. The stranger tilted his chair back against the wall, and I leaned on the bench.

'What happened to your hand?' he said.

'I cut it on the glass shelf yesterday,' I said, 'when I was defrosting the fridge.'

'There's a packet of Band-aids in the fruit bowl,' said my friend from the sink.

I stripped off the old plaster and took a fresh one from the dish. But before I could yank its little ripcord and pull it out of its wrapper, the stranger got up from his chair, walked all the way round the table and across the room, and stopped in front of me. He took the Band-aid and said, 'Do you want me to put it on for you?'

I drew a breath to say *what we say*: 'Oh, it's all right, thanks! I can do it myself.'

But instead, I don't know why, I let out my independent breath, and drew another. I gave him my hand.

'Do you like dressing wounds?' I said, in a smart tone to cover my surprise.

He did not answer this, but spread out my palm and had a good look at the cut. It was deep and precise, like a freshly dug trench, bloody still at the bottom, but with nasty white soggy edges where the plaster had prevented the skin from drying.

'You've made a mess of yourself, haven't you,' he said.

'Oh, it's nothing much,' I said airily. 'It only hurt while it was actually happening.'

He was not listening. He was concentrating on the plaster. His fingers were pale, square and clean. He peeled off the two protective flaps and laid the sticky bandage across the cut. He pressed one side of it, and then the other, against my skin, smoothed them flat with his thumbs, and let go.

Honour

'. . . THINGS MATTERED
AND LOVE, ANXIOUS LOVE
ROSE AND PUT FORTH ITS FLAGS.'
Chris Wallace-Crabbe
The Emotions are not Skilled Workers

On summer nights they walked through city gardens.

The air stood thick in their nostrils, a damp warmth lay on their shoulders. Water dripped somewhere, randomly, without rhythm. On the other side of the banked plants people were murmuring idly in a foreign language. Jenny's head swam in the heat: her pores opened for the sweat to break. She saw his face floating by the fleshy flowers, eager, sharp and gentle. She wanted to take him in through her skin.

'What is that tree? What is that plant?' he asked her, and she told him the names. He did not try to remember them much, asked merely to hear her say the words in her English accent.

'How is it you know their names?'

'Oh, my father. And there are days,' she said, 'when the only things that don't look sad to me are plants.'

'Why are women so sad?' said Frank.

22

'I don't know,' she said. 'I don't think it's catching. Is that what you're worried about?' She stopped walking and looked him in the eyes. Behind her an iron fence with spikes rose up against the sky, which was deep blue with points of yellow light.

'Maybe,' he said after a moment. She was looking at him. One of her eyes was set very slightly higher than the other, as in some Cubist painting he may have once seen. He stepped off the path and cartwheeled lightly away over the springy grass. Once he had seen his daughter, on a sandbank in a desert, do fifty cartwheels in a row under moonlight.

———

When Kathleen answered the phone, Frank's sharp voice said, 'Hullo. It's me.'

Kathleen laughed out loud. Only a husband would announce himself thus.

'What?' he said.

'Nothing,' she said, sobering up.

'Listen. Can you come over tonight? I'd like to have a talk.'

'Anything wrong?'

'No. Just some stuff I'd like to clear up.'

The front door of the long house was left open for her and Frank was writing something in his violent, swooping hand at the kitchen table.

'Time one of you swept the hall,' she said from the doorway.

'Well, I won't be here much longer.' His cackling laugh rang out among the teacups hanging from their shelf. He sprang up nervously, took two big steps around the table and leaned against the stove with his bare arms crossed. He stared down at his feet with an assumed air of perplexity.

'Listen, Kathleen!' He leaped forward, gripped the table edge with both hands and leaned over it, but kept his face turned up to where she stood on the step. She noticed with a small shock that his hair was quite thickly grey at the sides. He narrowed his greenish eyes and stretched his thin mouth sideways like a man at the start of a hundred yard dash. The familiar drama caused her stomach to start trembling with the desire to laugh.

'Things have got to change! They can't remain the same!' he cried.

She laughed in confusion. 'What, Frank?'

'Sit down. Do you want a cuppa?' He would bounce to the ceiling.

'You'd burn yourself. Spit it out.'

He gathered himself into a bunch and threw it at her. 'There's something I want. I want a divorce.'

He propped in front of the cupboard door to watch her cop it. She remembered suddenly how a dog they had once used to catch a thrown stick in his mouth — it stopped him dead at the moment of impact, *whack* between his black and pink jaws, but fitted: he regained his stride and ran on.

'See?' he burst out, pacing up and down. 'It won't be any different between us. Just on paper.'

'But — what's put this into your head?'

She looked down at the bandy curves of his legs, brown and stringy in baggy khaki shorts.

'It wasn't *my* idea.' He spun round as if accused. 'Jenny wants me to — sort of — clean up my past.' His laugh was high-pitched, he pulled his mouth down at the corners.

Kathleen turned blind with rage for two seconds. This time it took her a good moment to swallow it, spit from the caught stick. Frank squinted at her and the speed went out of him. He sat down at the table.

'That was a bit undiplomatic,' he remarked.

She stared, blank as blotting paper.

'Come and sit down, Kath.'

She needed to, and obeyed.

There was a pile of papers, written on, between them on the table. Frank shifted his feet on the matting. A meek breeze came down the hall from the open front door, slid loosely across the papers and confounded itself with the warm air in which husband and wife sat. The top sheet of paper lifted as if to move sideways. Frank dumped the sugar bowl heavily on to the stack. In the fluorescent light the grains glittered.

'You see,' he began in a gentler voice, with his head on one side, 'I've always thought I'd go on being related to you, for the rest of my life.'

Normal existence began to tick again. Someone had cleaned the louvre windows over the sink, and the panes gleamed darkly. In fact, the kitchen was full of shining surfaces. Frank was a great cleaner. When she was sick, even years after they had separated, he would burst into her room with broom, dust-pan and brush and whirl about, setting all to rights, placing objects in piles and at right-angles to each other.

'We will be, won't we? Because Flo will relate us.'

'Yes.' His face turned soft at the name. 'But Jenny – well . . . she hasn't lived like we have all these years. "Smashing monogamy."' He laughed bitterly. 'She wants things to be resolved. "Resolved" is a word she uses a lot.'

'You don't mean you want to get *married* again?'

'If I do, it'll only be to get European work papers,' he said hastily.

'I thought one reason why we never got a divorce before was so we wouldn't make the same mistake again! Remember what you always used to say? "Getting married isn't something you do – it's something that happens to you."'

'That's true. The first time, anyway.'

She hung dangerously, as if the other half of a high-wire act had failed to show up for work. He looked down at his hands.

'You know one thing she's done for me – she's made me cut right back on my drinking.'

'How'd she do it? She must have something I haven't got.'

'I've been living like a maniac for five years, Kath. Not just when you shot through with Perfect-Features – but afterwards – doing nothing but work, drink and fuck – look at my hair!' He indicated his grey temples with a gun-like gesture. 'Look at me! Thirty-two years old and grey as a church mouse!'

She laughed with a twist of the mouth.

'I've been bullshitting myself all these years,' he went on. 'I want a *real* place to live, with a back yard where I can plant vegies, and a couple of walls to paint, and a dog – not a bloody room in a sort of railway station!' Breathless with rhetoric, he sat smiling shyly at her, one arm resting on the tabletop.

'Does Jenny want that too?'

'Yes.' He might have blushed.

She would have to be mingy indeed to stay hard-faced against his hopefulness. 'What about Flo?'

'Jenny loves her. Can she come and live with us for a while? For a month or so? It would be a home. I'll drive her to school.' He looked eager, leaning over his arm.

'Does she want to go?' It was only a formality.

'Oh yes. I think so.'

Some splinter-self in the depths was twisting in protest: what about *me*? but Kathleen kicked the door shut on it. There were no demands or protests she might rightfully make. He had always treated her honourably. In five years she had never given it one moment's conscious thought, but had lounged on the assumption that she was still somebody's, even when she was most alone.

She looked up and saw a tiny liquid twinkling in the inner corner of Frank's left eye.

'Look!' he shouted, pointing to it. 'A tear! It is! I can still squeeze one out!'

———

Kathleen ran in from the glaring street. Through the screen door she perceived dim shapes moving at the other end of the passage. The wire smelled coldly of rust as she pressed her nose to it and rattled her fist against the wood. Jenny was calling back over her shoulder as she approached the door.

'So I told her I considered my contract fulfilled,' she was saying in a tone of such dry resoluteness that Kathleen envied her a firm life: orderliness, self-esteem. She saw Kathleen and said, 'Oh!'

They had never met, but stared at each other through the clotted wire with suddenly quailing hearts.

'I've just come for Flo,' said Kathleen.

'Would you like to come in? We're watching the news.'

Frank was hunched forward, elbows on knees. 'Come to check up on me, have you,' he said, not taking his eyes off the screen where a man's face opened and closed its mouth.

'Who's this clown?' said Kathleen, ignoring the jibe.

'Lang Hancock.'

'What's he on about?'

'Sssh!' said Frank.

'He claims,' said Jenny tactfully, 'that he flew through a radioactive cloud thirty years ago and that it didn't do him any harm – thus, that it's all right to mine uranium. He's brought his daughter along to show that his genes didn't suffer.'

'What! With that huge polka dot *bow* round her neck?' Kathleen started to giggle.

Frank turned round crossly and said, 'Sssh, will you? This is serious!'

Kathleen put her beach towel over her mouth and pulled a chastised face. She picked up a newspaper and flipped through it.

'My God,' she said. 'It says here that a lady went into hospital in France to have a baby, and when she came out of the anaesthetic they'd cut one of her *hands* off.'

Frank switched off the television. 'Do you ever read the actual news, Kath? Apart from Odd Spots, death notices and so on?'

'Of course,' said Kathleen.

Jenny stared at her, and thought in a blur of fear, 'Is it being a mother that makes her head racket round like that? Will this happen to me?'

The two women sat in similar poses, limbs arranged so as to appear casual. They did not perceive their striking similarity; they both made emphatic hand gestures and grimaces in speech, stressed certain words ironically, cast their eyes aside in mid-sentence as if a sustained gaze might burn the listener. Around each of them quivered an aura of terrific restraint. If they both let go at once, they might blow each other out of the room.

'This is a nice house,' said Kathleen recklessly. 'Why doesn't Frank just move in here, instead of both of you having to look for another place?'

The air bristled.

'Because then he would be living at my place,' enunciated Jenny carefully, 'and we would like to start off on equal terms.'

'We've found a place, anyway,' said Frank.

'I'll give you a hand to move then, whenever you like,' Kathleen charged on. There was a short hush.

'Will you have a beer, Kathleen?' said Jenny.

'No thanks. I was going to take Flo for a swim.'

'It's a scorcher, all right,' said Frank, shifting in his chair.

Light filtered through drawn curtains, the three characters floated in watery dimness. Pale objects burned: cotton trousers, a dress faded as a flour bag, a flash of eye-white in a turned head. There was a faint smell of lemon.

Flo ran in, dragging a white dog by its collar.

'I heard you talking, Kath. See? This is Jenny's dog. She *loves* me.'

'I bet she does. Come on – we'll go to the baths.'

'Come into my room and get your things, Flo,' said Jenny.

Flo took Kathleen's hand. 'Come and look at Jenny's things. She's got jewels, and a special thing like scissors for your eyelashes.'

The brown floor in the passage creaked under them. Jenny snapped on a lamp in the front room and the heavy double bed sprang into the light. Flo edged her way round its foot to reach the treasure box by the fireplace. The two women stood awkwardly, embarrassed by the meaning of the bed, but Flo turned round with a tweezer-like object in her hand and applied it brusquely to her eyelashes.

'Careful!'

'See? They make your eyelashes *curly*.'

Jenny laughed and flicked a glance at Kathleen to see if she disapproved. Kathleen did, but was also curious, and looked to see if Jenny had used the tool on her own eyes, which were brown and unevenly set.

'When are you coming here to spend the night, Flo?' said Jenny.

Flo looked shyly at her mother, not wanting to make her jealous. 'Can I, one day?'

'Of course.'

'I'll phone you,' said Jenny.

Jenny and Flo took a step towards one another and Flo raised her arms as if to kiss her goodbye. They both stopped at the same instant and looked at Kathleen with identical expressions: waiting for dispensation. Kathleen smiled and nodded, they kissed smackingly.

Outside the front door the hot afternoon folded them in its dry blanket. The gate disturbed vegetation and set free a wave of privet smell and the peppery scent of climbing roses.

Halfway down the lane Frank caught up with them and took hold of Flo's other hand.

'Hang on, Kath! I've got something to ask you. I have to go down to Mum and Dad's. Mum's a bit under the weather.'

'What? Why didn't you tell me?'

'I only found out last night. Dad rang up. Poor old blighter can hardly see to dial the number.'

'What's actually wrong with Shirl?'

'I don't know. Some sort of nervous complaint. Quite painful. She's had the doctor.' He lashed savagely at a hedge. 'I don't think Dad can manage by himself. He's never asked me for help before.'

They walked along in silence.

'Do you want me to come down with you?' said Kathleen. 'Unless you're taking Jenny, of course.'

'Would you? It'd get the load off me a bit. They haven't met Jenny yet. Mightn't be the moment to break that one to them.'

'Can I come?' said Flo.

'No,' said Kathleen. 'You can't miss school. You can stay home with the others.'

'Well, can I go and live with Frank and Jenny in their new house, then?' She was only flying a kite, barely listening for the answer, lining up her sandal toes with the cracks of the footpath so that the end of each fence fell upon an even number.

'Yes. If you want to.' Kathleen was trying to smile.

Flo seized her round the waist with her wiry arms. 'But what if you miss me too much? You won't cry or anything, will you?'

Her teeth were uneven and her forehead at this anxious moment displayed five horizontal lines of wrinkles so exactly like Frank's that Kathleen was all at sea.

'I can come and visit you,' she said. 'You can invite me over for dinner and we can both cook.'

Kathleen looked up from this bony embrace and saw Frank leaning against the fence with a strange smile on his face. 'He must be happy,' she thought. Flo pranced about. The parents' faces were stiff and their expressions inappropriate. Kathleen felt old, and perhaps bitter, but not against these two creatures whose separateness from herself, no matter how many times it had been demonstrated, she could never really bring herself to believe in.

Frank and Kathleen stood side by side like children in the doorway. Shirley was asleep, her head turned sharply to one side on the pillow, her mouth open as if she had just cried out.

'The doctor says it's called psoriasis,' offered Jack in the kitchen. 'She sleeps most of the time.' He smiled helplessly at them, bewildered, wanting to appease and be approved of. Age had shrunk him, and he hardly reached Frank's shoulder.

'What's the doctor giving her? I mean – she shouldn't be knocked out like that, should she?' Frank moved agitatedly about the room, pulling open cupboard doors and slamming them again without looking inside.

'Blowed if I know, Frankie,' said the old man. His knotty hands were resting on the back of a chair. 'The doctor's a young chap, 'bout your age. I s'pose he knows what he's talking about.'

'I wouldn't be so bloody sure. They're drug-happy, those blokes – eh, Kath?'

She nodded, watching.

'I was just going to wake her up and give her something to eat, when you two arrived,' said Jack. 'I had a snack a little while ago.' On the sink were a plate, a knife and a fork, rinsed.

'I'll do it, Dad,' said Frank. 'You sit down there and take a break. What'll we give her, Kath?'

They cobbled together a dish of yogurt and fruit, and Frank took it into the bedroom. Jack, legs crossed in his favourite corner chair, deerstalker cap pulled down over his bristly eyebrows and transistor whining faintly on his lap, began a soft tuneless whistle, tapping his fingertips on the armrests and looking out the window with elaborate casualness.

'Tum te tum te tum. Well . . .' he murmured. He sneaked a look at Kathleen and returned to his contemplation of a bush outside the glass.

'Think I'll pop out the back for a sec and have a look at the garden before it gets too dark,' said Kathleen at last, to put him out of his misery.

'Mmmm . . . there's quite a show out there. Pick some to take home.' One foot in its gleaming brogue beat rhythmically on air.

She made her escape and stood on the sloping lawn. A wind moved in the garden, very gentle and sweet: it shifted pleasantly among the leaves of small gums and roses past their season. The sky blurred upward, pearly as the inside of a shell, and in this delicate firmament there floated a perfect moon, its valleys and mountains lightly etched.

Shirley's voice rose sharply from the bedroom, and Frank's answered. Their words were indistinct. The footsteps thumped, and Frank burst out the back door and stood staring desperately into the massed hydrangeas. Kathleen stepped up beside him.

'I had to feed her with a spoon,' he said, grinding his teeth and sniffing. 'She didn't want me to. She only wants Dad.'

'She's probably ashamed.'

'What? What of?'

'Being weak in front of you. And she's probably worried about being ugly.'

'Ugly! I don't give a damn about that! I just want to know what drugs those bastards have got her on. I've never seen her as dopey as this!' He clenched his fists and let out a sob. Kathleen slipped one arm round his waist and tried to hug him unobtrusively. He was rigid and very thin.

'Does she know I'm here?'

'Yes. Go and say hullo. I think she might want a drink. I'll stay out here and calm down.'

The old woman struggled to sit up. 'No, don't kiss me,' she said in distress, moving her head from side to side as Kathleen approached. 'I'm all —' She pulled her night-dress together at the neck to hide the scaly patches of skin on her chest. Jack felt his way along the wardrobe and out of the room.

'I've brought you a drink, Shirl.' Kathleen stuck her hand out with the fizzing glass in it. After two sips of dry ginger, great runs of air rumbled up from Shirley's stomach, and she turned her face away, blushing and covering her mouth with her hand.

'I'm sorry,' she whispered.

'That's what fizzy drinks are for,' said Kathleen.

'I hate it,' cried Shirley passionately, still with her shoulder turned.

The bed-clothes were all skew-whiff, the sheets out of alignment with the blankets, the whole lot dragging on the floor.

'Will I tidy up a bit for you, Shirl?'

'Oh, it's too much trouble, love.' She fretted among the pillows, turning her head in abrupt movements like a bird.

'No it's not. I'll call Frank.'

Frank settled his mother on a chair while Kathleen took hold of the bed-clothes and yanked them away. A shower of silvery dead skin flakes flew out and fell in drifts on the polished wood floor.

'It's awful,' moaned Shirley, humiliated in her dressing-gown.

'Don't be silly, Mum,' said Frank. 'It's *not* awful, and you *must* accept being looked after.'

Kathleen worked away efficiently, shoving her hands between mattress and base and plumping up pillows. She remembered sitting thinly on a chair with her feet dangling while her mother 'made her bed nice'.

'There you are. Hop in here. I'll run the old sheets through the machine.' She gathered them up in her arms and forged out the door.

Shirley's splintery voice trailed after her. 'The second cycle, lovey – don't forget to open both the taps, and not too much soap powder . . .'

'She knows how to *do* it, Mum,' snapped Frank. Kathleen almost laughed. When Frank and his mother talked like that, things were getting back to normal. She blundered round in the laundry, unused to machines that worked without the introduction of coins, and got the thing going at last. Frank slipped in and shut the door behind him.

'What's Jack up to?' said Kathleen.

'Fumbling round in the study trying to find Mum's prescription.' Frank picked up a basket full of pegs and rattled it fiercely.

'I think this is probably the beginning of the . . . race to the end.' He grimaced, pointed one finger heavenwards and then down to the earth, and mimed sleep as children do, eyes closed and palms together under one cheek. They both laughed painfully.

In Shirley's kitchen the autumn sunlight was oblique and very bright. Kathleen squinted and moved constantly from one part of the room to another in search of an area of shade for her face. There was a blinding sheen on the table-boards, shafts of light sprang from cutlery, Frank's hair stood out like an aureole. The plastic cover of the photo album dazzled relentlessly.

'Look,' said Frank.

'I can't see.'

'It's my dog, a foxy I had when I was a kid.'

Shuffling footsteps came along the passage, and Shirley stood in the doorway with a mustard-coloured shawl wrapped round her.

'What are you doing out of bed, Mum?'

'Oh . . . I'm all right,' she insisted in her cracked voice, pushing past him and sitting down at the table. 'I'd rather be up and about.'

Frank clicked his tongue, but passed her the album. 'Look, Mum. Remember when Auntie Hazel used to stay in her caravan in our back yard?'

Shirley seized the album and shielded her eyes over it. 'Oohoo, that Hazel,' she crooned with a note of malice. 'Look at that dress she's got on! We said at the time, Brocade's as dead as a dodo, we said. We all knew what she was after when she latched on to Keith. There was the house in Kyneton, all his mother's things, you never saw such lace — and the furniture, a cheval glass she'd had made up for her by an old Chinaman up Ballarat way . . . Hazel hung on like grim death, but she only got hold of it a clock here, a chair there.' She turned the pages with a sigh, and they sat listening, half-hypnotised as she murmured. 'Ah, there's Jack as a younger man. He had a finely turned ankle in those days. It was the first thing I noticed about him. Why should I tell you all this? Dear God, it's life, I suppose.'

'I've got something to tell *you*, Mum,' said Frank suddenly. Kathleen looked up and saw him take the deep breath before the plunge.

'What, love.' Shirley hovered over the grey snaps like a map-reader.

'Kath and I are getting a divorce.'

The plastic page flopped under her hand, as if she had not heard.

'Now, we don't want you to get *upset* about this, Mum,' he said.

'What, lovey?' She turned the book sideways and bent over it.

'I might be getting *married* again, Mum. I'm going to *live* with someone.'

Shirley looked up from the picture book and spoke very clearly, with a note of world-weariness that they had never heard before. 'Oh, I don't give a damn. She can come down here. That couch turns into a double bed. I only ever wanted you, Kath, and Flo, but it's no use growling. I can't be worried about it now. Bring her down.'

Frank was shocked. Not only had he expected her to be outraged, but he needed her to be, so that he might define himself against her protest. It was perhaps the moment of his growing up. Before Kathleen's eyes the knot dissolved, and she watched him float free, feet groping, full of alarm.

Kathleen and Frank went walking down by the shore, under the avenues of huge cypresses rooted deep in the sandy ground. Perhaps they would have liked to walk arm in arm: there were historical reasons for the fact that they did not.

'I love it here,' said Frank. 'It seems so old. I bet Yalta on the Black Sea must be like this – flat and mournful. When I read *The Lady with the Dog* I imagined it happening here.'

On the pier their footsteps rang hollow and water slapped way below. Long ships, business-like, slid past on their way to the heads: a quality of absence in the air brought them unnaturally close. It was late afternoon, and a strange metal light intensified the dark greens and greys of the shore, and of the sad water that seemed to stream past them oceanwards. Frank, absorbed in his Chekhovian fantasy, planted himself squarely at the very end of the pier, slitting his eyes and loosening his coat to let it flap in the wind.

'There's going to be a storm,' remarked Kathleen, brushing dandruff off his shoulders.

'Have you no eyes, Kathleen?' trumpeted Frank. He fronted the brisk wind with a histrionic gesture. 'Look about you! Is there no poetry left in your soul?'

'Oh, I think there might be a bit left,' she said dryly. She stared past him.

The water was lashing at the encrusted supports of the pier, and the big lifeboat groaned on its pulleys. Their hair streamed back off their skulls and rain began to sprinkle on to their up-turned faces.

'Let's go, Frankie.'

'OK,' he grumbled good-naturedly, 'you old prune. I wish Floss was here. *She'd* play with me.'

They turned up their collars and let the wind hurry them back towards the car. On the dashboard Frank had sticky-taped a type-written notice which read, *This car should last another ten years.* He drove with nervous efficiency. As he drove he sang, accompanying himself with sharp taps of the left foot:

> *There's a trade we all know well*
> *It's bringing cattle over*
> *On every track to the Gulf and back*
> *Men know the Queensland drover*

and she joined in the chorus because she knew it would give him pleasure:

> *Pass the billy round boys*
> *Don't let the pintpot stand there*
> *For tonight we drink the health*
> *Of every Overlander*

Loudly and in harmony they sang, sneaking each other embarrassed, happy smiles, then laughed and avoided each other's eyes.

'I'm scared Dad'll go before I can get his story out of him,' said Frank.

'Didn't you start taping it?'

'Yes. But it's so hard to get him going. He's shy, and he gets mixed up.'

'Did you get the one about the carrot?'

Frank knitted his brows and mimicked his father's slow, musing voice: 'I was sitting on the verandah after work when Reggie Blainey came down the road dragging over his shoulder what looked like a *young sapling*. He got closer and I saw it was actually the fronds of a *giant carrot*. I says, Well, Reggie, that's the biggest carrot *I've* ever seen! And he looks up at me and he says, Listen, you reckon this is big? I dug for three hours — and the bloomin' thing forked at twenty foot.'

Under the rain, the lights of Geelong were coming on as they sped down the Leopold Hill.

Kathleen's brother-in-law opened the door to them in a flustered moment. An invisible child was throwing a tantrum in the kitchen, and from the stereo in the living room a string quartet was straining away loudly.

'Hul-lo!' he cried in amazement. 'What a treat! Come in! Pin was whizzed into hospital straight after lunch — the baby's overdue. We're just waiting for news.'

They followed him into the kitchen, where the benches and tables were covered in bright blue formica and the small window looked out over fruit trees and a chook pen. At their appearance the child on the floor ceased to beat his fists and sat up to stare, his cheeks puce and tear-stained.

'My goodness!' said Charlie. 'I haven't seen you two together for — must be five years! There's not a reconciliation, is there?' He clapped his hand over his mouth as if he had made a gaffe. Kathleen and Frank, whose lack of interest in divorce had given them a certain bohemian status in both their families, remained collected. Kathleen swept a mass of blocks off a chair and sat down. The two men stood about, Charlie flipping a tea towel, Frank grinning at the floor. The older boy appeared in the doorway as the string quartet reached its climax and resolved itself into one drawn-out, quivering harmony. Silence. Charlie sighed voluptuously.

'Wonderful, isn't it,' he said.

'When's mummy coming home. I want mummy to come home.'

'Yes dar-ling,' sang Charlie irrelevantly on two notes, his mind on something else but not soon enough, for a covered saucepan erupted on the stove and milk went everywhere. 'Damn. Blast it.'

Kathleen spoke up without forethought. 'I could stay for a few days, if you like, and give you a hand with the kids.'

'Oh, would you?' He spun round with the inadequate wettex dripping on his shoes.

'Am I neurotic?' thought Kathleen, already aware of a trickle of regret behind the smile.

She hurried the trolley along the bright shelves of the supermarket, Ben trotting at her side and Tom lording it in the seat above the merchandise. No matter how fast she moved, something horrible kept pace with her, ran smoothly along behind the ranged and perfect shining objects: something to do with memory, with time past she thought she had escaped, as long ago as childhood when she had striven to imagine her mother's life and her own future: meals, meals, meals: the meal as duty, as short leash, as unit of time inexorable into everlastingness. She dared not glance at other women passing lest she see confirmation of it in their faces. There was no word for this sickness in her, running alongside her, but *void*.

In the checkout queue she realised she had forgotten fruit.

'Will you stay here and mind the shopping while I run back?' Ben gripped her hand.

'I won't be long,' she pleaded. 'There's nothing to worry about – we'll go home and have some lunch.'

She wrenched herself free and bolted along the slick alley-ways, frantic to be by herself even for sixty seconds. She glanced back at them as she skidded round the great cabinets steaming with frost and saw Ben's pale face eyeing her and Tom's mouth opening to let out one of his leisurely roars. *I can't stand it, can't stand it,* a whining chipmunk voice began up in the back of her skull, it chattered at her, gibbered, she dived both hands into the pile of netted oranges, flipped them this way and that, mould whiffed at her, *the skull beneath the skin* pipped the voice, *shit shit shit,* two bags at sixty-five cents, she counted on her fingers a dollar thirty something, now where are those two little buggers? God help them, God send me back to Flo, how did I stand it when she was only two? Only three more days and I'll be on that train.

Outside, she trundled the pusher up the hill. It was quicker to carry Tom in it than to round him up on foot, but he was fat and the heavy shopping bags, one in each hand against the handle of the flimsy pusher, bumped clumsily against her legs and the wheels as she progressed. Ben gripped the handle, continually swinging the triple load out of line. She fought herself for patience. The sky was thick, big drops started, they had no coats. Tom began to bellow, 'Wet! Wet! Wet! Wanna det out!'

'Oh shut up, Tom!' she raged, wrenching hard to get the pusher wheel out of a crack in the pavement. Ben slid her a sly look.

'Will I shove a jelly bean into him?' he hissed.

'Where did you get 'em?'

'While you were paying the lady.'

The pathetic cavalcade struggled up the hill.

She sat on the back verandah cutting slice after slice off a rubbery ginger cake she had found in a tin and stuffing it into her mouth. The boys played in their sandpit. The sand was dark yellow but the rain had stopped. She remembered reading somewhere: only if you have been a child in a certain town can you know its sadness, bone sadness, sadness of the blood. *Every day the clouds come over*. She went and stood by the sandpit. The little shovels made a damp grating sound as the children sank them into the sand.

At teatime when Charlie came home from work, she served up for dessert a kind of pudding. Everyone but Tom ate it enthusiastically. Enthroned in his high chair, holding his spoon like a sceptre, he scowled into his bowl.

'Eat up, Tom,' said his father. He glanced at Kathleen and poked the pudding into a more attractive shape in the bowl.

'It's cake.'

Tom withered him with a look. 'That is *not cake*.'

His aunt and his father lowered their lying heads on to the table among the plates and laughed in weak paroxysms.

The baby came, a girl. Kathleen sniffed the head of the creature rolled tightly in its cotton blanket. Looking at her sister had always been like looking into a mirror: large forehead, eyes that drooped at the outer corners, pointed chin, small mouth. Kathleen laughed.

'What's funny?' said Pin, shifting uncomfortably in the hospital bed.

'I was looking at your mouth. It's exactly the same as mine.'

'Small and mean,' said Pin. 'Wanna see a cat's bum?' She pursed her lips into a tight bunch. They snickered in the quiet ward.

'You'll never go to heaven,' said Kathleen. 'You're rude.'

'Sit down here and tell me what you've been doing. The only way I can get away from the kids long enough to have a good talk with someone is by having another one.'

'Oh . . . I muck round. Read, you know. Clean up.'

'Charlie says Frank was down. You're not getting together again, are you?'

'Hardly. Too late for that, even if we wanted to.'

'What a shame. I always liked Frank.'

'So did I. Still do. I think he's the ant's pants. What've *you* been up to, apart from having babies?'

'Praying.' At Kathleen's polite attempt to conceal her disgust, Pin burst out laughing.

'How was the birth?'

'Oh, lovely. I mean – it would have been, if they'd left me alone. I was managing quite well, being a bit of an old hand, but I was probably making a lot of noise, because one of the doctors came in and mumbled something to the nurse, and next thing I know she's approaching with this big cheesy smile and one hand behind her back. Righto, Mrs Hassett! she says. I want you to curl up on the table with your bottom right out on the edge, just like a little bunny rabbit. No you don't! I said. No one's giving *me* a spinal – I was a nurse before I got like this. I *know* that bunny rabbit line – just get away from me, thanks very much. And I battled on, and voilà!' She indicated with a flourish the sausage-shaped bundle in the cot beside the bed. 'Anyway, Kath – 'scuse me for a sec. I'm going to stagger to the toilet.'

When Pin came back she was as white as a sheet. 'Here, help me back into bed, will you? I think I'd better call the doctor.'

'What, Pin?'

'I was wiping myself just now, and I felt something hard, right down low. I put my head between my knees and had a look. I think it's my cervix.'

They stared at each other. Pin tried to laugh. 'It's probably nothing.'

A nurse came. She slipped her hand under the bed-clothes. Kathleen wandered over to the window and looked out over the grey bay with its stumpy palm trees and, further away towards Melbourne on the endless volcanic plain, the two dead mountains, rounded as worn-down molars.

The nurse said, 'I'll go and call doctor.' Her expression was respectful as she padded away on her soft white shoes. Pin grimaced and shrugged.

'Oh Pin. What a drag.' Kathleen sat down on the bed and took hold of her sister's hand with its heavy silver engagement and wedding rings. 'Are you still playing the piano?'

'Yes, and I'm getting better too.' Pin grinned defiantly. 'My teacher said, "For a thirty-five-year-old with a rotten memory, you're not doing too badly".'

Across her mouth flitted a stoicism, a setting of the lips, still well this side of martyrdom.

⸙

The house was at the bottom of a dead-end road with narrow yellowing nature strips, and a railway line running across its very end like stitches closing a bag. It was twelve o'clock and there was no one around.

Jenny came out the front door and saw Kathleen dawdling by her car, arm along brow against the strong sun. She looked small, dwarfed by the big blue day, and unusually hesitant, leaning there looking this way and that, squinting up her face so that her top teeth showed. Jenny felt a throb of tenderness towards her: a spasm of the heart, a weakening in the pelvis. She darted out the gate and stopped in front of Kathleen, seized her wrist. With force of will she kept the other woman's hand, studied with a peculiar flux her sun-wrinkled eyes, the marks of her shrewd expressions. They could even smell each other: flower, oil, coffee, soap: and under these, warmed flesh, dotted tongue, glass of eye, glossy membrane, rope of hair, nail roughly clipped.

'Welcome,' said Jenny.

Perhaps they would never dare again. They stepped out of each other, frightened.

'There's nothing here to drink,' called out Frank on the verandah. 'I'm going to find a pub.'

Jenny turned away from Kathleen, distracted. 'I'll come with you.'

Kathleen waited, still leaning against her car, until they were out of sight, walking slowly in the heat with their arms round each other. Two ragged nectarine trees fidgeted their leaves in the scarcely moving air. Her head was faint in the dryness. She heaved herself up and turned to tackle the house.

Its facade, a triangle on top of a square, was slightly awry and painted the aqua colour favoured by Greek landlords. She ducked under an orange and green blind rolled up on rotted ropes at the outer edge of the verandah, and turned the key in the handle-less front door. In the tilting hallway she walked quickly past two or three small rooms with brown blinds half-drawn and opened the door into the kitchen, in which a combustion stove, painted white to indicate its decorative status, crouched in the chimney place, superseded by a gas cooker, itself forty years old, standing in a nearby corner alcove. Someone had slung a blanket across the window on two nails to keep the hot day out: its woollen folds muffled all movement of air and absorbed the knock of her footsteps.

She stood still in the bare centre of the room, on boards, in dimness. The heat was breathless. A drop of water bulged and quivered under the tap.

The back door was shut. It was made of four vertical strips of timber, also painted white, and closed with a loose brass knob. The timber had worn thin top and bottom, like the business end of front teeth, so that the dry brightness off the concrete outside was felt in the room as two insistent, serrated presences of light.

She opened the door, stepped down into the dazzling yard, and walked along by the grey wooden fence and through the green dried-out trellis door into the wash-house with its squat copper and pair of troughs under the window never meant to open. She placed her palms lightly on the edge of the troughs. They were grey, forever damp and cool, clotted of surface and rimmed lead-smooth in paler grey; she had been bathed when very small in troughs such as these, and her mother had let her play with the wooden stick that she used to stir the copper, a stick with a face on the knob. The wash-house smelled of wet cloth and blue bags, and she could not climb out of the high trough by herself, so she was obliged to sit there nipple-deep in cooling water waiting for her mother, gazing blankly out the blurred window panes to the corner next to the dunny where the tank stood on its wooden stand, up to its ankles in grass even in summer, and if you tapped its wavy sides it would not give out a note for it was full to a level higher than you could reach, and its water was clear and swirly with wrigglers, baby mosquitoes that would not hurt you if you guzzled fast enough, and she sang out, 'Mu – um! I've fi – nished!' but her mother did not hear, for she was outside in the yard at the clothes-line putting a shirt to her mouth to see if it was dry enough to be unpegged and taken in for ironing.

A bike clattered against the front fence.

'Kath – leen!' shouted Flo.

Kathleen slipped out of the wash-house and halfway down the yard came upon a rotary clothes-line rusting away on an angle, a skivvy faded to sand-colour hanging by one wrist from its lowest quadrant, like a flag left tattered and forgotten after a rout. She took hold of the body of the shirt and, without think-ing, raised it to her lips in that gesture of mothers, breathed in its sweet dry weathered cotton soapy perfume; and at that moment saw a to-and-fro movement behind the wash-house window panes. It was Flo waving to her.

She dropped the skivvy and plunged on towards the back fence, beyond which cicadas raved endlessly in trees bordering the railway line. The faint voices of Flo and Frank, a little duet for piccolo and banjo, were still behind her in the back of the house. She stood at the end of the yard, almost off the property. A door banged somewhere else, water ran loudly into a metal container, fat hissed in another kitchen. The sky, without impurity, went up for miles.

It was the house of her childhood. She knew its impermanent, camp-like feeling. When front and back doors were open, the house would be no more than a tunnel of moving air. Under rain, its roof would thunder and its downpipes rustle as you turned in your sleep. Heat in winter would have to be generated inside and cunningly trapped, in summer repulsed by crafty arrangements, early in the morning, of curtains and blinds. Unlike stone or brick, its weatherboard walls would not absorb the essence of its inhabitants' existence: they were as insubstantial as Japanese screens: disappointment and anxiety, hope and contentment would pass through them with equal ease and rapidity. The house laid no claim to beauty. It was humble, and would mind its own business.

The last piece of furniture to be persuaded through the narrow front door was an oval table missing all four castors. They worried it into the kitchen, pulled up chairs and sat around it.

'Didn't this used to be our dining-room table back at Sutherland Street, Frank?' said Kathleen.

'Yep. Four dollars at the Anchorage, remember? That was when I cornered the market in cane chairs, too.'

'Come off it! We only had three.'

'Yes, but the price had doubled by the following Saturday.'

The fridge was already whirring behind the door. Jenny passed out cans of beer and sat down next to Frank. He smiled at her, but Kathleen's opening line had launched him on a tide of domestic memory and he was away.

The impromptu performances that Frank and Kathleen put on at kitchen tables and other public places were the crudest manifestation of the force-field that hummed between them: an infinity of tiny signals – warning, comfort, rebuke – flashed from one to the other ceaselessly and for the most part unconsciously. In its most highly coded form it passed unobserved in a general conversation; in public garb it called others to witness, embraced them as audience or participants in embroidered tales of a common past. It was hatred, regret, pity; it was respect and the fiercest loyalty. They could no more have turned it off than turned back time.

Jenny was left striving for grace, for a courteous arrangement of features while they recited, delighted in the ring of names without meaning for her. Frank put his arm round her bare shoulders, but she kept looking at her beer can and fiddling it round and round, letting her curly hair fall across her face to shield her. There was a short silence in the room, during which Flo could be heard splattering the hose against the side wall of the house. They had opened the door and taken down the blanket as the afternoon drew on and the sun shifted off the concrete outside the kitchen, but the heat was still intense.

'Give the concrete out here a bit of a sprinkle, love,' Frank shouted. Flo did not answer, but a great silvery rope of water flew past the open door and whacked against the bedroom window.

'Down a bit! Down! Don't wet all our stuff!'

The dog, saturated and hysterical, darted into the kitchen and ran about in a frenzy. At the same instant they heard the first signs of life from next door, a rat-tat-tat of voices in a language they did not understand.

'Is that Greek?' said Jenny.

'Might be.' Frank was absent-mindedly stroking her neck. His dreamy smile sharpened into a cackle of laughter. 'Hey Kath – remember Joe and Slavica?'

'Oh God.' She turned to Jenny. 'They were a Yugoslavian couple who lived next door to us when we were first married.'

'We got on fine with them for a while. They used to ask us in for dinner and force us to drink till we were falling off the chairs. We'd sing all night, it was great.'

'Yes, but poor Slavica,' said Kathleen. 'She didn't even score a place at the table. We'd arrive and there'd be three places set. Slavica would be out in the kitchen like a servant.'

'You mean – she actually *ate* out there?'

'Standing up. We used to have to drag her in and make her sit down.'

The two women exchanged their first straight look. Frank galloped onwards, heading for the drama of it.

'Anyway, Joe got crazier. He used to come home from work with half a dozen bottles and drink the lot all by himself in front of the TV.'

'About ten o'clock one night we heard him start to curse and smash things –'

'Their little boy nicked over our back fence to hide.'

'He couldn't speak English. He let me cuddle him.'

'And then we heard the back door crash, and Slavica was

locked out in the yard. She called out to us very softly, and we passed the kid back over the fence.'

'He didn't want to go back.'

'And straight away we heard Joe rush out into the yard and abuse her —'

'He *thumped* her!'

'And he dragged the kid inside and left her in the yard all night, she told us later. She slept in a corner near the chook pen.'

'Didn't you *do* anything?' said Jenny, horrified.

'*We* were scared of him, too!' said Frank. 'He was big! He was a maniac! We rang the police, but they didn't want to know about it — a domestic.'

Frank was on his feet now, his narrow eyes alight. 'But one night Kath was driving home and she caught this ghostly figure in the headlights. It was Slavica running across the road with no shoes on. He'd kicked her out in the street. So Kath brought her into our place and she slept on the couch.' He made two stabbing motions with his fore-finger towards the living room. 'That couch in there, the white one. She said he was crazy because he suspected her of having an affair with the lodger. How corny can you get?'

'The lodger was a classic. A real lounge lizard. He gambled all his money away and couldn't pay the rent. He had a pencil mous-tache, slicked-back hair, the lot.'

'Well, next morning we waited till Joe went to work and then sneaked out to see if the coast was clear. It was raining, and there were all the lodger's pathetic belongings chucked out on the footpath — a tattered suitcase, a pair of pointy two-tone shoes, a couple of lairy shirts —'

'Slavica dashed in and got the kid,' said Kathleen. 'I took them down to the People's Palace.'

'The Salvation Army?'

'We didn't know where to take them, and it wasn't safe at our place.'

'But wasn't there a Halfway House or something?'

'Not back then!' said Kathleen. 'This is Australia, mate!'

'Oh.'

Frank was poised to continue, bouncing on the balls of his feet. 'Anyway, Kath found her a room in a house in Northcote run by an older Yugoslavian who said she'd been through the same story, and on Saturday morning Kath drove Slavica home to pick up some kitchen things.'

'I pulled up out the front in this old VW we had at the time, and Slavica ran in and came out with an armful of pots and pans. She was too scared to go back for her clothes. Joe was on the front verandah with this terrible smile on his face, his arms were folded and he'd laugh – God it was awful, a sort of mad, bitter cackle – I said, Get in, Slavica, we have to get out of here. She jumps in, I'm trying to start the flaming car, the kid in the back with eyes as big as mill-wheels – and at the last minute Joe comes tearing out with a long piece of string and a saucepan, and ties it on the back bumper bar, like people do at weddings.'

'My God.'

'I get the car into gear, he's raving and shrieking and half the street's hanging over their front gates watching – and just as we take off he gives the back of the car an almighty kick, and away we go with the saucepan rattling behind us. Talk about an undignified retreat! I stopped about four blocks away and tore it off.'

Kathleen, out of breath, laughed nervously and glanced at Frank, who took up the tale. 'Well, so Slavica was OK, but from then on we got no rest at night. He'd drink himself off the map after work, then at ten o'clock he'd start this awful yelling.'

'Not yelling, exactly,' said Kathleen. 'Worse. More like loud whispering. Right under our bedroom window, which fortunately was on the first floor.'

'What did he say?'

She mimicked it slowly and dreadfully. ' "Australian — bitch — cunt. I make you trouble. I burn. I kill." And so on.'

There was a silence.

'Was I born then, Kath?' said Flo from the door. She was holding the dripping hose in her hand, and the dirt round her mouth made her look as if she were grinning.

'You were born all right,' said Kathleen. 'You slept in a basket, and we were so scared of him that we kept you in our room all night, just in case. Point the hose the other way.'

'In fact,' said Frank, 'we were so scared of him that I started drinking too.'

'Is *that* why you started?' said Jenny dryly.

'I kept a sort of wooden club thing on the shelf above the front door.'

'And you used to prowl around the house brandishing it and saying —'

' "*He's strong, but I'm clever!*" ' The ex-couple chorused it and burst into a roar of laughter.

'Why doesn't Jenny tell a story now?' said Flo, carefully directing the dribbling hose down her leg and off her ankle on to the concrete.

Faces relaxed, a softer laugh ran round the table, Jenny let her shoulder lean against Frank's and turned up her face towards Kathleen. They were, after all, people of good will.

Soon Frank and Flo wandered outside to inspect the site of the vegetable garden and the two women sat shyly at the table, touching the same boards with their bare soles, the same table-top with their forearms, but clumsy, a thousand miles from the moment of blessing which had united them that morning.

Jenny spoke. 'I was —'

'Frank's mother gave us those willow pattern plates,' gabbled Kathleen, without hearing her. 'You haven't met Shirley, have you? I'm glad you've got my old kitchen cupboard. It used to belong to my best friend when *she* was married. And those knives, see where they're engraved JF? Those are my grand-father's initials.'

Jenny, sick of it and too polite, fell back. What hope was there? Tongues were wagging stumps before such entanglement, such opaqueness of desire.

Out the back, in the long sun of late afternoon, Frank and Flo saw a bird hop extravagantly off the concrete, with a worm in its beak. They laughed, and with one accord folded their arms wing-like behind their backs and mimicked its irresistible self-satisfaction.

Flo in baby's bonnet and mosquito bites; Frank bearded like a Russian and wearing a sheepskin coat; Kathleen looking embarrassingly plain, her hair pulled back harshly off her fore-head, her mouth drooping ill-temperedly; Frank chest-deep in a swimming pool with Flo perched on his shoulder; Kathleen squinting suspiciously, walking away from the camera with a huffy turn of the shoulder, standing against bare asphalt in a silly mini-skirt. Then Frank and Kathleen grinning carelessly, open-faced and confident, audacious almost, shoulder to shoulder as if nothing would ever trouble the effortless significance of their being a couple.

Jenny shuffled the photos back into their box and knelt there among the cartons. Which was worse: her utter non-existence at that moment when they had been happy, or her twinge of pleasure at Kathleen's plainness? She was disgusted with herself. She slid out the painful photo again and indulged the pang, like a child shoving its tongue against a loose tooth. She turned the photo over and read *Perth February 1970* in a round slanting hand. In February 1970 she had had no meaning to them, neither flesh nor spirit, no voice, no form. She was nebulous. She wrestled with her anonymity, tried to force herself into premature, retrospective existence. Serenely there on the glossy sheet they laughed up at her, brown-faced. Their being flowed oblivious beyond her. It was as outrageous to her spirit as if she had tried to imagine life continuing after her own death.

'Snoopers never find out anything nice,' said Frank behind her.

She jumped and shoved the picture away as if it had burned her.

'I used to snoop on Kath's diary, years ago,' he said. 'Know what the worst thing about it was? I never even got a mention.' He laughed out loud, cheerfully. 'Look. I brought you something.'

He held out his closed hand to her. Inside it something whirred loudly. She shrank back, dreading a prank, but he shook his head and kept proffering it to her.

'No. Look. It's a cicada.'

'Will it bite?'

'No. They sing!'

He opened his hand cautiously and took hold of the insect with thumb and forefinger. It goggled at her.

'*La* cigale et *la* fourmi! Par Jean de la Fontaine!' chanted Frank.

He was charming her, and she laughed. 'Let it go, Frankie. It might have a tiny heart attack.'

Frank wandered off down the hall to the back door, holding the dry creature up to his face and murmuring to it. He said out loud, 'Take this message to the Queen of the Cicadas!' and opened his hand: away it soared into the blue evening. He had forgotten Jenny, imagining that she had gone back to her unpacking, but when he turned he saw that she had followed him softly into the kitchen and was watching him. He laughed uncertainly, caught out in his game, afraid of being thought foolish. He stood poised in the doorway waiting for judgement. She did not know if she could speak.

'I love you,' she whispered.

'Do you?' The light was behind him and she could not see his face. 'I hope so. I want you to.'

At the moment where day passed into night, the house and yard were still.

'You remind me of a lizard,' she said, blushing. 'You remind me of a lizard on a tree trunk.'

He laughed. 'Pommy. I bet you've never even seen a lizard, let alone one on a tree trunk.'

'I have so. I saw it on television.'

'Come here,' he said.

They sat on the step and she put her head on his knee.

'Let me smell your neck,' he said. 'Mmmm. Sweet as a nut. A nut-brown maiden.'

'Do you think we should make a meal?'

'Sooner or later. Hey. Kath and I were a bit hard to take today, weren't we. Talking about old times.'

'It was worse when you were outside and she formally surrendered the crockery and furniture to me. She reminded me of the mother of a bloke I used to live with in England. "Jen – nee! You *do* know how to defrost a fridge, don't you?" She was the closest I ever came to having a real Jewish mother-in-law. She was so generous I kept thinking, "Look out – there's something else going on here."'

They laughed.

'Well,' said Jenny, 'maybe I'll be able to talk with Kath one day, just the two of us.'

'What for? You'll find out what's wrong with me soon enough.'

'No. Not for that.' She sat up and pushed her back into his shoulder. There was still a faint slick of sweat between their skins. 'It's risky, isn't it, what we're doing.'

'Yes. Very.'

'And not very fashionable, either.'

'No. There are quite a few people around who wouldn't mind seeing me slip on a banana peel.'

'Not Kathleen.'

'No. I mean the opinion-makers. The anti-marriage lobby. Of which I remain one of the founding members, as if anyone needed another contradiction.' He let out his sharp, cackling laugh. 'I'm game, if you are.'

She thought she was probably game. She twisted herself round to smile at him. Her teeth were white and good, with a gap between the front two.

'Your teeth are like Terry Thomas's,' he said. 'I saw him once, walking along Exhibition Street. He was wearing a loud check suit. And he said to me, "Hel – lo! Would you laike to go for a raide in mai spawts car?" '

'He did *not!*'

'Actually it was Kath who saw him, not me. Is there any beer left?'

They stepped up into the kitchen and began rummaging for food.

They were waiting for Frank.

Flo's half of the children's room was quite bare, once they had put things in piles and packed up her belongings to go. She had few clothes but dozens of books. The room echoed. They stood by the stripped bed, not sure what to do next.

'Want to draw?' said Flo.

They settled down at the table with the box of Derwents between them and coloured away companionably, discussing patterns and the condition of the pencils.

'Gee I'll miss you,' said Kathleen. 'I'll miss that awful piercing voice going "Kath? Kath!" '

'And I'll miss you going "Psst – psst – hurry up!" ' said Flo.

They smiled at each other and got on with their work.

'Kathleen,' said Flo after a while. 'Have I got perfect teeth?'

'Who has.'

'Some people do.'

'Mmmm.'

'Kath. Is there anything . . . sort of . . . *special* about me?'

'Yes. You've got a wart on your elbow.'

'No! Really.'

'I don't know, Floss. Lots of things, probably.'

'Will you tell me the true answer, if I ask you a serious question?'

'Sure.'

'Am I adopted?'

'Not exactly. I found you under a cabbage.'

Flo drummed her feet, trying not to laugh. 'You said you'd be serious. Am I?'

'No, sweetheart.'

'How can I be sure?'

'*I'm* sure, for God's sake! I lugged you round inside me for nine months, and I had you in the Queen Victoria Hospital, with several witnesses present.'

'Did I hurt, coming out?'

'Yes . . . but it's not like ordinary pain. You got a bit stuck, after trying to come out for about twenty-six hours. The doctor had to help you out with a thing called forceps, like big tweezers.'

'Yow.' Flo had heard this story at least fifteen times before, and never tired of it. 'What did I look like? Was I cute?'

'It was hard to tell. You were a bit bloody.'

'*Bloody?*'

'There was blood on you.'

'*How come?*'

'Inside the uterus there's lots of spongy stuff partly made out of blood, which you lived in for nine months. And they had to make a little cut in the back of my cunt, to make it bigger and let you out.'

'*Poor Kath*,' said Flo luxuriously.

'Oh no — that part didn't hurt, because they gave me an injection. And then they cut the cord and washed you and wrapped you up in a cotton blanket and let me hold you.'

'Aaaah,' said Flo with her head on one side.

'And then I cried with happiness.'

'Aaaah.' Flo dropped her pencil and came round the table. She backed up to Kathleen and sat on her knee. 'I love that story. It's my favourite story.'

'I'm pretty keen on it too.'

'Guess what — Jenny might be going to have a baby.'

'What?'

'Hey — I can hear a car.' She sprang off her mother's knee and went racing out into the hall. Very carefully, Kathleen began to slide the pencils back into their right places.

Kathleen stood outside the front gate with a forgotten jumper in her hands. In the oblong back window of the diminishing car she saw a brown blob become white: Flo turning to look back. A child would be born to which Frank would be father, Flo half-sister, and Kathleen nothing at all. With a sharp gesture she shoved her hands down the little knitted sleeves.

Jenny and Frank hardly slept, for days, in their house. He lay with his arm under her neck and round her chest so she was folded neatly with her back against his wiry flank, her right cheek resting on his upper arm.

'Tell me, tell me,' he said.

Stumbling at first, finding a pace, she talked to him about her childhood. He asked and asked for details: what sorts of trees? what did you look like? what was on the table? and while she talked he saw again, richly, his own small town, Drought Street, the oval behind the house, the white tank on its stand beside the school, the dusty road, the dry bare leafy dirt of the track home.

'In our marsh there were snipe,' she said.

'We ate monkey nuts,' he replied.

'I sat under a tree, in a striped dress of silky material.'

'A boy had his mouth washed out with soap for swearing.'

'My father had the best garden in the village: people passing in buses admired it over the hedge.'

'I ran a sharp pencil down the big river systems on a plastic template of Australia.'

'My grandmother took me to London for tea. A long white curtain puffed in the wind on to our table: when it fell back there was jam and cream on it.'

'On the first day of school it was so hot that the door of the general store was shut because of the north wind and the dust. I went to buy an exercise book off Mrs Skinner and I sat on the doorstep waiting.'

'My father did his accounts at night, and light came through a hole in the wall up near the ceiling, into my room.'

'On the track between the ti-tree the air ticked, and there was a smell like pepper.'

'Were you happy?'

'I don't remember.'

'I don't remember.'

Sleep, what was it? Sometimes Flo stirred or cried out. Someone next door was awake, a white night; they heard soft footsteps, a door closing quietly, a restless person moving. There were hours, it seemed, of lying perfectly still, wide awake, flooded into stillness by the melting of their skins. Secretly, each of them dreamed that Flo was their common child, that they were lying close to each other in some inexpressible dark intimacy of bodies and of history.

After dinner Jenny set herself up with her exercise books at the kitchen table. Flo edged in with a red tartan shirt in her hand.

'Jenny. Is it you who mends my stuff now?'

'Me or Frank. I expect. What is it?'

'I ripped it on the equipment at school. I could ring up Kathleen,' said Flo.

'Um – no, don't do that. Go and hop into bed. You can read till nine o'clock.' How briskly should she speak? Her voice rang falsely in her ears.

'Kath always lets me read till about ten o'clock. Five to ten,' said Flo, speaking rapidly and keeping her eyes on the ground.

'*Flo.*'

'Well, she did! Sometimes!' Flo turned up her face defiantly and went very red; her gaze sheered somewhere to the right of Jenny's. Jenny blushed too.

'Give me the shirt, Flo.'

Flo shoved it at her, darted into her room and sprang into bed. She began to read immediately so as not to think of her failed manoeuvre. Jenny was not sure whether she should go in and kiss her goodnight. She dropped the shirt on to the kitchen table and started twisting a handful of her hair, flicking the springy ends between her fingers and letting her eyes blur. Frank would never notice the tear in the shirt. She could do it quickly now without saying anything, thus adding a drop to the subterranean reservoir of resentment that all women bear towards the men they live with, particularly the ones they love; or she could point it out to him in a *pleasant tone* and they could discuss it like *civilised people*. Why did they always have to be bloody trained? She stuck a piece of hair in the corner of her mouth. She heard the front door slam, and sat down quickly at the table. He came in whistling with eyes bright from the street.

'Frank. There's a problem.'

'What?' He stopped.

'There's a tear in your daughter's shirt.' She pointed at the red garment on the table.

'Oh!' He picked it up by its collar. 'Is it my job, then?'

'I think so.' She was solemn as a judge at the head of the table. 'Also, I've got some other work to do.'

'I can do buttons,' he said doubtfully, 'but I've never been too hot on actual tears.'

She said nothing, hooked her bare feet on the chair rung and fought the treacherous urge. He darted her a quick sideways glance.

'Well!' he said with a rush of his determined cheerfulness. 'I'll see what sort of a fist I can make of it.' He hurried out of the room and returned with an old tea-tin which disgorged a tangled mass of cotton, buttons, coins and drawing pins. Jenny turned back to her books and began to mark them, looking at him every now and then. Frank leaped to the task. He spread the patch over the rip, fidgeted it this way and that, clicked his tongue at his clumsy fingers.

'There! Got the bugger covered. Now for the pins. Heh heh. Just a matter of applying my university education, in the final analysis.'

He looked up. Pen poised, she was gazing at him in that state of voluptuous contemplation with which we watch others at work. With joy he sank the needle into the cloth.

'At the school I went to,' said Jenny in a little while, 'we had an hour of sewing every day. One person read out loud, and the others sewed. We even had to use thimbles.'

'Sounds like *Little Women*,' said Frank, negotiating a corner with his tongue between his teeth. He was sewing away quite competently now. 'Didn't kids muck around?'

'No. It was very peaceful, actually. We all wanted to be nuns for that hour.' She laughed.

'I'm glad it was only an hour a day, then. Otherwise we might never have met. Well – aren't you going to read to me?'

'What shall I read?'

'I'm not fussy.' He was round the corner and on to the home stretch.

She opened a book at random and read, '*Her Anxiety*. Earth in beauty dressed / Awaits returning spring / All true love must die / Alter at the best / Into some lesser thing / Prove that I lie.'

Frank, paying no attention, was holding out the small garment to show her. He was as pleased as Punch.

~

In her room, for days, Kathleen found traces of Flo everywhere: half-filled exercise books, a slice of cantaloupe skin with teeth marks along its edges, a skipping rope with wooden handles. She picked up her night-dress and Flo's little flowery one dropped out of its folds.

She wandered out to the kitchen and sat at the table cutting her fingernails. She sat sideways on her chair looking out the windows at the very clear air. A gum tree over the fence flashed its metallic leaf-backs in the wind. A bird flew across the yard in patchy sunshine, its wings gathered as it coasted on air; it disappeared behind the bamboo which was being jostled by the wind. Kathleen's eyes filled with tears.

'I feel unstable,' she said. 'Not *bad* – just –' She made her flat hand roll like a boat. The other woman at the table looked up over her glasses and nodded, saying nothing.

She worked, throwing away page after page and plugging on, sharpening the pencil every five minutes. The floor around her was sprinkled with shavings. At three thirty she knew it was no good. For four years she had been programmed to stop thinking at school home-time, and will was powerless against this habit. She got under the eiderdown with the most boring book she could find and tried to read herself into a doze so she could get through the moment when Flo would not push open the door and stand there grinning with her school-bag askew on her back. In a little while she got up and sat at the table again and kept forcing.

She went for a walk up to the top of the street to the old people's settlement. There were yellow leaves everywhere. She leaned against a gate-post, dull, feeling nothing in particular. An old woman came out her back door to empty a rubbish bin and saw her standing there.

'Hullo dear,' she called. She had a silver perm and knobby black shoes and an apron which lifted a little in the wind.

'Hullo.'

The woman moved closer. 'Anything wrong?'

'Not really. I'm missing my little girl.'

'Oh.' The old woman knew what she was talking about. Kathleen wanted to ask her the imponderables: what do you understand that I don't? Does it get easier or harder? If she had dared she would have asked something simpler: will you invite me into your kitchen and let me watch you make a cup of tea?

'Do you do any gardening, dear?'

'No.'

'I've found that a great help,' said the old lady. 'My gardens have got me through two nervous breakdowns.'

The old woman was small and wrinkled, and her large ear-lobes had become floppy with the weight of the gold rings that hung from them. Her skin looked waxy, and on her cheek-bones were several enormous blackheads. Her dark blue crêpe dress, unlike Kathleen's, had probably been owned by the same person ever since it was bought. She was not looking at Kath-leen, perhaps so as to spare her from social duty, but simply stood beside her, following her gaze to the turbulence of coloured clouds behind the trees in their fullness, the upper sky veiled with pale grey, the parsley trembling in thin rows, the worn-out tea towels showing their warp and woof on the line. In a little while she heaved a sigh, and gave Kathleen a quick look from her bright eyes. 'Well. Back to work, I s'pose. It'll be teatime d'rectly. Ta ta!'

'Bye,' said Kathleen, and walked on.

Flo's voice sounded very high-pitched and childish on the phone.

'How's everything over there, Flo?'

'Oh, great! We have roast pork, and Jenny makes these *great* noodles.'

'Are you getting to school OK?'

'Well . . .' She gave an adventurous giggle. 'Frank said not to *say* but most mornings I'm late, because Frank and Jenny don't wake up as early as you do.'

What mean satisfaction she derived from this. 'I bet you drag the chain, do you?'

'A bit.'

A pause fell. Flo was making crunching noises.

'What are you eating?'

'A carrot.'

Kathleen felt shy and importunate. She had no small talk.

'Kath? Know what I wish?'

'What.'

'I wish we could all live together.'

'Who?'

'You, and me, and Jenny, and Frank.'

'Hmm. I'm afraid that's almost certainly never going to happen.'

'But *why*?'

'There's not a room for me over there, for a start.'

'You could sleep in my room, with me.'

'I don't think so. I don't think I'd be very . . . welcome.'

'I *wish* you could!' cried Flo urgently.

'I could come and live in the broom cupboard, and every time Jenny or Frank opened it I'd pop out and sing that song that goes, "Ullo! I'm a reject / Does one arm 'ang down longer?"'

'Don't talk like that, Kath.' Flo's voice was heavy with disapproval. 'You're trying to make me not like Jenny.'

'Excuse me,' said Kathleen. 'What a nasty thing to say. And not even historically correct.'

'Never mind. I didn't think you really meant it. When are you coming to visit? So you and I can cook, and have the meal ready to surprise Frank and Jenny?'

'I could come on Tuesday. You go and ask Frank now if that's all right.'

Flo muffled the phone with her hand. Tuesday was all right. There was nothing else to say so they hung up.

Before Tuesday could come, the old man died. He stepped out of the bath and his heart simply stopped.

The ground they stood on was untended, unlawned, littered with fallen gum leaves and unruly twigs. The trees gave no sign of autumn in the bush cemetery, but it was in the light, its doubtful angle, its mildness on the skin. Shirley's eye rolled on that strange warm day but she gave Flo a thick bunch of roses to hold in her two fists beside the grave. Beside the grave in order stood: Shirley, trembling and smiling into space like a vague hostess; Frank, frowning and clearing his throat and standing with his heels together and daylight between his knees; Flo, wishing the coffin lid might open a crack so she could see a dead body; Kathleen, folding herself, putting herself away now, decorous as a spectre; Jenny, almost wife but fighting it, singed from behind by the inquisitiveness of Frank's cousins and (to Frank, who saw how her brown smooth skin made her lips seem pinker) suddenly resembling Flo, as all people we love at moments resemble each other.

At the house people laughed more than they had thought they would, or ought to. Against a clock stood a very old photograph of Jack as a boy in a striped suit with short pants and lace-up boots; his face bore the good-natured, musing expression he had never lost.

'It's a beautiful photo, Mrs Maxwell,' said Jenny.

'I'll bet he hated that suit!' cried Shirley with the shrill laugh of someone right on the edge.

'Poor Papa,' agonised Flo, who wanted there to be more tragedy in the occasion. 'He was a good man, wasn't he, Nanna. He led a good life.'

'He certainly did, sweetheart. Oh, he was the kindest of men.'

Shirley seized Flo in her skinny arms and they hugged eagerly, their eyes full of tears. 'The first time he asked me out,' she went on in a conspiratorial tone, glancing around her as she spoke, 'we drove out into the country. There we sat among the bush irises – flags, we used to call them – white and blue – and Jack asked me if I wanted a drink!' Her laugh cracked in the middle. 'He must've thought I drank! Well, I did, I suppose – and he said he had a bottle of beer in the car. I thought, Oh good, this is nice. And he got the bottle out of the car but he didn't have an opener because *he* didn't drink! So he knocked the top off the bottle against a tree. And I've often thought, later, we could've died. One piece of broken glass.'

Over by the window, behind the couch on which the three women and the child were sitting, one of the cousins was hissing to Frank, 'Who's the new one, Frankie? Got any legal advice?'

Frank tossed his empty glass from palm to palm, smiling furiously and whistling through his teeth. 'We're all *reasonable people*, Brian,' he replied in a light, tense voice.

'Ah yeah . . . that's what they all say.' The cousin laughed loosely and looked away. He planted his feet wide apart and tightened his thighs like a footballer. 'You'll end up paying a packet in alimony, mate,' he predicted comfortably, draining his glass.

Shirley, Jenny and Kathleen walked down to the beach in their funeral clothes. Their heels sank and they sat down in the sand, Shirley in the middle, and watched the water, the oceanward rushing of the tide, the tiny waves crisping helplessly towards the leftover line of dried seaweed that ran crookedly all along the water's edge. The younger women, set about the older one like a pair of brackets, did not know each other, did not know what they were protecting the mother-in-law from, but felt their positions to be proper.

'What am I going to do now?' asked Shirley.

Nobody answered. The sea ran by. The day seemed very long to them all.

———

Flo dangled maddeningly over into the front seat and whistled and called to the dog. 'Come! Come! Come in the back with me!'

'Don't treat the dog like a toy, Flo,' said Jenny, irritated. 'She wants to stay in the front with me.'

'It's all right for you two!' burst out Flo, flinging herself back into her seat. 'There's plenty of love in the front seat, but none in the back.'

'Are you jealous?' said Frank. He winked at her over his shoulder.

'*I am not jealous,*' cried Flo in a fury. She slouched in her corner and stared out at the trees. 'I haven't got anything to *do.*'

'We told you if you came away with us there'd be no whingeing,' said Frank.

'I am *not whingeing.*'

'Look out the window, then.'

'There's nothing to *see.*'

Jenny glanced back over her shoulder and caught an odd cast to Flo's scowling face: a snubbing of nose, a stretching of eyes, a rising of top lip. She looked sinister. The word passed instantly and was forgotten.

The wind tore steadily past the house, racing off the sea and over the sandhills and up the gravelly drive and through the scraggy hedge. All day the house groaned and shook in the wind, which relented a little at nightfall, leaving pinkish clouds looped neatly above the drab green humps of ti-tree. They were all sunburned in such a way that the sides of their fingers looked silvery-white, as if they were underwater.

On the clifftop the wind still blustered fitfully. On the ocean beach they made a fire, and Frank and Flo ran half a mile beside the cold white and green surf, still clear to Jenny's eyes no matter how far they ran, so empty was the air. She wrapped herself in a sleeping bag and waited for stars, roasting her face and chilling her back; before it was dark the others came panting back to her through the soft sand. The first planet swung for them, burned pink and green like a prism, spinning idly in the firmament.

The wind blew itself right out in the dark, and next morning sun was flooding quietly into the beach house when they awoke.

Five in the afternoon was the appointed hour, but when Kathleen crossed the creaking verandah and knocked at the front door, the house was silent. No dog barked. She tried the side gate, but it was locked from the inside and had no hand-hole by which she might have climbed it and gone down to the back door. It was quite shocking to her to be locked out of the house of people she knew. She was aggrieved and hurt and cross. It was hot. She sat bad-temperedly on the verandah and swore to herself. Surely they couldn't have forgotten her.

After ten minutes she got up and tried the front window. It slid up obediently. Jubilant, she crawled in, closed it behind her and ran down to the kitchen where she filled the kettle and set about making herself a drink and a snack, the ingredients for which she found in abundance in the fridge. She opened the back door and sat contentedly on the step, chewing and swallowing.

Half an hour later a key rattled in the front door and they were upon her: the dog yapping, Flo leaping on her back with cries of welcome, Frank looking preoccupied, Jenny frozen-faced and very sharp-footed. At the sight of Jenny, whose eyes avoided hers after the first obligatory greeting, Kathleen realised that something was badly wrong. She scrambled to her feet, noticing that her shirt was covered with crumbs. Jenny opened the fridge and began to forage in the lower shelves.

'There's a fresh pot of tea made,' said Kathleen, performing a dance of appeasement behind Jenny's back. Flo was dragging at her, and she followed into the girl's bedroom.

'What will we make for dinner?' Flo was saying, sitting up importantly at her table. 'We could have a tomato salad, and ice-cream.'

Kathleen knew that everything she said would be overheard in the kitchen, where the silence was being broken only by the movement of feet and chair legs on the wooden floor. She felt miserable, superfluous, and would have disappeared as impolitely as she had come had it not been for oblivious Flo with her pencil and paper, waiting eagerly for her reply.

'Hold your horses, Flo,' she said quietly. 'I don't think we're going to be able to make the dinner after all.'

'But why?'

'Because . . .' She heard Jenny's heels go out of the kitchen in the other direction. 'Because maybe Jenny or Frank would rather do the cooking here. I'm a guest – guests aren't supposed to act as if they owned the place.'

Flo could see her plans slipping out of her grasp again, sliding away for reasons that would be carefully explained to her in words of one syllable, adding to the load of childish trouble not of her making that she must lug about with her. She let out the eternal cry of childhood, prelude to resignation: 'It's not fair!'

At that moment Frank stepped into the room. He was smiling awkwardly. 'Kath – look, don't get excited – I want to talk to you for a minute. There's a crisis on here.'

Kathleen's face was burning with resentment. She knew what was coming, and stuck out her chin to cop it.

'Now listen –' He was unconsciously making calming movements with his flat hands. 'Jenny's feeling extremely . . . *uncomfortable* that you're here.'

'But I was invited!' she cried. She sat there on the edge of the bed, spine erect, hands under thighs, feet dangling.

'Yes, yes, I know. But – you didn't – *wait*. You –'

'I know. I came in the window. Well, what am I going to do now? I came to see Flo. That's why I *came*.' Although this was true, she had a nasty feeling that it was not the whole story. She saw that Frank was floundering out of his depth, did not know what was the right thing to do, hated carrying the bad news between the two women who were too cowardly to face each other. She was full of disgust for herself, and pity for all of them.

'We're going to have to talk about a few things,' said Frank. 'Can you meet me and Flo at the school in the morning? Eight thirty?'

'OK.' She got off the bed.

'You're not going *home*, are you, Kath?' Flo too was in over her head.

'Let's go out in the back yard, Flo, just you and me,' said Kathleen desperately. 'And we'll think what to do.'

They shuffled outside past Frank, and squatted against the fence at the very bottom of the yard. The little dog nosed about them, and Flo scratched its woolly coat and squinted up at her mother, waiting for enlightenment.

'I made a mistake, Floss. I shouldn't have climbed in the window when there was nobody home.'

'But there's nothing wrong with climbing in someone's window. We used to always get in the window at Sutherland Street, if we forgot the key, and so did everyone else.' There was a moral in here somewhere, Flo knew, and she wrestled to get at it.

'Yes, but Jenny's never lived like us, in big open houses where groups of people live and anyone can come in and out in the daytime and the night. She doesn't agree with that sort of way of living. Most people would be mad if they invited someone to dinner and came home and found them already making themselves a snack in the kitchen.' She felt quite giddy and disoriented, trying to remember ordinary social formalities. 'Also,' she went on, forcing herself, 'there are sometimes funny feelings between an old wife and a new one.'

'Jenny isn't Frank's wife. You are.'

'That's true in one way. But Jenny lives with Frank now, and I don't any more, so it's sort of the same, really.'

The little girl squeezed the struggling dog in her arms. 'I don't like this,' she said stubbornly. 'I asked you to come and visit, and nothing's working out like I want it. It's not fair. I don't think grown-ups should fight when children want to have a visitor.'

The back door banged and Jenny, who had taken off her shoes, was coming down the yard towards them with a glass of wine in her hand. She crouched down three feet in front of Kathleen and offered her the glass. The two women looked each other steadily in the eyes, and their mouths curved in identical grimaces of embarrassment which they could neither conceal nor turn into smiles. It was the best they could manage.

Kathleen leaned against the school gate from eight thirty till nine o'clock when the siren cleared the yard of children and only a few papers blew about in the dust. She was wondering whether it was time to panic when she spotted Frank and Flo, walking hand in hand and uncharacteristically slowly, coming round the building from the other side. She rushed up to them.

'Where were you! I've been waiting for half an hour.'

'We said at the *gate*,' said Flo, her face straining against tears. 'We've been at the *gate*, we got there at half past and you weren't *there*.'

'Oh Floss! We were at different gates.' She dropped to her haunches, but the child stood stiffly holding her father's hand, unapproachable.

Frank was darting agitated looks about him. 'Let's get out of here. We could go to the espresso bar.'

Kathleen took Flo's other hand and they crossed the road and sat at the window table of the café, Flo in the middle, one parent at each end. Kathleen began.

'I know I shouldn't have climbed in the window. I'm not in the habit of climbing in windows.' Her voice sounded huffy, and Frank let out an impatient laugh.

'Windows, windows! What we should really be talking about is getting this bloody divorce.'

'*Divorce?*' Flo burst out sobbing. 'On no! I don't *want* you to get a divorce!'

'Come and sit on my knee, Floss,' said Kathleen wretchedly.

'No!' She fought them both off and sobbed in the exact middle of her side of the table, refusing to touch either of them, battling for honour.

'But Flo!' said Frank. 'Divorce is no different from how me and Kath have already been living for years!'

'I don't care! Oh, I want us *all* to live together, in the same house. Can't we all go back to Sutherland Street? I *know* it would work! Oh, can't we?'

She wept bitterly, in floods of grief: she did not touch her face, for she was sitting on her hands so that neither of her parents might seize one and sway her into partiality. The tears, unwiped, splashed off her cheeks and on to the table. The Italian waiter behind the espresso machine turned his face away in distress, his hands still clinging to the upright levers.

'It's just – it's just *life*, Flo,' stammered Frank, the tears standing in his eyes. 'We have to make the best we can of it.'

They sat helplessly at the table, survivors of an attempt at a family, while the little girl wept aloud for the three of them, for things that had gone wrong before she was born and when she was only a baby, for the hard truth which they had thought to escape by running parallel with it instead of tackling it head on.

———

By nightfall there was nowhere else to go.

Jenny opened the door in a night-dress, red pencil in hand,

curly hair pinned back off her forehead. With her shoes off she was the same height as Kathleen.

'Oh. I was working. Frank's out.'

'It was to see you. Excuse me for coming without being invited.'

'Oh Kathleen. I'm not a monster, you know.'

'Neither am I.'

'Come in.' She stood aside. Flo was curled up on the floor. The book had slipped sideways from her hand, and her mouth was open. A little trail of dribble had wet the cushion. The women sat down on two hard chairs.

'I came because, because things are a bit much for me, right now. I'm a mess, in fact.'

'You, a mess?'

'Do I have to break plates?'

'No. I shall try to see for myself.'

'All this is very painful for me. I can't get used to living without Flo.'

'I thought Frank said you wanted to work.'

'I *do*. But it's so long now that I've had to make my life fit around her – it doesn't make sense without her.' She twisted her face, trying to make a joke. 'I'm bored. I don't get any laughs.'

'I have the impression that you judge the whole tenor of your life by whether or not you're laughing enough.'

'You could say that.'

'I don't know if that's a good criterion.'

'Know any better ones?'

'Why is it so important, laughing?'

'Look, I've got this sign stuck on my bedroom wall. It's by

Cocteau. It says, *What would become of me without laughter? It purges me of my disgust.*'

'What disgusts you?'

'Oh, my whole life, sometimes. Things I've done. Things I haven't done. My big mouth. My tone of voice. The gap between theory and practice. The fact that I can't stand to read the paper.'

They looked down uncomfortably.

'Sometimes the only person I can stand is Floss here. For years I've thought I'd be glad to see the back of her. Now I don't know what to do with myself. I roam around. Try to work. Think about falling in love. I can't help thinking of all the horrible things I've done to Flo and Frank.'

'What things?'

There was a long pause.

'I've never told anyone about this.'

'You don't have to.'

'Once, a long time ago, I ran away with another bloke. I was crazy about him. I didn't care about anything else. I felt as if I'd just been born.' She blushed and pushed her clasped hands between her thighs. 'One night, walking along the street, I told him I loved him more than I loved Flo.' She laughed. 'I even thought it was true. Pathetic, isn't it.'

'No.'

'Anyway. I wanted to go away with him. Frank, Frank cried, he got drunk and broke all the windows upstairs, kicked them in. I was so scared I fainted and fell down the stairs. It was the middle of the night. One of the girls downstairs picked me up and dusted me off. Frank was out in the street by that time chucking empty milk bottles around. She said, Frank's being ridiculous.

But he wasn't.' She breathed out sharply through her nose. 'I went away with the other bloke. Flo was only about two, at the time. One morning I came back, on my way to work. I walked in the front door and in the lounge room I saw Flo sitting up in front of the television. She must have just woken up. She was all blurry and confused. She didn't see me. She was sitting in an armchair with her feet sticking out, all by herself in the room. It was *Sesame Street*. And Frank came into the room with a bowl of Corn Flakes for her breakfast. He had this look – his face was – I can't talk about this.' Kathleen put her face on her arms on the back of the chair, lifted it up again, and went on. 'He was trying to get ready for work and feed her and do everything. He was *running*.'

Neither of them spoke.

'I suppose it doesn't sound like much,' said Kathleen.

'Go on. I'm listening.'

'Of course, I was absolutely miserable with this other bloke. I used to type his fucking essays for him. Jesus. He had this way of looking at my clothes. I couldn't do anything right. He told me I was like a bull in the china shop. Of his heart.' Again she tried to laugh. 'I don't know why I'm telling *you* this. There are some things I'll never forgive myself for. That morning I was talking about. Never. I don't know if you . . .'

Jenny leaned forward and spoke very clearly. 'Listen, Kathleen. I'm nuts about Frank. *Nuts* about him.'

Flo, who had turned over on to her back with her knees splayed like a frog, drew herself together with a start and sat up.

'Oh! I dreamed! Hullo Kath! Did I go to sleep? When are we going?'

'Going where?' said Jenny.

'Down to the park to play on the swings, like you said at teatime.'

'That was hours ago, Floss. It's nearly ten o'clock. And I'm only in my nightie.'

'What if we all went down,' said Kathleen. 'Just for quarter of an hour.'

'I only said that because I thought mothers were supposed to,' said Jenny. 'If I put a belt on, it will look like a dress.'

Outside the gate Flo galloped ahead with the dog. The two women came along slowly in the almost-dark. The sky, which was indigo, had withdrawn to the heights as if to make room for a sliver of moon, dark dusky yellow, rocked on its back like a cradle.

'Kathleen? I don't feel disgusted. Kath? When I met Frank, I knew he liked me, because he kept his body turned towards me all the time, wherever I was in the room. We were in a room with some other people. I didn't know him.'

'Frank and I had a dog, once,' said Kathleen. 'But he got a disease. He was going to die. I carried him to the vet wrapped up in an old blue coat. I put him on the table and they were going to give him an injection. We went walking in the Botanic Gardens, after we left him. We were both crying. Then we saw a bird hop in a bush.'

'I dreamed about you and me becoming friends. I've been in Australia two years now, and I haven't got a good girlfriend.'

'But I was unbearable, the day we moved the furniture, and climbing in the window.'

'You were always barging on to my territory.'

In the park, beside the concrete wall of the football ground, the women sat down close together on the shaven grass. There was a strong scent of gums, and earth.

'Are you having a baby? Flo told me you might be.'

'I thought I was pregnant, but not yet. I'm going to. I want to.'

Flo and the dog were tearing about in the thickening darkness, over by the swings and slides. They saw her leap up and grab the high end of the see-saw.

'Hey! Come over here! Jenny? Kath? Come over!' She was beckoning.

They got up and picked their way barefoot off the grass and across the lumpy gravel.

'It's a game,' said Flo. 'You two get on.'

They hesitated, glanced at each other and away again. Flo was nodding and smiling and raising her eyebrows, one hand holding the ridged wooden plank horizontal. They separated and walked away from each other, one to each end. They swung their legs over and placed themselves gingerly, easing their weight this way and that on the meandering board.

'Let go, Floss.'

The child stepped back. Jenny, who was nearer the ground, gave a firm shove with one foot to send the plank into motion. It responded. It rose without haste, sweetly, to the level, steadied, and stopped.

They hung in the dark, airily balancing, motionless.

Other people's children

Madigan was a great lump of a fellow with yellow eyes, who bunched his thick fingers together in front of him when he entered a room, and walked with legs that seemed too heavy for the top of his body. His eyes bulged behind warped plastic-rimmed spectacles; his eyelashes pressed against the lenses. Kin to Madigan were auto-didacts who transcribed reams from reference books in public libraries, sniffing and murmuring and grinding their teeth, wearing huge black vinyl gloves as they pushed the biro.

He lived with some hippies in a cavernous, ivy-covered house south of the Yarra. His room was a converted shed that sagged against the back fence. Madigan hid in there. Sometimes he would grit his teeth and go inside for a couple of hours to the kitchen where the others sat round the table under the hanging light bulb rolling joints and drinking Formosan tea, talking about massage and colonic irrigation, agreeing with each other, complaining soothingly in soft voices. He secretly despised the way their voices went up at the end of each sentence, as if they waited for approval before continuing. When they talked, when they sighed 'Ama-a-azing!' he felt like a fox living in a chicken coop. But he needed them, for company, for human presence near him in the chilly house, and to buy food and cook it; and because without them he wouldn't have had a room at all and would have had to offer himself to some soft-hearted feminist who would give him a roof and a side of the bed in exchange for his helplessness and the occasional surprise of his cutting humour.

They were kind people, though; vague, and years younger than he was. They patronised him and deferred to him and discussed him behind his back.

'Madigan's pretty well unemployable?' they reassured each other. 'He'll probably never get his shit together?'

The women worked at odd things, tolerated the three children of one of them, cooked huge, ill-assorted vegetarian meals, and listened respectfully to the opinions of the men, all of whom were musicians of one stripe or another. If the men wanted meat, they had to go round the corner to the Greek's.

Every second Tuesday Madigan dressed himself neatly, combed his colourless hair, and strolled to the dole office. When he got his cheque, he handed over to Myra his share of the rent and food money as faithfully as a good husband on pay day.

Madigan sat outside the State Library at lunchtime, watching for normal life. His anxious nature, knotted as a mallee root with scruple and doubt, yearned towards a grey-haired man of fifty on a bench who bent earnestly over the hand of a woman, clasped her fingers with earnestness, leaned forward over their clasped fingers; all the while seagulls jostled rudely round their ankles, keeping up a chorus of ill-tempered cries and squawks. The woman stared straight ahead in her yellow cardigan, her mouth closed over false teeth, her feet in cheap sandals balancing stiffly on their heels, her toes pointing upwards at a forty-five degree angle. Was the man saying 'Come back to me'? What had the man done, that she would not look at him on this public bench? Madigan turned away discreetly.

He mooned round milk bar windows looking for hand-lettered signs. He dreamed up small agonies over *Wanted: one kitten preferably fluffy please call at number 5 Park Street* and *Mrs Day wanted: canary whistler will give good home*. He passed the pubs in Gertrude Street and heard them, through the open door, singing *Cuando cuando cuando cuando*.

In the Eye Hospital Out-patients, the hooks of other people's conversations lodged themselves amongst his nerves.

'Cor,' croaked a woman opposite him, noticing a mistake in her knitting. 'Right in the flamin' neck.'

'What's that woman?' said her friend.

'Vietnamese?'

'Japanese.'

'Could be Malay.'

'No. Can't be Malay. She hasn't got the hair. Malays have got curly hair.'

'See that girl over there who needed an interpreter? Well I think she's from Italy. 'Cause she's got Italy written on her bag.'

Madigan was from a town on the south coast of Queensland

and he wished he could go back, he longed to go back, but he had to stay now, might as well, because he had lugged all his stuff down and was thinking of unpacking it, and because Margaret had finally been driven off the edge by his dithering, and because he was a professional, and he was going to work, though nobody down here had heard of him yet.

The last time he went up north to visit his parents, he hitched, carrying the harmonicas in an old cotton pillowcase. A fat, stupid couple picked him up. They stopped for petrol somewhere in the middle of a starry night. Madigan, thinking to be a guest, stepped out into the thick warm air, crossed to the roadhouse and bought three cans of drink. He went to the window of the car and offered a can to the man, who gave him a suspicious stare and shook his head. Madigan put the cans in his bag and returned to the back seat. The fat, stupid man screwed himself round to speak over the seat.

'Funny thing happened,' said the man. 'Bloke just come up to me window and asked me if I wanted a tin of drink.'

Madigan's mother was squat, bow-legged, fearful, dim. She believed that everything wrong in the world was due to the influence of some cult or other. His father worked for the local council. Madigan borrowed twenty dollars from his mother one morning after his father had left for work, and wandered up to the main street, carrying his harps and wondering if he had the stamina to busk. He went into an espresso bar to think about it and sat down at the table next to the tinted window, with the twenty dollars in his pocket. As the cappuccino popped its creamy bubbles pleasantly before him, a rhythmic movement low down on the footpath outside the window caught his eye.

He glanced down and saw his father crawl past on his hands and knees. He was smoothing out fresh concrete.

Drinking coffee made Madigan nervous, anyway.

He was back in Melbourne for the next dole day. They gave him a job, which he accepted willingly, washing dishes in a restaurant. He told the others at home that he was pearl-diving, giving it a weary professional ring. They laughed fondly. Myra imagined him standing at the sink in his dream, up to the elbows in greasy water, the shrill thunder of the restaurant kitchen battering round his ears. He wouldn't last three days in a job where you had to work fast. She leaned across the table to give his arm an affectionate press. He saw the hand coming, the fingers stained green by cheap copper rings, and jerked back out of her reach with a look of panic, then tried to transform his reaction into a suave movement towards the teapot. He thought Myra was probably on the look-out for a man in her life, a responsible chap, someone to look after the kids. Or maybe she even wanted to fuck him. Oh God. He bolted out the back and into his shed and under the eiderdown. His hands were all wrinkly and ridged from the hot water. Maybe he should buy some rubber gloves. He could think about that tomorrow.

———

In another kitchen four or five miles up the Punt Road bus route, a match scratched and the little flower of gas blossomed. It was six thirty in the morning. No one would have been fool enough to address Scotty before the first coffee had coursed in her bloodstream. She stood sternly at the stove in her loose pyjamas and waited for the kettle. She rolled out the griller and saw mouse-marks in the chop fat; on the bench ants thronged round an open jam jar. She clicked her tongue, lowered her imposing brow, and massacred the ants with a hot, wrung-out dishcloth. Then she seized a red texta and a sheet of butcher paper from the table drawer and wrote in a smooth teacher's script:

I wish people who were 'into' midnight 'munchies'
would develop an ant *and* mouse *'consciousness'.*

She sticky-taped the notice to the glass of the back door so that everyone would see it on their way out to the lavatory, and stepped out on to the bricks. There was a small bony moon very high up in a clear sky. The sun itself was not yet visible but was casting a pink light on to the underside of leaves. She planted her feet in the grass, rolled the pyjama pants up to her knees, and began to bend and stretch. She was a straight-backed, dark-haired girl with firm flesh on her and plenty of it. Her feet were high-arched, her ankles hollow. She thought she was too fat, but she was flexible as she bent this way and that, her movements severely graceful. Her round face, which fell habitually into a disgruntled expression, smoothed itself with concentration. Sweat began to gleam on her broad forehead.

Someone came out the door behind her. Scotty stopped, doubled over with her legs wide apart and her head hanging between her knees. It was Ruth, with a guilty expression and a white china potty in one hand, heading for the lavatory. She hurried past.

Water rushed in the wooden stall and she emerged.

'I know I should walk out to the dunny at night, like you do, Scotty,' she called, risking it.

'Oh, don't defer to me, Ruth. I make myself sick. I'm such a fucking puritan.' Scotty straightened up, flushing. 'I hate those house-meetings. They're just fights with somebody taking notes.'

Ruth came across the grass, her smooth, Irish-jawed face confused with sleep and troublesome thoughts, her thatch of reddish hair standing on end. They looked at each other for a moment, without expression.

'I'm sorry, Ruth,' said Scotty.

'So am I. I get that wild with you I don't know what I'm saying.'

'I hate it when we fight. Specially about the kids.'

'So do I,' said Ruth. 'I heard you go out the door last night. I started wondering if there's something about me that makes people go out in a rage and slam the door. Jim was always doing it.'

'I was miserable.'

'Miserable? I thought you were just mad, and sick of me.'

'Of course I was miserable! Look at my tongue — it's covered in ulcers! Jesus, Ruth — what do you think I *am*?'

Ruth looked down at her bony feet in the grass. 'Sometimes I wonder what you're feelin'. Or even *if* you're feelin'. You're always so rational. You've got the gift of the gab. I can't keep up.'

'I've been *trained* to have the gift of the gab,' said Scotty, 'and that's what you liked about me at the beginning. You thought because I could talk I must know more than you. And so you wanted me to tell you what to do — be your mother, a bit. And now you see I'm just ordinary — got feet of clay — you sort of can't forgive me.'

In Ruth's eyes shone a beam of dogged loyalty to old friendship. 'I got nothin' against clay,' she said. 'It's what our plates are made of – what we eat off every day.'

Scotty laughed. 'You should write songs.'

The sky rippled with smooth bars of pink and gold. People were stirring inside the house. A door slammed, a child's voice was raised in anger, or mirth.

'The lines aren't drawn yet, are they, Scotty?'

'I hope not.'

'What if we blow it?'

'I dunno.'

'Here, Scott. Give us a hug.'

They were dissolved. Ruth was tall enough for Scotty's head to lie on her shoulder. Such hopes they had had! It was a moment of grace, beyond will or reason, and might never be repeated. They let go.

'Where'd you go?' said Ruth.

'Oh, I ended up at Alex's gig,' said Scotty. She recommenced the exercises and her voice came and went among her limbs, punctuated with sharp expulsions of breath. 'I met this guy.'

'Oo, hoo! Did you go home with him?'

'*Hang* on! I met this guy, who Alex knew, and we had a drink, and after the gig we drove him home, and he was weird.'

'You didn't go home with him then?'

'I didn't get out of the car. Thank goodness.'

'Aaaah.' Ruth was disappointed. She was a one-man woman, and when she went out it was to visit friends in familiar houses, or to talk politics in pubs, or to meetings, not to dance and drink too much whisky and stagger home with strangers.

'I'm not a hooer, you know.' Scotty stood up at last, her cheeks shining and damp. 'I'm not a band moll.'

'I didn't mean *that*,' said Ruth hastily.

A raffish grey dog bounded into the kitchen, followed by a girl in a pink dressing-gown. The dressing-gown cord was tied in a neat bow round her portly little torso. She had thousands of freckles and the pale, blinking countenance of the bespectacled. Her large feet were shod in pink slippers with pom poms; and she had tried to flatten the waves of her hair with series of bobby-pins crossed at strategic points. Something matronly about her, at eight years old, pierced grown-ups' hearts, but her eyes were watchful with the plain child's pride. She went straight to a chair and sat holding the dog's head between her knees and picking the crusty sleep out of the corners of its eyes.

'Good morning, Laurel,' said Scotty.

Laurel looked up. 'Polly's silly,' she remarked. 'You give her a b-a-l-l and she chews it to bits. You give her a b-o-n-e and she just buries it.'

'What's a b-o-n?' said a thick voice at the door.

'Bone, Wally, you idiot,' cried Laurel in sudden rage.

'Don't call your brother an idiot,' said Ruth.

'Yeah. Shut your face, fatty,' said the boy. 'Come on, Poll.' He clapped his hands in front of the dog and it began to leap off the ground as high as his shoulder. At the height of each leap it seemed to hang for a second in mid-air, ears flying, legs dangling, like a jelly-fish in deep water. It emitted sharp yips.

'Get the dog outside,' said Scotty, in the level voice of someone accustomed to being obeyed.

Wally looked up resentfully, but he had felt the flat of Scotty's hand before when his mother was not about, so he ushered the dog out and slammed the screen door behind it.

Whenever Ruth washed herself with Johnson's baby soap, she remembered when Laurel was a baby. They lived in a tall, dark terrace house with a yard full of useless sheds, behind which, when they moved in, she had found stuffed dozens of blood-soaked sanitary pads, dry and crackly and blackened. In the kitchen were two old troughs. She brought hot water in from the bathroom in a plastic bucket. The floor was of brick. Once the dog had surprised a rat among the paper bags in the cupboard under the sink: the dog bristled and roared, Ruth screamed, the rat thrashed about among the bags (they could only hear it) and shot suddenly into view through a crack, up the wall and out through a gap in the timber round an ill-fitted pipe.

With the Johnson's baby soap she ran her slippery hands gently over Laurel's solid body; the water in the plastic tub lapped sweetly, her hands slid and met no resistance; the baby's head lolled in her palm, her hands moved effortlessly at the child's flesh.

Jim was never there, except for dinner when he would cheerfully ram food into his large mouth, kiss her and dash off out the front door. He came home at four in the morning smelling of beer and sometimes perfume. He had crowds of friends at university. He told her he had set himself up at a table in the union building behind a sign saying *Any questions answered 20 cents*. He sat eagerly, cross-legged, talking, talking, talking. He even stole from her her own stories: once she had woken in the night, feeling something was wrong; she ran into the baby's room and found Laurel sitting up in the cot, clinging to the bars and staring at the overturned radiator which had already burned its way right through the matting and one layer of lino – flames were starting to lick up round it. Bullshit, he said with a laugh. There weren't any flames! And I got there first. There was only a lot of smoke and you panicked. He never told her she was stupid in so many words, but she felt he thought so, and she became stupid, frightened of words of more than one syllable, thick-thoughted, easily confused by anyone with a ready tongue.

They never went anywhere, never went out into the country looking for firewood or mushrooms, never went drinking together in pubs, for he was always in company and none of them liked her. Once he shat his pants from laughing. He swaggered in bow-legged, still grinning, and dropped the stained jeans and underpants on the bathroom floor for her to wash them. Once, when she cried about her life, stuck there in the house with Laurel and the dog, he had taken her with him to the pub. She slid herself behind the long table, and the talking faces swung towards her for a second, summed her up and – worse than dis-missed – smiled blankly. She knew one of the women from her own cut-short university days. The woman nodded to her. Ruth drank in silence, holding the baby on her lap, as the voices shrieked around her. Some of them were doing a play and seemed to be conversing in lines from the script, which made no sense to her but set the others roaring. One of the men, in a pause in the talk, raised his glass and stared at Ruth and said in a loud, hearty voice, 'I see some of us have brought their wives with them tonight. Let's hear it for 'em' – and farted with his pursed lips. No one said anything. Then Jim sprang to his feet and seized the man's collar in mock rage.

'Come on – let's step outside,' he said. The man laughed and they exchanged joking cuffs to the ear, then sank back into their places, honour satisfied. The volume of sound swelled again and Ruth was forgotten. She sat with flaming cheeks, and blushed and blushed until the backs of her eyes sang.

When Jim woke up, it was too late. She didn't love him any more. She didn't love anyone. She had the other child and breast-fed him in a dream; she weaned him and washed the milk off the front of her clothes and lost two stone and sat all day in one of the downstairs rooms reading pamphlets. Now it was her turn to be out all the time. She was mean, he said. She said, 'If you're not here to take the kids on the dot of ten tomorrow you won't be seeing them again.' He danced about in a kind of hysterical sulking. She stood unmoved by the door. He saw she meant it. He was there on the dot of ten, but she wasn't. She was round the corner at a friend's place, waiting for ten fifteen before she came home. If there was one thing Ruth understood, it was the power of absence. Away he went in the old Holden with Wally asleep in his basket on the back seat and Laurel waving out the side window. When they weren't there she didn't know what to do with herself. She wandered round the city in darned clothes that hung off her, staring at herself in windows. In a big shop full of silky dresses she heard a man singing in a high-pitched, yearning voice, which entered unobstructed into her hollow head,

'Helpless, helpless, help-less . . .'

She didn't think about the words, but tears ran down her face.

She told Jim to go. He cried, 'But I still love you. What am I going to do with the love?'

It was a word that neither of them had yet learned the meaning of.

She was quite calm inside, watching him writhe flat on his face on the bed. Hadn't he ever cried before? His sobs were like vomiting, it was so hard for him to bring up grief.

'It's too late, Jimmy,' she said. 'I'm sorry I'm hurting you, but it's too late.'

'You're not keeping *both* the kids, are you? *Oh*,' he wept. 'Let me take Wally.' He sat up and wiped his eyes. Wrinkles she had never noticed before fanned out from his eyes, cut like brackets round his mouth. 'I promise, I promise I'll look after him. I couldn't bear it if you kept them both.'

Laurel was the one she had been lost in, lost with. While Ruth had roamed the empty rooms, unreachable, Laurel had plodded after her; once, while Ruth raged to herself, Laurel had punched herself in the head with a dull rhythm. They were bound together in that history. Jim took Wally, who was still not much more than a baby, and they went away over to the west in a big red ambulance he bought with his university pay. He would live, somehow. He didn't live anywhere, with the kid. They slept in the red ambulance, picked up other travellers, camped on beaches under squares of flapping canvas, were dirty and bitten and, finally, happy.

Once Wally walked barefoot along a hot, terrible beach north of Perth, trailing after Jim who was looking for a creek. Wally had forgotten his hat and his father hadn't noticed. That night the little boy was in fits, spewing; his body was racked, his eyes

rolled back in his head and Jim was seized with mortal fear, less
of death than of the dumb face of Ruth. He threw the child into
the ambulance and sped to the nearest town, his heart beating
and stinging in the backs of his hands, glancing sideways at the
flat creature beside him on the front seat. The doctor took one
look at the ragged man, wild-haired and burnt black, and said to
the nurse, 'Give the kid gamma globulin. It could be hep.'

It wasn't. Wally had a history now: 'Once I walked a hundred
miles in bare feet,' he would relate long after to his mother, who
had many times imagined him ill, wrapped sweating in rags on
some stranger's kitchen floor while his father ranted at the table
behind him; 'and I got heat inzaustion and they gave me three
needles in my bum.' Wally was thin and dirty with little muscles
like string and pearly down in elegant whorls along his backbone.

Meanwhile, Ruth knew that if she were not to take out her
guilt on Laurel she must find company, people to pick loose the
threads that tied the burden to her. She dragged the kid in her
glasses to the big house she had heard talk of. She walked in the
back gate and saw a woman, a solid brown-skinned big-muscled
girl in a flowery dress, bending over the vegetable garden yank-
ing up weeds. They had seen each other at one of the meetings,
perhaps. The dark woman looked at Ruth.

'Help,' said Ruth. 'Can I come and live here? Have you got
a . . .'

The dark woman stood there with her feet balancing squarely
on two great blocks of bluestone, an uprooted weed dangling
from her left hand.

'Come inside and we'll have a cup of tea,' said Scotty.

Logically, Jim got busted for dope. There was no one with the money to bail him out, and they would have taken Wally away from him had Ruth not got on the train and come for the kid. He was a wild little boy. He had never eaten off a plate in his life: he knew that the most reliable joy to be had was a packet of hot chips against the chest. He was burnt to a crust, and his foot-soles were thickly calloused. His blue eyes penetrated. He had reverence for nothing, as his father had taught him. His response to discipline was to show his bum. But when his mother came to get him, a strange thing happened. They took one look at each other and fell in love. He would sit on her lap while she smoked, and slip his grubby little hand under her shirt and flip her breasts this way and that, his face a dream of contentment. He would stroke her face with his hard paw, sing to her in his croaky voice: 'Woothy, my Woo,' he sang, swooning on her bosom.

Laurel was too big to be cuddled and too proud to ask for it. She stood about wretchedly in doorways. Scotty tried. Scotty loved her, there was no doubt, in the tentative way in which we love other people's children, fearful of rejection, even of mockery, loving without rights, thanklessly. Scotty's love was awkward, and intellectual. Laurel would bring to Scotty the teacher her difficult questions.

'Scotty, is Robinson Crusoe a myth or a legend?'

'Scotty, got any idea how to draw a hamster?'

'Scotty, do you believe in changelings?'

'In what?' said Scotty, who was reading the paper.

'Changelings. When a baby is born and they swap you for another baby and nobody knows.'

'I don't think they make mistakes like that in modern hospitals.'

Laurel made a quick movement of impatience. 'Not in *hospitals*,' she said. 'Fairies come and take you away. And put an ugly fairy baby or goblin instead.'

'Better not let your mother hear you talking about fairies,' said Scotty casually. She looked up at the girl's round face on the other side of the table.

'I was reading this book,' pursued Laurel, 'and it said, Once there was a mother and goblins had stolen her child out of the cradle. In its place they laid a changeling with a thick head and staring eyes who did nothing but eat and drink.'

Scotty laughed, then saw her false step. Laurel's face was stricken. 'Are you worried about it or something?'

'It sounds like *me*.'

'Oh Lol.'

'It *does*. A thick head and staring eyes.'

'I love the way you look.'

'You're only saying that to make me feel better.' Laurel's gaze was relentless.

'I once heard another story,' said Scotty carefully, dredging it up from memory, 'about a man who had two children. I think he was an Arab. One child was handsome and charming and popular, and the other was plain and clever. And another man came to visit, and while he was there he saw the two children and noticed how different they looked, and he asked the father, "Which of your two children do you find more beautiful?" thinking he would have to say "The elder". But the father thought a while, and finally he said, "He whom the heart loves is ever the most beautiful".'

Laurel said nothing, looking steadily into Scotty's eyes, but

Scotty could see the flexing of iris as thoughts passed through her solemn head.

'I also eat too much,' said Laurel at last.

'You are *not fat.*'

'My *face* is fat.'

'It's puppy fat.'

'Yours wasn't.'

'I still eat too much,' said Scotty, whose empty plate was encrusted with muesli.

'Why do some people eat a lot and stay thin, like Wally, and other people eat the same amount and get fat, like you and me?'

'I eat more when I'm miserable,' said Scotty. 'Anyway we are *not* fat.'

'Wally said I was fat. He said it at school.'

'Wally is a shit.'

'No he isn't.' Laurel went red. 'He just doesn't want me to be his sister when there are other kids around.'

'Well, isn't that shitty?'

'He probably can't help it,' said Laurel. 'He's not proud of me.'

'*I* am.'

'But you're not in my *family.*'

'I can't change that,' said Scotty, and looked away.

'No matter how much you love me,' Laurel bored on doggedly, 'you can never be my real mother.'

'I know,' said Scotty.

Breakfast fiddled with, lunches in brown paper bags, the two children straggled off across the park, Laurel casting looks over her shoulder to where Ruth and Scotty stood at the gate watching, still in their nighties. The Italian boys from over the back came jostling round the corner and absorbed Wally into their group, leaving Laurel to drift on alone. The red ribbon on her top knot shone at them until she turned the corner past the milk bar and disappeared. The women sat down on the stone step.

'Remember when we had only Lol?' said Scotty. 'And I taught her to read, and we did the comic books, and she used to come and sleep with me?'

Ruth gave a brief laugh. 'No good thinking about that now.'

'But isn't it weird how Wally's changed everything. Lol used to be a happy kid. Now she moons round after you all the time. It's so important for Wal to be tough – he won't have a bar of her. I think it's sad.'

Ruth scrambled over to her open bedroom window and reached in for the packet of Drum on the table. The effort of forging thought into speech made her short of breath. Whenever she spoke of the troubles of her life, her accent broadened and she clipped her words off short. Her face came forward bearing the mirthless grin of resignation, neck awaited the yoke. 'Wal's lived most of his life on a beach,' she said. 'He's not used to girls, or havin' a sister.'

There was a silence. The school siren went for nine o'clock, and the sunny street was empty. What a fine pair they looked to the boiler-suited gardener turning on the hoses in the little park across the road: one short, one tall, sitting carelessly on their front step dressed in cotton, forearms resting on knees, feet bare on the smooth brown-and-yellow-tiled path. The man waved good morning to them and they saluted back.

'Another hot one?' he sang out, bending down with his spanner to the hidden taps.

'Looks like it,' they chorused.

The man moved across the park, setting free one after another dense mists of spray shot through with faint rainbows, mauve, yellow and green. Through the floating cloud slashed the postman on his bike and held out a fan of letters to them at the gate.

'Whacko! Pension day,' said Ruth. She hung the cigarette from her bottom lip and ripped open the narrow envelope, scanning the cheque for deductions.

'Money for nothing,' joked Scotty, drowsy in the sun and late for work. 'I should have had a kid after all. Given up teaching.'

'You call that nothin'?' snapped Ruth. 'Bein' a mother in this society?'

Scotty did not like being corrected. 'Hmmmm,' she said in her wry voice. 'Just the same. It would have been different for me, if I'd had a kid now. It's a different kind of decision these days from what it was before the women's movement, when you had yours. If you had kids before the penny dropped, you're in the clear, aren't you. Proved yourself both ways.'

'What do you mean?' said Ruth suspiciously. She drew hard on her cigarette, baring her teeth and hissing in the smoke.

'Just a thought.' They paused, in a slight tension. 'Anyway,' Scotty went on, 'what about the idea we talked about last night, before we started fighting? Why don't we collectivise the house money?'

Ruth extended one long leg off the side of the path and poked about in the dirt with her toes. 'I dunno.'

'I think we ought to. I feel ashamed that I never realised before how much more I get than you.'

Ruth fired up at once. 'Ashamed? I don't *want* you to feel ashamed!'

'Well I do! I feel ashamed! Aren't I allowed? Is feeling ashamed counter-revolutionary or something?'

Ruth clamped her hand to her jaw and removed the cigarette. All the life went out of her voice as she said, staring out across the sunny road, 'I'm sick 'n' tired of havin' my hand out to the rest of you.'

'Tsk. Don't look at it like that.'

'It's a bit hard not to.'

'Why don't you get a job?'

'Nah,' said Ruth. 'I have to *be* here when the kids get home. The hours are no good. They can't come home to an empty house.'

'We could organise it,' said Scotty. 'That's all it needs – organisation.'

'Nah. When it comes to the crunch, the only people you can trust with your kids are other people with kids.' Ruth flicked away her butt, stood up and stretched, thrusting her chin forward as if presenting her face to the elements, and showing the thick sandy hair under her arms. In that position she looked like a ship's figure-head.

'Life's a struggle,' she recited, letting out a sharp sigh and dropping her arms.

'All shall be well / And all manner of things shall be well,' quoted Scotty, to sustain the philosophic moment and to conceal the sting of hurt from Ruth's last remark. But Ruth darted an irritated look over her shoulder as she opened the wire door and said, 'I hate that sort of religious shit.'

The cease-fire was over.

⌁

Alex believed the whole of western civilisation to have been justified by the invention of the saxophone. He played rhythm guitar in a rock and roll band. He was small and neatly made, with long, hard fingernails, pink Jewish lips, and bags under his eyes which, when he was very tired, tinted themselves a delicate shade of lilac. He drank too much coffee, too black, and read and practised all night because he couldn't sleep: his blood was nervous and alert. Sometimes, past midnight, Ruth would hear him beating away softly with one foot in time with his playing. He liked there to be a guitar in the room, even if it was only leaning against a wall. In the kitchen, if he wasn't playing, he was shelling peas into a saucepan, sharpening the knives, or gouging away with a rag at the tin of dubbin to polish his old brown shoes. He was never bored. Wally, who broke things and ran outside, made Alex quiet and wary, but Laurel he took into the room where the piano was and taught her to pick out a bass line with one finger.

'Frequency means . . . often-ness,' he would explain to her.

'Often-ness,' repeated the little girl thoughtfully.

'Why don't you teach her *Botany Bay*?' said Ruth, sticking her head round the door.

'I don't know it.'

'You've been culturally imperialised.'

'I know,' he said. 'I bet I have more fun than you do.'

After Ruth had stamped out of the house meeting and banged her bedroom door behind her, Scotty and Alex had been left at the table staring at their hands. The stillness of the dry yard crept in through the back door. A cricket scraped in the mint round the gully trap.

'She can't stand you, Scotty, can she,' said Alex.

Scotty, who had turned very red and stiff during the argument, forced out a high, difficult laugh. 'We used to be like *that*,' she said, holding up one hand with two fingers tightly crossed. 'She'd put food in my mouth so I didn't have to get sticky fingers.'

'What happened?' Alex tilted back his chair, reached behind him for the acoustic guitar, and began to pick at it.

'She started hating me.'

'But these things are never one-sided. There must have been a reason.'

'You tell me and we'll both know,' said Scotty with a stubborn, ill-tempered grimace. 'She doesn't like my tone of voice, she says.' Scotty disliked analysis; she wanted things to be just so, and for everyone to agree with her without wasting time.

'Is it something to do with this house? You found it. You got the upstairs room.'

'*She* could have had the upstairs room if she'd wanted it.'

'You run a pretty trim ship, Scotty. Signs on the wall and so on.'

'Anyone can put a sign on the wall.'

'Yes, but they don't, do they?'

'There's nothing to *stop* them.'

'Don't do your block.' His hand shivered to make vibrato.

Scotty twisted her mouth, half closed her eyes and drummed her fingers on the table in a pantomime of irritation. 'You know something?' she said. 'When the other big house got sold, Ruth cried for a week. I said to her, "Ruth, you *must stop crying*. We have to *do* something." And she'd say, "Oh, don't talk about it. I can't even bear to think about it." She was *hopeless*. She was talking about squatting and being a stay-put widow, and that sort of bullshit. Everyone but her and me had full-time jobs, so I had to go out looking by myself. And I couldn't find anything big enough for the whole seven of us, so we had to split up. And you know what she said to me in one of these fights we're always having now? She said, "I'll never forgive you for the way you were at the end of Rowe Street. You were so cold and efficient — you didn't seem to care. And for me it was the end of the world." I was stunned.'

'What *was* good about that house?' said Alex. He kept on picking away, his face open and attentive.

'Oh . . . for Ruth it was special, you know. She dragged herself out of that mess with Jim, and he took off with Wally. She fixed up her room, and planted her vegetables, and started up a new women's group. It was a big household. Rosters. Telling life stories. Signs! *When was the last time you saw a man round here with a broom in his hand? Revolution begins in the kitchen.* The kids were everybody's kids — Laurel and Sarah's daughter used to call each other "my sister". We thought everything we'd theorised about was coming true. Breaking down old structures, as we used to go round saying in those days.'

'It almost sounds old-fashioned,' said Alex.

She laughed awkwardly and turned her face away from him. 'It was a home, I guess,' she said. 'We were always laughing and singing and drawing pictures of ourselves. We loved each other. We couldn't wait to get home at night.'

In the quiet, the steel strings quivered and the guitar belly resounded warmly.

'I'm jealous,' said Alex.

'Don't worry. You pay later,' said Scotty bitterly. 'Look at us now.'

~T~

Madigan accepted the cigarette because he thought that was what people probably did. He puffed amateurishly at it, roving round the room and expelling the smoke in a flat slice over his chin. He felt blunderous, as if he were occupying too much of the available space. The conversation was not successful: his voice seemed to him too loud, or too tentative, or too emphatic. In desperation he darted his myopic eyes round the kitchen in search of a new tack.

'What's in that bottle?' he bellowed. 'Gin?'

'It's Scotty's,' said Alex. 'She calls it a mood improver. Pretty dangerous one for someone who's in a bad mood as often as she is.'

Madigan gave a hoot of nervous laughter.

'Sit down,' said Alex. 'Make yourself at home.'

'I will in a minute,' said Madigan. He sat on the very edge of a chair, lumped his legs under the table, and rested his large fore-arms in Sphinx position across the cloth. His cigarette was at last sufficiently consumed for an attempt to be made at graceful disposal. He stabbed it into the ashtray and withdrew in relief, brushing one hand against the other. He had butted it imperfectly, however, and it continued to smoulder, releasing a thin grey column of smoke to the ceiling, betraying his discomfiture as surely as cooking smoke betrays the outlaw to his pursuer. Alex reached out one hand and crushed the butt against the china.

Madigan edged over to the record player and squatted down beside the pile of records. 'Hey! Billie Holiday! Whose is this?'

'Scotty's,' said Alex.

'They all belong to all of us,' said Ruth at the same moment. She was crouching down to sort out rotten oranges from good in a wooden crate under the kitchen bench.

'No – I mean who bought it,' said Madigan.

'Nobody in particular,' insisted Ruth. 'They're everyone's.'

Madigan, with his back turned, rolled his eyes and clenched his teeth. He squatted there on his large haunches for ten minutes, working slowly through the stack, examining the covers, making a light hum of attention to the task.

'I hear you're making a record,' he said at last.

'Yeah, that's right,' said Alex.

'Who's producing it?'

'Bloke called Everett Walker.'

Madigan let out a snorting laugh. He stood up and drifted back to the table where Alex had picked up a biro and was doing the *Age* crossword. 'Do you *like* Everett Walker?'

Alex looked up. 'Do you mean personally, or his work?'

'Any way you like,' said Madigan hastily, confused.

'He's all right, I suppose. We haven't got much choice, at this stage of the game.'

Madigan pointed his lips and put the fingers of one hand on the tabletop, keeping the other safely in his jacket pocket.

'I don't – there's something – he talks too much,' he said. 'He's got one of those mellow voices that seem to grow on you, like moss.'

Alex laughed.

Madigan drew a deep breath. 'Don't you think he's a bit – sort of –'

'What?' said Alex, interested.

'I can't stand him!' burst out Madigan. 'He gets hold of bands like yours, that have a rough, human sound, and he makes them sound like a hospital trolley!'

'Wow! You're a master of simile!' said Alex, in genuine admiration.

Madigan looked at him sharply. 'Do not patronise me, my handsome young fellow,' he said with a peculiar frowning smile, 'or I shall lash you with my clever, cutting tongue.'

Alex started to laugh, and gestured with his hands palms upwards.

'But how can you *work* with a bloke like Everett Walker?' cried Madigan in another spasm of agitation. 'I mean – how do you prevent him from riding rough-shod over you?'

'Oh, you just give him the steely smile and the cold shoulder,' said Alex airily. He picked up his guitar and held it across his lap.

'You old softie,' said Ruth, who had been taking in this male pantomime. 'You never gave anyone the cold shoulder in your life.' She laughed.

'I did so,' said Alex.

'Who?'

'Oh, I dunno. Someone.'

'Everett Walker actually came to our house once,' said Madigan.

'Into your actual *house*?' said Ruth.

'And sat at our actual table, in our actual kitchen, and drank an actual cup of tea.'

'Gosh,' said Ruth.

'I thought you couldn't stand him,' said Alex.

'Oh, he didn't come to see *me*,' said Madigan. 'He was talking to Tony about some deal or other. Anyway I tipped the sugar bowl over his head.'

'You *what*?' Alex stared.

'Oh, he started bandying about words like Zen and off the wall and laid-back and talking about Jah, and everyone was listening to him so idolatrously that as usual I was at the end of my tether. So I grabbed the sugar bowl and tipped it over his head and ran out of the house.' His eyes quivered behind the lenses, like fish in a tank.

Ruth and Alex laughed with new respect. They had gathered closer to Madigan where he sat and were gazing at him with such shameless curiosity that he edged further away and fidgeted the salt and pepper about on the table. Alex ran off a few absent-minded riffs. 'Well,' he said, with a turned-down smile. 'That answers the question I was going to ask you, I guess.'

'Which one was that?'

'That's why I asked you over, as a matter of fact. I thought maybe you'd like a bit of – you know – session work.'

'Who, me?' said Madigan. 'You mean, on your record?'

'Yeah.'

Madigan uttered an incomprehensible sound somewhere between a laugh and a shriek. 'That'll teach me to keep my smart cracks to myself,' he mumbled. He flung up his arms and clasped his hands behind his head, squeezing his eyes shut and opening his big mouth very wide. As they stared, his face became quite peaceful. The grimace relaxed, a smile curved the lips, the eyes opened as if he had had a refreshing sleep.

'Want to have a blow?' he said, colouring up. Ruth went back to the sink and put the plug in.

'OK. Have you got your harps?'

Madigan leaned down behind him and produced the pillow-case from its hiding place round the corner in the hallway. 'What'll we play?' he said. 'Down at my place they always want to play *Rose of San Antone*.'

'Don't know that one,' said Alex.

'Play *Love Hurts*,' said Ruth.

'That's American imperialism, isn't it?' said Alex.

'Yeah. But it does, doesn't it. Hurt,' said Ruth.

Alex laughed. 'I wouldn't know. Would you?' He looked at Madigan who was burrowing among the metal.

'Love's just romance, isn't it?' said Madigan uncertainly. 'Hollywood, and that?' He chose a harmonica from the jumble and ran it back and forth between his thrust-out lips. 'We don't have to play a song,' he said, sipping at the instrument. 'Let's just mess around. You could do hand-claps, Ruth.'

'Go on! Do *Love Hurts*!' cried Ruth. She flung the dishcloth into the sink. 'You know how it goes, Alex! Like on the record!'

Alex nodded, planted his feet against the table edge and chopped out a deliberate rhythm for her, which Madigan, inspired by Ruth's exuberance, punctuated with elegant flourishes of breath.

'*I know it isn't true / I know it isn't true / Love is just a lie / Meant to make you blue*,' sang Ruth. She was smiling with half-closed eyes; she twirled around on the red concrete floor, clapping her hands and swinging her long limbs with a lively vigour and cheerfulness. Was this the same Ruth? thought Alex; the one who wore the harness of gloom? She was moving like a queen, light-footed, open-handed, full of pleasure and grace.

'*Love hurts / Love hurts / Love hurts . . .*' Ruth's voice faded out, just like the record, and the three of them laughed and looked away from each other in that mixture of embarrassment and almost tearful joy that comes after wariness has been shed.

'That was nice!' said Madigan. 'It's like those country pubs you go to up the backblocks of New South Wales – they always have a blond woman with big tits and a microphone, and she sings like this' – he threw back his head and bawled – '*LA International Airport! / Where the big jet engines roar!*'

Before Ruth could react, the door opened and into the room stepped Scotty in her crêpe-soled shoes, home from work and not in the mood. She stumped silently across the room heading for the loaf of bread.

Madigan looked up, blinking. 'Hullo!' he said brightly. 'You must be Scotty. I've heard about you!'

'Have you indeed,' said Scotty, hacking away at the bread.

Madigan stared at her in puzzlement. No one spoke, but Alex

saw, with a quickening of the heart, the blade of light that flashed from Ruth's eyes into Scotty's heedless back.

'We were just having a blow,' said Madigan. 'Want to join in? Sing a bit?'

'You don't give up, do you,' said Scotty, keeping her eyes on what she was doing. She slammed the fridge door shut with her knee and tramped out of the room with a bulging sandwich in her fist.

'Yikes!' said Madigan. 'Did I say something wrong?'

'The boss comes home,' said Ruth.

'I thought you didn't have bosses in these sorts of houses,' said Madigan.

There was no answer. Madigan could not read their expressions, and chattered on regardless. 'Still, I suppose it must be hard to cater for everyone's tastes, in a commune. One person's under the shower singing *Old Father Thames* and all the others like new wave.' He laughed, looking from face to face.

'It'd take too long to explain,' said Alex.

'Here come the kids,' said Ruth.

———

'Know what there is on the way to school?' said Wally, getting reluctantly into the bath.

'No. What,' said Scotty.

'A big drawing on a wall. Of a great big dick.'

'Oh.'

'With balls 'n' everythink.'

'And sperm coming out?'

'No. Just a little hole at the end. But guess what. I come past there with Laurel, and guess what. I said, Look at that great big dick. And *she* said, That's not a dick, that's a *thumb*. Even with that *knob* on it 'n' everythink!' He laughed, screwing up his face and hugging himself with glee.

'Oh well,' said Scotty. 'Here. Wash your face.' She wrung out the washer and held it out to him.

'Has it been on your cunt?' said Wally with his slow, insolent smile, not taking his hands out of the water.

'No,' she said.

'Do you know my dad?' said Wally.

'No. I've never met him.'

'He's *great*.'

'Is he?' She shook the washer, waiting for him to take it.

'He wouldn't like you,' said Wally.

'How do you know?'

'Oh, he just wouldn't.'

Scotty looked at him meditatively. She took one step forward and stood over him, the washer steaming in her hand. He seized it hastily, but his rapid wipe did not erase a knowingness which made Scotty glance behind her to the empty doorway.

'Get a move on, will you?' she said. 'I have to go and pick up Laurel from tap. You can stay here. But listen to me. You are *not* to go down to the creek, do you hear me?'

'Aw. Why not?'

'Because you're clean, that's why. And because the creek's polluted.'

'Big fat bum,' whispered Wally into the washer.

'What did you say?'

'Nothin'.' He stood up, gripped the side of the bath with both hands, and clambered out on to the mat. He shook himself like a dog, his little penis flipping up and down.

'Where's Ruth?' he said.

'At the laundromat. She'll be home any minute.'

'*Good*,' said Wally daringly. He took the towel from her hand and buried his grinning face in it.

To the watery strains of *On the Good Ship Lollipop* and the tremendous reverberating thunder of forty little girls in metal shoes, Scotty climbed the stairs of the warehouse and lined up with the mothers in a damp corridor. The music stopped, the big door opened at the end of the hall, and out streamed a river of children, their heads at breast-height to the waiting women; they flowed steadily along through the narrow run, shoving like sheep in a race. Scotty searched for Laurel, but all the faces pointed with determination in the same direction, not looking up, the elbows working like pistons. There was Laurel's big red ribbon.

'Lol!' Scotty put out a hand and tapped the child's shoulder. 'How was it?'

Laurel's face was trying hard not to collapse. 'Awful,' she said. She inserted herself between Scotty and the wall and sheltered there from the surging bodies. Scotty took her hand and looked down at her pink-framed glasses, her large feet in the shoes with their jauntily tied ribbons.

'What do you mean, awful?'

'I couldn't do it.'

'But it was only your first time.'

'They went too fast for me. They put me in the back row and

told me to copy the girls in front, and I couldn't see the teacher, and the kids next to me knew how to do it and they *laughed* at me.' She buried her face in Scotty's belly.

The crowd was dispersing rapidly. 'Bloody shits,' said Scotty. She was ready to kill. With her arms round Laurel she threw up her head and stared round for the teacher. Out came a little old woman in tap shoes, clacketing along the floorboards. She saw Laurel and Scotty and a look of concern changed her face under the thick creamy make-up.

'My dear!' she cried, clicketing and clacketing up to them. 'Oh, you're crying! I *thought* you weren't having much fun. Is this your mother, darling?'

'Yes – I mean no,' sobbed Laurel, taking her face off Scotty's trousers and trying to wipe her eyes.

'But don't worry about crying!' said the teacher, tremulously dabbing at Laurel's cheeks with her hanky. 'It's good that you cried! It shows how much you care about doing it well!' Her legs were hard with muscle, but quivering with age and fatigue. Her eyebrows were plucked to the thinnest line and lipstick had leaked into the wrinkles round her mouth. Beside her Scotty was a giant in her flat runners. Laurel's freckled cheeks were flushed, her glasses awry, but she had stopped crying; her curiosity at seeing the teacher at such close quarters distracted her from her humiliation.

Scotty said to the teacher, 'We'll be all right. We'll probably be back next week.'

Laurel squeezed her fingers imploringly.

'If we feel up to it,' added Scotty.

The teacher nodded and watched them anxiously as they went, padding and clacketing, along the empty hall.

Laurel heaved a sigh. 'I thought it was going to be fun,' she said.

'Aren't you supposed to take off the shoes?' said Scotty, as Laurel clattered down the stairs and out on to the footpath, holding her hand.

'I don't even care,' said Laurel. 'I hope nobody thinks I'm ever coming back here. Because I'm not.' She tore off the shoes and flung them into the back of the car.

'Adversity is very character-forming, I'm told,' said Scotty. They got into the front seat.

'What's adversity?' said Laurel.

'Hard times. Hard life.' Scotty turned on the ignition.

'Can we go and get a souvlaki?' said Laurel.

'You'll get fat, like me, if you don't look out.'

'Oh, why do you even *worry* about it?'

~~~

On a balmy, greyish afternoon when autumn breezes buffeted, Madigan dozed the hours away under the eiderdown. Each time he woke he was surprised to find he had been asleep: the angle of the light had shifted along his flecked wall, the household noises had ebbed into silence; into his mouth ran the sweet taste of fresh saliva. After school when the stampeding feet woke him for good, he stumbled down to the park with two of Myra's boys and played kick-to-kick with them till teatime. Their cries were mysterious to Madigan, who winced and shied away from their rough bodies because of his spectacles. 'Jezza!' they shrieked, plunging after the tight leather; 'Thommo!' with a dying fall.

'You boys better get home,' said Madigan at last. 'Myra will be wondering where you are.'

He was always surprised when they obeyed him; he did not realise that they liked him because he addressed them in exactly the same tone of seriousness that he used in talking to grown-ups, instead of acting out for other adults present the little play called 'Talking to Children'. They pelted off ahead of him, and he saw them ripple over the zebra crossing and vanish round the corner.

When they had gone the air was utterly still. Swallows passed like a handful of flung pebbles. Darkness swarmed under the thick-leafed trees. It was as if darkness and not light were the force. The orange gravel of the intersecting paths was lurid with the struggle of darkness against light. The water of the lake was not water but some thick, gluey substance incapable of move-ment. Ducks forced their way across its surface, moving in formation, dragging a wake of arrowheads. Madigan began to walk quickly home, keeping close to the fence.

He reached the hollow lighted kitchen with relief. Myra was standing at the stove with an apron tied round her waist. She was talking with animated gestures to one of the unfairly glamorous girls from over the road whom Madigan privately referred to as 'the girls with the bee-stung lips'.

'It had this great big skirt?' said Myra, stirring, 'made with —' (she groped for the word) '— *abundant* material?'

Madigan always felt like bursting into applause when he witnessed one of Myra's raids on the inarticulate. He sat down at the table and unbuttoned his jacket.

'Madigan,' said the smallest boy. 'When we start eating, will you keep sitting next to me?'

'Why, Harry?'

'Because I like you, and I like you to sit next to me,' said Harry.

'All right.'

'Thank you,' said the boy in a soft contented murmur, and leaned against Madigan's side.

'Don't mention it.' Madigan blinked and blinked, half-dazzled by the bare bulb which dangled over his head. The great chimney-place opposite him was stuffed with old newspapers. The girl with the bee-stung lips drifted out of the room in a patchouli cloud, layers of worn crêpe swaying round her booted ankles. A faint odour of dope clung around Myra's solid person as she delivered the steaming pan to the centre of the table.

'Oh, not soup *again*!' groaned the eldest boy, putting his spoon down with a crash and turning away in disgust to rest his face in the palm of his hand.

'You should be grateful to your mother,' said Madigan severely. His glasses fogged up in the steam that rose from his plate. He began to transport the soup to his mouth, tilting the bowl at the correct angle and closing his lips round the spoon so as not to make slurping noises. Myra served the three children and herself. 'Mmmmm! Flavoursome soup, Myra!' said Madigan in the cheerful, encouraging tone of a husband in a television commercial. Blinking rapidly, he pursed his lips for the next spoonful. The bored boy, watching Madigan's exemplary table manners, suddenly laughed out loud. His mother dealt him a ringing blow to the side of the head.

'Get to your room!' she shouted, flushing with embarrassment and rage. 'How dare you?' She glanced at Madigan who was

staring, bewildered, spoon raised, dimly aware that this unpleas-
antness had been provoked by some oblivious act of his own.
Harry had dozed off against Madigan's arm, and the middle boy,
having seen the lie of the land, was shovelling soup into his
mouth as silently as he could, darting his eyes left and right as his
brother left the room red-faced and furious, holding back tears.

The children were dispatched and the two grown-ups finished
the meal in silence.

'Where *is* everyone?' said Madigan.

'I'm here,' said Myra, looking into her empty bowl.

'No, I meant the others. Tony and the blokes.'

'I don't know. Gone to play, I guess.' Myra went over to the
sink and turned on the tap.

'Don't wash up,' said Madigan vaguely. 'I'll do it later.'

'It's all right. Don't you get sick of washing up, doing it all
day?'

'They sacked me, didn't I tell you?'

'What for?' Myra already wrist-deep in water, reddened again
with indignation on his behalf.

'Oh, I'm a pretty slow worker,' he said. 'They don't have to
give a reason. Probably got someone with ambition.' He laughed
and rolled his eyes at her.

'Well, I think that's terrible.'

'Who's staying home with the kids tonight?' said Madigan.

'Me.'

There was not even a hint of resentment in her voice. Her
patience drove Madigan to distraction. Why didn't she jack up?
Blokes never did anything unless forced. He'd better buy her a
book, or something.

'Are you going out?' she said.

'Oh, I might. Later on.'

She ground away with a piece of Jex at the saucepan bottom. Madigan looked at her feet in the loose sheepskin boots, patiently parallel at the sink, and felt like tearing his hair.

'What about a game of Scrabble?' he said with effort. Myra turned round with a shy smile. She must have been pretty once, but her face had puffed up and her belly had gone and she was always announcing diets and then lying about it: the bee-stung girls would walk in and find her giggling guiltily behind the kitchen door with a slab of carrot cake in each hand and crumbs all round her mouth. Her eager kindness excruciated Madigan. Someone like him couldn't afford to be around sadness like hers.

'I'll play,' she said, 'but I'm not very good at it.'

Madigan turned away to hide the gnashing of his teeth, and pulled the maroon cardboard box out of the drawer. Myra wrung out the dish-mop, banged it firmly to separate its white strands, and hung it on the tap under the sign Tony had put up saying *Washing glasses in soapy water makes the beer go flat*. She sat down opposite Madigan, blushing with pleasure, and Madigan laid out the board and the little wooden racks with his thick graceless hands which always trembled slightly, and they played a slow game, painstakingly placing the creamy tiles in their squares, cogitating without haste, for neither of them possessed the killer instinct. The alarm clock sat upon the table with a woollen tea-cosy to muffle its tick; its face looked foolishly askew up the spout-hole.

From the front bedroom came sounds of struggle, fierce giggling, feet running away. The big front door slammed violently and Harry set up a wail. Madigan glanced up but Myra, soothed

by mental effort and adult companionship, went on placidly contemplating her move, one eye squinted against the smoke of the
joint which Madigan had declined to share. Harry's weeping,
moving very slowly closer, was becoming heart-rending.

'Is it good for him to cry like that?' said Madigan, shifting in
his seat.

'Of course,' said Myra briskly. She did not take her eyes off
the board.

'But — to go on forcing it out, long after there's nothing left?
So his whole body aches?'

'He'll stop when he's sick of it.'

Harry sidled in, swollen-faced. 'I got no one to play with, and
no one to look after me,' he said thickly.

'You're not the only one with that problem, me lad,' said
Myra, chin in hand, still not looking up.

'Steady on, My!' said Madigan, shocked and impressed by her
tough tone.

Harry slid up to his mother's legs. She took him on to her lap,
one hand outstretched with a tile ready to place. She slipped her
other hand up under his jumper and tickled his sweaty back. He
took a big quivering breath, let it out again and relaxed against
her. Madigan winked at him and clicked his tongue, but Harry
was not ready to smile.

'Would you pay CON?' said Myra.

'Oh . . . I don't think so. I don't know,' said Madigan, who
was slipping, himself, into a dream of comfort.

'Tsk. Come on. Don't be wishy-washy. Would you *pay* it?'
She swung her head up to look at him, her eyes blank with
concentration.

'Harry,' said Madigan. 'Run up to my room and get the dictionary, will you?'

'He can't read,' said Myra.

'It's a big thick book with red and yellow stripes.'

Harry trotted away and returned with the right book.

'Good on you,' they cried.

He smiled tremulously and slipped back on to Myra's knee. Absently she soothed him, playing all the while.

'Those big boys are bullies,' she said, 'sometimes. It's one of the things I should try to knock out of them.'

'Maybe the events of their lives will knock it out of them,' said Madigan.

'*I'm* an event in their lives.'

Madigan sat hypnotised by her certainty, her deft handling of what to him were looming imponderables: children's distress, their nastier character traits, the future. He recognised the danger signals in himself: a slight swooning sensation, a physical comfort drawn directly from the fact that she achieved this balancing without even looking up from the game. He pulled himself together and stood up abruptly from the table.

'I think I'll go out,' he announced.

Myra looked up, aware that by some false move she had forfeited his company. 'Thanks for the game,' she said, completely without irony.

'*Don't thank me*, Myra,' he ground out, and bolted from the room.

Dennis shot things at weekends. He told Ruth she lived with dilettantes who were up themselves. His smile looked more like a snarl. Ruth took pride in being the only one who could handle him when he was drunk. Once Scotty had walked into Ruth's room without knocking and seen them lying together: Dennis's face was turned towards her over Ruth's shoulder, his white teeth were bared, his eyes glazed. For a second Scotty thought there was murder: then she realised they were fucking. His pale blue eyes looked at her but did not see. She ran.

Dennis never stayed for breakfast, but slipped away to work as soon as it was light. Anyone who had left a bedroom door ajar might at the instant of waking glimpse the loose dangle of his arm, sense the quiet disturbance of his passing, a blondness, thread of tobacco smoke, sponge of boot-sole.

Dennis was always leaving. Ruth, who longed to be his ally in a struggle larger than their own lives, who longed to be like him (blunt-minded, phlegmatic, wary of easy levity — virtues, she imagined, of his class), did not protest; but sometimes when he knelt over her to say goodbye, when he searched her face, she felt herself swell and grow puffy with sadness. She reproduced, not consciously but by the osmosis of desire, his ungrammatical speech, his flat vowels and truncated cadences. She called people 'mate', professed impatience with subtleties: 'I can't stand all this stuff about colours,' she would declare, folding her arms over her flowered apron. 'All this shit about "Is that puce?" "No, it's more like magenta", when it's really just purple or dark red.' She roughened up her manners and her childhood memories, so that one Sunday when her father came to call, Alex and Scotty were agape at his rounded, jovial tones, his casual bandying of literary references.

Ruth waited for Dennis at night, long after Laurel and Wally had dropped off and the ironing was done and the kitchen set to rights. Towards midnight her ears were tuned to the scrape of the back door on the matting. She would put on her flannelette nightie and her glasses and get under the blanket and open *Labour and Monopoly Capital* and begin the plodding task, the mountainous journey she conceived between her history and his. He would come in and find her asleep with the light on, the book still upright on her chest between her loosened fingers.

She captured him one Sunday.

'Stay,' she said. 'Oh, go on. I'll get your breakfast in bed.'

Half laughing, half frowning, he gave in. She kicked off her felt slippers, galloped to the shop for milk and bread, trotted to the kitchen and set up the little wooden tray for him. Scotty stumped in and cut up a grapefruit with a serrated knife, facing straight ahead to discourage conversation. Ruth was in the state of silly over-cheerfulness seen in those whom love has made happy. She swung her hip to bump against Scotty's as they stood side by side at the bench and hissed, 'Been fuckin' all night. Stink like an alley-cat on heat.'

'Charming.' Scotty, who had slept the righteous sleep of the loveless, turned a slow look of distaste upon her. 'What was that crash on the front verandah at one o'clock this morning?'

'Oh that!' said Ruth with a grin. 'Dennis was a bit pissed 'n' we had a fight 'n' he ran out 'n' jumped on me pushbike. Bent it.' She giggled. 'He give me some money to get it fixed, but.'

Scotty's mouth curled in disgust. 'What an oaf,' she said. 'I hate men.'

'Get yourself a real one,' said Ruth cheerfully. 'Not one o' them soft-talkin' Carlton types.' She hoisted the tray breast-high and strode out of the room.

'Yoo hoo!' she yelled. 'Tea-oh!' She pushed the bedroom door open with one knee, and stopped. Dennis had slipped back into slumber. A narrow strip of sunlight lay across his broad face, across the pillow and the cream-coloured blanket with its faded blue stripe. His hair was messy and yellow. A grey shadow fell around his eyes, described a curve across the breadth of his cheeks. He was breathing very quietly.

Bunches of dried flowers (dead flowers to Scotty, who had no use for souvenirs) hanging from the curtain rod along the kitchen windows were symbols, for Ruth, of what had been and what she alone was faithful to. Where had the laughter gone? In the old house they had laughed till they ached, in convulsions of hilarity: joints before breakfast, spiky electrocuted haircuts, improvisations in foreign accents, gentle family jokes (Laurel trying to remember Moby Dick and coming up with 'Dick Shark'), acid trips when the little girls had clowned to entertain them and Ruth and Scotty had lain against the furniture weeping with laughter, dying with laughter.

The institution of Telling Life Stories had gone swimmingly at the old house, once a week, in each of the bedrooms in turn: the cups of tea, the packets of Iced Vo-Vos and Chocolate Royals, the knitting, the open fire, the horror stories that any childhood will turn up: 'My father read my mail and found the contraceptive pills.' 'He was driving so fast I thought I could just open the door and jump out.' 'When I got home from school my mother . . . my mother . . .' 'He came into the bathroom and I was in the bath with my sister and he said, Who did it?' 'They took her away and I never saw her again.' 'I was afraid to open my mouth.' 'She died.'

For Scotty, this was over. They had been through it once, once was enough; the sound of her own voice droning the ossified facts disgusted her. But Ruth wanted it again, to show Alex how it was done; she wanted to keep something alive, to build a bulwark against the draining away of the recent past through neglected channels. Scotty gave in ungraciously, Alex out of curiosity. Ruth went first. She told and told, with that dull gleam of eye, mirthless smile, slow mastication of detail: and Scotty fell asleep, a crime for which Ruth would never forgive her. 'I was drunk,' said Scotty afterwards, grinning with shame. 'I got bored! I slept for two hours and when I woke up you were still in grade three.' Alex gave an embarrassed laugh, and flipped a tortoiseshell guitar pick between his fingers. Ruth glared at the floor. Scotty, trying to make amends in the name of domestic peace, offered to tell her own story the following week. She produced an elegantly edited version of her thirty years, studded with ironic jokes against herself and tailored stories of travel in countries the others had never been to: 'The music went on for three days and three nights; I had pneumonia and a nun looked after me; we crossed the river at dawn; I went into this room and there was more coke on the table than you'd ever dream of seeing in all your life; when I got to his place and saw the mattress on the floor I thought, Let me *out* of here!'

At the end of it the others sat in silence, frustrated and confused. They were none the wiser about Scotty's personality – or
rather, she had not given away any little weaknesses, which was
of course the unspoken reason for these sessions: let us bare our
weak points so I won't have to be afraid of you any more.

Scotty was seriously bored. It had much less to do with Ruth
than Ruth imagined. She suffered from boredom as a condition.
She would sink into it, would be up to her neck in it, without
having a name for it. She had no way of concealing it, of making
herself gracious in spite of it. At school her kids held it at bay:
their sexual restlessness she understood, and they made her laugh
with their strangled English; but at home it came creeping into
the marrow of her bones. She ate too much, furtively devoured
Easter eggs, muffins, half packets of Vita-Weats thick with butter
in the middle of the night on her way back from the lavatory.
After these binges she would fade into anxious sadness, an obses-
sion with the deed; guilt, shame, lack of energy; a desire to turn
back time, to sleep away what she had done, to be free again of
the load taken on; fear of ugliness; weariness; despair; self-disgust
at the failure of will. It was part of the condition that she could
not talk about it. She would wander round her room, try on all
her clothes, grieve because none of them hung loosely on her; she
would unbutton her overalls, drop them to her ankles and dully
examine her body in profile, holding her shirt up under her
breasts. She longed miserably to hack off the offending flesh, to
have it surgically removed in some secret clinic. If Ruth came
striding into her room while she was lying there after work,
black-faced, struggling with this loathing of herself, hiding behind
a book, if Ruth sat down and sighed comfortably and pulled out

the packet of Drum, Scotty's discourteous grunt of greeting was the best she could do. She wanted to scream, *Shock me!* but she couldn't be bothered. Ruth would take the crude hint, gather up her tobacco and papers and matches and go quietly, closing the door behind her. It was all on Scotty's terms. Nothing Ruth said succeeded. Scotty was sick of the old fooleries. She wanted nastier mirth, to say the unforgivable, to purge herself of her disgust. With her ignorant certainties she rudely crushed Ruth's stirrings of intellectual curiosity.

'The Great Wall of China can be seen from the moon,' said Ruth.

'Oh bullshit,' said Scotty crabbily. 'It can't, can it, Alex?'

'Why don't we buy an encyclopaedia?' said Alex the science graduate, the diplomat, refusing once again the unenviable role of Solomon.

When Scotty went on the night train to Mildura for her term holidays, she bought a postcard at the station of a certain local geological formation called The Walls of China and sent it to Ruth with the inscription, 'Reckon you can see this from the moon as well?' Ruth was hurt and cross; but some dregs of rough affection in the message touched her obscurely, and she looked at the postcard front and back for a long time and then stuck it in *Labour and Monopoly Capital* as a bookmark. None of them ever looked up the disputed factoid. Indeed, the peculiar angle of the dismal little piece of information made it hard to classify: Wall? Moon? China?

Ruth enjoyed starting sentences with 'us deserted wives', 'us single mums', invoking with a sniff and a twisted grin the sisterhood of adversity. Into her bones had sunk wisdoms such as *All good things must come to an end,* and *Life's a struggle.* With casual relish she related tales of disaster and pain. 'If there was one thing Sarah didn't need, it was a caesarean, after the childhood she had.' 'They took one look at him and he was full of it – they just sewed him back up again.' Over the morning paper she narrowed her green eyes, pursed her lips, drew in hissing breaths, gave ironic nods of suspicion vindicated, and made vague political predictions. 'The pressure's buildin' up,' she would say, ominously. 'The lid's gonna blow off any minute.'

'We had the radio on while we were fuckin',' she told Alex in the kitchen. 'An', the news come on and they announced the PKIU only got a five dollar rise. Dennis's cock went all limp. We couldn't go on.'

She gave an odd, triumphant laugh of excitement, her eyes gleaming dully.

'Wouldn't it have been better to fuck more, instead of less?' mumbled Alex, who was flossing his teeth. 'That way you would have been defying the badness, if you see what I mean. Making a stand for human contact.'

'What are you, a hippy?' said Ruth.

At that moment Alex noticed Dennis, eyes down, coming up the path between the kitchen door and the lavatory.

'Look at that blond head,' Alex remarked to Ruth. 'I always think blonds are more . . . sort of *blessed* than other people.'

Ruth stared. 'What sort of an idea's that? How can a Jew come out with a thing like that?'

'There is a faint flicker of Nazism in it, isn't there,' said Alex, sawing away with the waxy cotton.

'More than a flicker!'

'I nearly said *holy*, actually,' said Alex, laughing. He was not fazed by ideological rebukes, though goodness knows he had enough of them to contend with in this household, of every conceivable brand.

Alex and Scotty came out the front door on their way to the gig. Ruth's bedroom light was still on.

'Bloody house meetings – just an excuse to get stuck into each other.'

'No wonder she hates you,' said Alex, stowing his guitar in the back and buckling his seat belt. He revved the motor and they swooped away on to the road. 'Look at you – all dressed up to go out on the town, and she's in her room bawling.'

'Oh, don't *you* start!' said Scotty. 'Why does everyone think I've got no feelings?'

'You do seem to cope,' said Alex.

'*Somebody* has to cope! And once you start, they expect you to cope for them as well, and you're never allowed to drop your bundle ever again – and then the buggers hate you and tell you you're authoritarian!'

'Maybe that's why we hate our fathers,' said Alex in his maddeningly reasonable tone.

'Oh shut up.' Scotty stuck her elbow out the window and slouched in her seat. The car, open to smooth streams of night air, cruised down Punt Road and crossed the river.

Outside the back door of the pub, Scotty said, 'I might just hang round out here till it starts.'

'Don't be silly. Come inside and talk to us.' Alex was standing sideways on the step with his guitar case in his hand.

'No. I don't want to look like a moll.'

Alex laughed and went in without her. She leaned against the wall and looked up and down the street. A tram passed, light and square as a cage, making the asphalt tremble under her feet. She thought about Ruth at the meeting, her grim face and set jaw, her determined pessimism, the way she dragged on the cigarette as she ground into words the grist of her resentment. Strung tight as new fence wire, Scotty's shoulders ached with self-control. She let out a mean sob.

'Shut up, idiot,' she snarled out loud.

Under the rows of knobbily pruned plane trees came three Aborigines, a man and two women, stumbling cheerfully home. The man saw Scotty leaning there in the dark with her hands in her pockets, knee bent, one foot back against the wall, and sang out, 'Hul-lo my son! How you going?'

'Good thanks,' she called back.

'Ooooh! It's a girl!' shrieked one of the women, and they all went off into gales of laughter. 'Sorry!'

'It's all right,' said Scotty, blushing.

'Good night love!' They rolled on by, a jolly trio smelling pleasantly of beer.

'Good night,' said Scotty.

She turned on her heel and went round the corner and into the pub.

It was crowded and red-dark inside. She shouldered her way to the bar and ordered a scotch, propped herself with her back to the bar, and downed it in one gulp. Ruth swam away. Scotty hated parties, but liked pubs, for here she had no social responsibilities: everything was paid for and the deal was clear. She did not like social drinking, or beer, or wine. She liked to get rapidly and effi-ciently drunk on something hard and dance it all off and go home alone, and anything more was just somebody else's fantasy. 'Drink-ing is between me and the bottle,' she had said once when Ruth and Dennis offered her a beer at the kitchen table. 'No one else has anything to do with it.' The memory of this remark made Scotty flinch with shame. She hated talking about herself, and imagined such statements being repeated mockingly behind her back.

She found herself a spot between the bar and the cigarette machine and drank quietly through the first awkward, cold bracket, when the speckled concrete floor was bare and she was not going to be first. She watched the roadie's blond head gleam green in the light over the desk, the swing of his arm as he brought the cigarette to his lips, his hands hovering over the board sneaking the volume up with each song; she saw the band one after another twist in their ear-plugs as the sound turned bitter and clattered tinnily among the rafters; she drank scotch until the taste of it no longer withered her and it started to do its job on her stiff righteous joints; she drank scotch and ice, and by the break she was oiled up and loose. She waited.

She felt the ripple of attention run through the crowd, a turn-ing of heads and bodies towards the lit stage, and away they went again on a riff she knew by heart from hearing it a thousand times through her bedroom floor at night. She battled down to the front of the band where she could watch Alex, whose face took on a resoluteness, a sweet grimace of concentration: her feet were lifted surely off the sticky floor and she was dancing, whisked up and washed away in the oceanic commotion of sweating bodies, in the same unfailing bliss engendered by hot swimming pools full of screaming kids. She heard Alex pick up the riff and his teeth flashed as he began to grin to himself and she was grinning too and before she closed her eyes she saw sweat flying round the drummer's head like a little net cap sewn with pearls and she closed her eyes, she was herself for herself with no skin to hold her in, and to the wincing man in distorted spectacles standing pressed against the side of a speaker box her face was as open and tender as that of someone *blissed out* on some *mind-expanding drug* — that naked face and powerful body — better steer clear of her, she looked dangerous.

Watching her, Madigan suddenly thought of a film he had once seen, *Gentlemen Prefer Blondes*, in which two women, one dark, one fair, both big and graceful as racehorses, strode like colossi among puny millionaires or muscled giants whose personalities had been pumped into their biceps. An odd run of expressions passed across Madigan's face: sourness, envy, admiration, suspicion. She wasn't stupid, that girl dancing with her eyes shut: she had just slipped her moorings, and he wished he could do the same.

The music stopped and she opened her eyes, giddy, not knowing which way she was facing. She had her back to the stage and tears on her face, and there was someone standing in front of her talking to her, a Hawaiian shirt and glasses and shoulders hunched inwards.

'Do I know you?' she asked stupidly.

'I came to your house once,' he said. 'To visit Alex.' He was peering down at her through ugly spectacles. His eyes were watery and seemed to want to burst through the glass: his lashes spread against the lenses. She thought perhaps she remembered him, his childish shoes, feet pointing straight ahead.

'Why are you looking at me like that?'

'I'm not,' he said. 'It's the curse of all bespectacled people. People think you're looking at them funny, or sexy, and you're really just trying to see who they are.'

'I'm having a bit of trouble with that question myself at the moment.'

'Which question?' He stared right into her eyes, perfectly serious.

'Oh, never mind. You wouldn't understand.'

'You're not crying, are you?' He glanced nervously left and right to see if anyone else had noticed.

'Want to make something of it?'

He laughed a peculiar gusty laugh, hyuk hyuk, too loud, as if someone had formally told a joke. His breath smelled sweet. 'Oh, I wouldn't take *you* on,' he said.

'Why not?' she said in a pugnacious tone.

He composed his features into a debonair expression. 'I keep running into strong women who are looking for a weak man to dominate them, as Andy Warhol said. Although I hate Andy Warhol and all that New York stuff.'

Scotty laughed. 'I'm looking for someone to flatten, actually.'

'You can flatten me.' He spread out his arms. 'It'd be easy.'

'Don't be a dag.'

'Well, buy me a drink, then. Please.'

She looked at him sharply. He had a very thick, white neck. 'On the bite, are you.'

He nodded and blinked.

'The direct approach always works on me.' She wiped her cheeks with the back of her hand and he followed her to the bar.

'Do you actually like this sort of music?' His oyster eyes, distorted by the spectacles, narrowed as he raised the glass of beer.

'Of course,' said Scotty indifferently. She sucked a mouthful of scotch through the ice.

'It's not to my taste,' he said. 'At least . . . I don't think it is. Still . . . everyone's much more professional in the city. Specially this side of the river.' He stuck out his chin, expecting contradiction, but she merely replied, 'Why don't you get proper glasses?'

'I had some once. Gold.'

'What happened to them?'

'I had this girlfriend up north, and at the vital moment I failed to make a declaration of passion, so she jumped on my glasses and went to Europe.'

Scotty laughed. She looked him up and down. He stuck one hand in his pocket and with the other tilted the glass so that a few drops of the beer ran down his throat. He pretended to whistle, looking behind him.

Alex came shouldering through the mob, sweaty and shiny.

'G'day, Madigan. What's the matter, Scotty? I saw you crying. You looked really small.' He grabbed the back of her hair and yanked at it.

'I'm OK,' said Scotty. She nodded at Madigan. 'He's not sure if he likes the music all that much.'

Alex turned to him. 'Oh yeah?'

Madigan took a deep breath and rushed it. 'It's too New Yorkish, and violent. And decadent. What's it got to do with

Australian people's lives? Why don't you play music for ordinary Australians?' He was panting, staring earnestly into Alex's face.

'If you want to see some "ordinary Australians",' said Alex, controlling himself with difficulty, 'come out to a Saturday night gig in Ringwood sometime, mate.'

Madigan fixed him insistently with his protruding eyes. 'No, not them. I mean the mums and dads. Mr and Mrs Normal.'

Scotty butted in, clenching fists and teeth. 'Mr and Mrs *Normal*? This is rock and roll, you *dag*.'

She cast Madigan a look that would have floored him had he not summoned up all his nervy, scrupulous tenacity to deflect it: he was older than Scotty, and more romantic, and probably even more bitter. Their stares locked, then dropped apart in a kind of hostile respect. Scotty turned abruptly and strode away towards the lavatory. The men raised their eyebrows at each other.

'I like Scotty,' said Madigan who, to Alex's stupefaction, now showed no sign of agitation. Completely composed, breathing in a regular rhythm, Madigan held up thumb and forefinger a hair's breadth apart. 'That cool she's got – it's about *this deep*.' His attention wandered. Alex saw his gaze blur, slide, then suddenly sharpen and focus. 'Any chance of a blow with you blokes?' he said in a fresh tone, hearty and humble.

Scotty sat fully dressed on the lid of the end toilet, scowling into her fist. On the back of the cubicle door some ignoramus had printed *I hate the overalls brigade lesos and all dumb womans libb chicks*. Scotty drew a black texta from her front pocket and replied *Perhaps if you wore overalls yourself it might reduce the pressure on your spleen signed Miss Piggy Veterinarians' Hospital*. She stood up, rested one knee on the toilet and raised her face to the rigid louvre windows which gave on to the playground of the crèche next door to the pub. Through the chicken wire she stared at an abandoned swing: it moved on dull silver chains, clinked faintly in the apricot night air.

The outside door of the lavatories, flung back by a drunken hand, crashed against the basin, letting in a bright blast of music. A harmonica squealed. Scotty sprang up, ran out the door and plunged back into the red crowd.

It was Madigan working away at the centre microphone, a stooped, shock-headed, self-possessed figure, both hands to his mouth, the lead wagging: his eyes were squeezed shut behind the flashing lenses, his fingers flicked open and cupped shut. He was peeling off high, sheer ribbons of sound. Everyone was dancing.

When the crowd straggled out, it took with it the fragile romance of two a.m. Without the music, everything showed its decrepitude. The carpet was hopelessly stained and damp, worn thin as skin between the tables. The musicians, their glamour turned off with the lights, stood about randomly looking ordinary-sized and ill-tempered, cheated again of emotional recompense for their outlay. Scotty leaned against a wall and watched two girls in vinyl pants and lurid make-up loitering with intent between the stage and the door of the band room. The girls were in the way of the roadies who staggered round them, knees bent under the shared load, muttering curses. Scotty stepped up to Alex.

'You be long?'

'Don't think so. I'll just pick up my pay.'

'What's the matter with Whatsisname?' She jerked her head at Madigan who was crouched at the side of the stage.

'Not feeling the best.'

'Is he OK?' Scotty stared at him. Alex shrugged and made a motion of playing a violin. Scotty approached the hunched figure. He saw her feet and jumped. 'Are you all right?'

'Sort of-ish.' He looked up.

'Are you ill?'

'Probably got flu. Or something.' He straightened up with a confused attempt at a laugh.

'Let's go,' said Alex, coming up behind. 'Want a lift home, Madigan?'

'Well . . .' He looked around him. 'Do you think anything else is going to happen here?'

'Oh for Christ's *sake*,' said Scotty. 'I have to go to work tomorrow. Yes or no. Don't drag the chain.'

Madigan followed sheepishly, dawdling past the closed door of the band room with its strip of light along the floor.

When they stepped out on to the esplanade, the clock on the pillar said two thirty. A line of palm trees held up their stiff fingers against dark blue air which smelt of fish and salt.

Madigan had begun to shiver dramatically. Scotty shot him a cross look.

'Let's drop in at the Greek's for a coffee before we take you home,' said Alex. 'Are you too sick for that?'

Madigan shrugged, knowing he did not have a choice. He twirled the pillowcase this way and that; the harmonicas clacked.

Alex was greeted familiarly by the owner of the café as he served them at the high glass counter.

'Do you always come here after gigs?' said Scotty.

'Always. It's open day and night.'

'The whole twenty-four?'

'Yep. It's a *rock and roll* café.'

Scotty thought of the morning to come, children in the kitchen and the classroom, and longed again for the exhausted camaraderie of night workers.

'Now you know why I'm always half stunned in the mornings,' said Alex, tipping a sparkling river of sugar into his cup. He glanced at Madigan, this spectre he had invited to the feast, and tried to kick things along. 'This is a rare moment,' he said, 'seeing Scotty awake in public at this hour of night.'

Madigan did not reply. He looked quite pathetic, hitching his thin jacket and the collar of his lairy shirt up round his chin.

'Comes on sudden, doesn't it,' said Alex. He stirred his cup with a vigorous motion.

'Come and stay at our place,' said Scotty on an impulse, half to make Alex laugh, half meaning it. 'We'll look after you till you're better. What are you doing out on the streets at night in this condition? Don't you get looked after at your place?'

'Are you kidding?' said Madigan.

'Bloody hippies,' grunted Scotty with a righteous expression.

'They're all right. They're not running a hospital, you know.'

'It's the test of a collective household,' said Scotty primly, 'whether you get looked after when you're sick.'

'Ah yeah. They told me over in Prahran to look out for people like you,' said Madigan. 'Communes, and that.'

'What would they know about it,' said Alex with a blithe laugh. 'They're hopeless, south of the river. Sit round the kitchen table blowing joints all day, nothing gets done.'

'Come to us, then,' said Scotty, beginning to clown. 'We'll make you a little bed, won't we, Alex? All nice, with clean sheets smelling of mothballs. Freshly squeezed orange juice. Fizzy vitamin pill.'

'Yeah, that's the stuff,' said Alex.

'And we'll put the orange juice through the – what is it, Alex? – the *sieve*, like Ruth does, so it won't be, you know, too *strenuous* to drink.'

Alex tipped his chair back and laughed out loud, but Madigan, unable to gauge the exact edge of her tone, watched suspiciously. 'I think I'm probably too weak for the treatment,' he said. 'Maybe you'd better just drop me off home. I'll get something at the chemist tomorrow.'

'Get stuck into the ginseng, pal,' said Scotty, swilling the dregs round in her cup and not looking at him. 'Isn't that the big cure over your side at the moment? Or is it comfrey?'

'What's wrong with comfrey?' Madigan rallied. 'Myra at our place makes fritters out of it. I *like* comfrey.'

'Myra makes 'em, does she?' said Scotty. 'And what do *you* make?'

'Me? *I* can't cook,' he said, caught on the hop.

'Know what the first thing is?' continued Scotty smoothly. 'Learning how to boil water. Or – no. First you have to find the kettle.'

Nobody laughed.

After they had dropped Madigan home, they turned into Punt Road and flew back across the river.

'Bit rough on him, weren't you?' said Alex.

'Rough! He was just trying to provoke me!'

'No he wasn't! Listen, I've been to his place. You ought to go down there. Un–believable.'

'What happens?'

'They couldn't even get a market roster going. The men objected to being asked to come to a meeting about it. The blokes sit up at the table like Lord Muck while the women run round waiting on them.'

'You're starting to sound like a lackey of the feminists,' said Scotty. 'Are there any kids?'

'A couple, I think. It's the sort of house where you hear terrible sickening bangs and screeches from the other room. And their mother never goes out at night.'

'What a horror show!' said Scotty, gasping with enjoyment. 'You mean that actually still happens?'

'Look, Scotty – it's time you got out of Fitzroy! Nothing's changed, in the outside world!'

<hr>

Ruth drove, and Scotty and Sarah crouched at the back doors of the Holden poised to spring out at the chosen spot. The first couple of times they were jerky with fear and excitement. Ruth sat behind the wheel, leaning forward eagerly to watch the dim figures bobbing up and down against the wall like buoys struggling in water. By the fifth time, out in Hawthorn, far from home, their actions had become fluid and swift. Up came Scotty's arm, sprayed the huge words in her elegant left-handed script, while Sarah squatted, hopping crab-wise along behind her underlining in one smooth continuous flow. They sped away from each finished sign in a euphoria of silent laughter. It was like falling in love again in the dark. All their antagonisms dissolved, their eyes shone.

'Don't you want to have a go, Ru?'

'Oh – I'd be too slow. I haven't got such nice writing as Scotty,' said Ruth shyly, dying to.

'You do the next one with Sarah,' said Scotty. 'I'll keep watch.'

'Here's a nice white bank,' said Sarah. Ruth swung the car into the side street and turned off the motor. 'Come on, Ru.'

Ruth grabbed Scotty's can and slipped out after Sarah. She was so eager that she started without checking that the nozzle was facing away from her, and squirted herself on the face and neck.

'Eeek!' she screeched, brushing pointlessly at herself.

'Leave it, leave it!' said Sarah. 'Go on! Your turn!'

Scotty heard them and glanced over. At that moment the divvy van flashed past along Glenferrie Road. None of them saw it. Sarah and Ruth, weak with laughter, were stabbing away with the cans at the punctuation which Scotty insisted be perfect. Scotty neglected her watch again to check the spelling, and round the corner swept the divvy van.

'Get in! Get in!' yelled Scotty, twisting the key in the ignition. Sarah tumbled into the back seat and Ruth ran to the driver's side, pushed Scotty over and took hold of the wheel. Of course it was too late. The van blocked their exit from the narrow street, its lights blinded them, its doors burst open and two policemen strode down upon them, huge in the blaze of white and flashing blue.

'Oh God, look at 'im,' whispered Ruth. The first one was blue-faced, big-jawed, eyes invisible under the peak of his cap. He shoved his hand through the window and seized the keys out of the ignition.

'Whose is this car?'

'My husband's,' said Ruth.

He saw immediately that there were no men in the car, and his tone changed. The younger one stood silent on the other side of the car.

'Where *is* your husband? Does he let you out on the streets after midnight, does he?'

'My husband's in jail,' said Ruth, staring straight ahead through the windscreen with narrowed eyes. 'And I wouldn't ask his perm—'

'I see. And where are your children while you're out at night engaged in this sort of activity?'

'At home. Well looked after. *Mate.*' Ruth turned her black-streaked face up to him with a stare of concentrated hatred.

He met her gaze. 'I'm Inspector Nunan, of Glenhuntly CIB,' he said. 'We'd like you to follow us to the station.'

He passed the keys back to her and she snatched them rudely.

The divvy van sped away and they followed.

'Our rights. Our rights. What the fuck are our rights?' hissed Scotty. 'I knew we should have read the Civil Rights booklet before we left.' She began to giggle.

'Shut up, Scotty,' said Ruth. 'This is serious.'

'What a disaster,' said Sarah, whose freckled face in the helmet of curls looked white and small. 'We didn't even finish the sign.'

'Forget that now,' said Ruth. 'That's the cop shop there, isn't it? He's goin' in. Well, what *are* our bloody rights? Do we have to say anything? You two are the fuckin' intellectuals round here.'

'We can't very well *deny* anything,' said Scotty. 'They did catch us red-handed.' She and Sarah were on the verge of a fit of laughter.

'Can't you two shut up?' said Ruth, furious.

'I thought *you'd* know all that stuff about rights, Ruth,' said Sarah. 'I thought communists knew all that stuff.'

'I'm just a fuckin' deserted wife, mate,' said Ruth grimly, pulling up next to the divvy van outside the town hall. 'That's all I know about.'

'Well don't start bloody playing the violin about it, for Christ's sake,' said Scotty.

'What are we going to *say*?' said Sarah.

'I'll do the talking,' said Scotty.

The young policeman had inspected the boot of the car and was standing beside it with the keys in his hand when they came out the door to go home. They nodded to him and got into the car. Ruth backed it out of the drive and made a big U-turn.

'Look at that dingbat,' said Sarah. Scotty glanced back and saw the young cop standing with one arm raised, waving goodbye to them like an idiot country boy waving to a train. The two of them began to giggle weakly, disgusted with themselves. Ruth took no notice. She planted her foot and away they went.

〜

Ruth stumbled out of her bedroom and heard shouts of laughter from the kitchen. Scotty was transforming the night's debacle into a comic turn for Alex's entertainment.

'And round the corner, to put it bluntly,' she was saying, 'came Inspector Nunan of Glenhuntly.'

'To put in bluntly,' said Ruth from the doorway, 'we made fuckin' idiots of ourselves. In the cop shop we were pathetic.'

'Oh, come on, Ruth! It's not all that serious!' said Scotty. 'Can't we even get a laugh out of it?'

'It's all right for *you*. You've got enough money to pay the fine.' Ruth slopped coffee into a cup. 'Where are the kids?'

'Out in the street,' said Alex. He stood up from the table, picked up his bowl and ran it under the tap.

Ruth took a tearing drag on her cigarette and breathed out a long plume of smoke. 'Did they get anything to eat?' she said to nobody in particular.

'No,' said Alex. 'I'll go and call them.'

'Oh, don't bother,' said Ruth with a sigh. 'I'll do it in a minute.'

'*I'll* do it,' said Alex.

He could be heard yelling at the front door. Ruth and Scotty drank their coffee with downcast eyes.

'I'm goin' down the Prom for the weekend with Dennis,' said Ruth. 'An' I'm leaving the kids here.'

'All right,' said Scotty ungraciously.

With a great stampeding the two children ran in at the door and flung themselves at the table. Alex went about the business of serving them, singing to himself to cover the dismal sound of burnt toast being scraped. Laurel seized the plate of toast, divided the pile into two equal parts and shoved one in front of her brother. The red bow on top of her head wobbled vigorously as she ate. The children crammed the slices into their mouths and chewed loudly with much smacking of lips and champing.

'Why don't you two shut your mouths when you chew?' said Scotty in a surly tone. 'It nearly makes me sick to listen to you.'

They glanced up at her, puzzled, and went on gulping and gnawing.

'Lay off 'em Scotty,' said Ruth. 'Just lay off 'em.'

'I *live* here,' said Scotty. 'It's awful, the way they eat. Why don't we teach 'em?'

'Don't be so fuckin' bourgeois! You never used to think table manners were important!'

'Things change,' said Scotty. 'They're not babies any more.'

'*You've* changed!' said Ruth. Out came the Drum, the tense rolling. 'You know what's happened to you? You've turned into a boss. You're an individualist.'

The children stopped eating. Wally kicked Ruth under the table, and pointed at Scotty.

'She's fat,' he announced.

'Shut up, Wal,' said Ruth. Her mouth flickered, and Scotty had to turn away to hide a tremor which passed across her lips. 'I'm goin' away for the weekend, you kids. Scotty 'n' Alex are goin' to mind youse.'

'Ohhhh! Ru – uth! Why can't we come?' cried Laurel.

'Cause you can't, matey, 'n' that's that. Come up to my room 'n' talk to me while I get my stuff ready.'

The family trooped out the door into the hallway, keeping their eyes down.

Alex, who had observed this scene from the other side of the bench, came and sat down beside Scotty at the devastated table. Their eyes slid sideways and met. Scotty gave in.

'Fat, am I,' she said.

'Miss Piggy,' said Alex.

The pair of them lolled there, faces to forearms on the table-top, and laughed till tears came to their eyes.

'Oh God this house is gruesome,' groaned Alex. 'It's driving me nuts.'

'Don't say nuts. I might want to eat some.'

'Driving me bananas, then. Oh, sorry.'

Fresh spasms bowed them down.

When they looked up, Wally was standing on the kitchen step, half hiding in the doorway.

'I'm gunna make a rabbit hutch,' he said.

'But you haven't got a rabbit,' said Alex.

'But one day I might save up and buy one, from selling bottles.'

Laurel pushed into the room behind him. 'Are you going to make it now? I know where the hammer is. Can I make it with you?'

'Sure,' said Wally magnanimously, heading for the shed. 'You can hold the nails.'

Laurel's face dropped. She looked back at Scotty and Alex sitting at the table. They were speechless, but Scotty raised one clenched fist and shook it encouragingly. Laurel ran out the back door with a single-minded expression.

'Starts young, doesn't it,' said Alex.

From the shed came the splintering of wood and voices raised in eager discussion.

'See youse,' shouted Ruth from the front door, and crashed it shut.

'I think she's going down to the beach to make up her mind,' said Alex.

'What about?'

'Whether to leave or not.'

'*Leave?* Oh Christ. I thought we'd made up our minds to stay here and knuckle down to it.'

'It?'

'It, it, IT. The flaming collective necessity.'

'Oh, I'm sick of talking about it,' said Alex. 'I'm going into my room to have a little practice.'

———

People were setting up a fair on the scrubby football oval at the northern end of the gardens. Scotty pedalled across the lumpy grass and propped in front of a display board at which a girl with her back turned was struggling to pin some flapping posters to the caneite. Scotty, still holding on to one side of her handlebars, leaned across to help the girl restrain the poster. The girl glanced at her.

'Miss,' she said in a very soft voice. 'Remember me, Miss?'

Scotty stared. The girl was young, only about nineteen. Scotty remembered something . . . faces and desks flicked past like pictures in a book, a fine dust of chalk entered her nostrils and fizzed there, chalk dust packed the whorls of her fingertips. The girl was dressed anonymously in jeans, a dark blue windcheater and cheap running shoes. She looked Greek. Not one of the beauties. A blunt face, lips permanently parted, a mouth breather. Eyebrows clumsily plucked and half grown back. Back row on the right, under the map. Not Effi. Effi's friend.

'Soula, Miss.'

A great, rare smile broke over Scotty's face. 'Soula.'

They were both laughing silently, looking right into each other's eyes. Then they stood still and studied each other.

'Miss. If anyone ever asks me about teachers, I say, Miss Scott was the best one I ever had.'

'Oh Soula.'

'Really Miss! I loved your class. I learned stuff.'

'We had lots of laughs, anyway.'

'Miss! Seriously!' A shadow of earnestness passed over her face.

'It must be seven years ago,' said Scotty.

'Long time, Miss.'

'Yeah.'

'Miss. Do you remember when you took us to see *The Summer of '42?*'

'Yes. And remember when we went on the excursion to the tombstone maker and Vito dropped the big block of marble on his toe?'

Soula turned aside to laugh, covering her mouth with her hand.

'What's everyone doing down here in the park?' said Scotty.

'It's the Tribune fair, Miss.'

'You can call me Scotty, you know.'

'Sorry, Miss — I mean —'

They laughed.

'It's the Tribune fair, Miss. I work for the Party.'

'Oh yeah? How long?'

'Three years.'

'How did you get involved?'

'My parents.'

Scotty stood over her bike and nodded. Soula's plain, direct, un-ironic gaze took in Scotty's pink trousers, the black shirt, the frivolous New York badges, the sparkling combs that held the hair back over her ears, the ears themselves pierced in several places with rings and studs. Scotty, at this casual mention of the Party, felt the beginnings of the same envy she swallowed every Friday night when Alex went home to his parents for dinner, to be present at the ritualistic lighting of certain candles in ways mysterious to her, exclusive.

'Do you ever see any of the old grade?' said Soula.

'I ran into Vito, actually, at the market, just before Christmas,' said Scotty. 'He told me he had to leave when he was in second form. Because some kids beat him up, or something.'

'He dobbed someone, Miss,' said Soula severely.

'Oh.'

'Miss, do you remember Tony Petridis?'

'Of course.'

'Well he's a junkie now.'

'*What?*'

'He's a junkie.'

'You mean a bad junkie, a real one, or just the odd . . .'

'Real one. He's a pusher.'

'But I only saw him —'

She had seen him a year before, loafing on the footpath outside Johnny's Green Room at two o'clock in the morning. She was drunk, staggering home after some gig or other, on her own and fearless with whisky. She would have walked straight past without recognising him had he not stepped forward and called to her, 'Miss!' He was huge, strong as an ox, a muscle builder, bursting out of his white T-shirt, but in his face still shone a calm seriousness, the courtesy and intelligence of the strictly brought-up Greek boy. His three friends stood quietly behind him in the shadow, watching. Exactly as she and Soula had done, laughing and then soberly curious, Scotty and Tony Petridis examined one another quietly and without haste, up and down. Each of them echoed with oblique shafts of memory, with the pleasant ache of old sexual imaginings, always contained by decorum and long ago forgotten. She had watched him from the high staffroom window. His soccer player's body – the triangular torso, low hips, short powerful legs – wove and swayed, graceful as a slow dancer, down in the rainy yard. Oh Tony. He reached out his arms to her that night: he took hold of her tenderly in his huge arms under the sickly neon of the poolroom, he held her firmly against his great chest and kissed her on the mouth. A perfume of hash and sweat hung about him.

'You should see his hair,' Soula was saying. 'It's right down to *here*. And you know how he was always big? Well now he's *fat*. Do you remember Effi? She's a junkie. She's got a baby, even. The doctor reckons it might have been born with an addiction. It's like a cat, real skinny, sort of deformed. She can't get off it, Effi. We try to help her. She doesn't *want* to stop. But we won't let her go.'

Stupid with shock, Scotty listened to this litany, spoken with the same dull, gleaming-eyed fervour with which Ruth told her bad news. Who was this *we*? There was no *we* with power to prevent the rot.

'Do you think the posters look good, Miss?'

She tried to look. The posters, firmly attached now to the vertical board, showed what might have been expected – forests of fists raised, a banner-crowded sky, a suckling mother bran-dishing a machine gun: the whole panoply of worn-out symbols from which Scotty, like the rest, had learned to hope.

'Do you like it, Miss? Is it all right?' Soula's damaged eyebrows made an inverted V of anxiety.

'Yes, it looks great.' The teacher's tone of mechanical encour-agement rolled off her tongue. Soula's face relaxed and she stepped back from the board.

'Thanks, Miss.' She was smiling. She was content.

When Scotty got home she climbed the narrow stairs to her room and lay on the bed. The air was as grey and dirty as if she had been told of a death. Some birds were singing unnaturally loudly on the tiles outside the window. She tried to cry; but she had talked herself out of that, too.

—⫯—

The beer glass was empty. No need for Madigan to feel in his pockets: that was it.

I like them, at home. Of course. I like them naturally of course. No one's ever allowed to dislike anybody these days. I do like them. I do, I do! But not when they play. They don't know how to build up a feel. It goes sloppy on them. God sometimes I feel old. I'm too old for dope, that's certain. Thank goodness. I must make a list. A list. I hereby resolve till further notice to avoid having lots of options. OK. A list. I wonder if I can get that old bloke down Gertrude Street to sell me the guitar case with-out the guitar in it. The neck is bent as any fool can see. If I practise more. Two hours every morning. Before breakfast.

He printed PRACTISE 10–12 DAILY on the first page of the exercise book. He crossed out 10–12 and replaced it with 11–1. Under that he wrote BE REALISTIC. Then GET SLIPPERS, PILLOW. He scribbled out SLIPPERS and printed THONGS.

Might be a couple that match in one of the boxes. VACUUM ROOM. Vacuun roon. Moon. Loon. Tune. BUY RHYMING DICTIONARY. They say they've never managed to find a rhyme for silver, or orange. Funny. Both colours. Oh well, substances too. Objects. Ob*jects*? Mister Otis regrets. That he won't be around. Unnggggggg. I didn't like to just not turn up or say nothing, but ouch! By the time I'd contacted her I was a nervous wreck. I lost interest. She lost interest. Interest was lost. Hell, I wrote her a funny letter with drawings, surely that's reasonable enough value. BUY STAMPS. I try against ingrained habit and prejudice not to talk in riddles. BUY ENVELOPES. DO NOT TALK IN RIDDLES. PULL BED OUT AND LOOK UNDERNEATH. *I moved my bed into the middle of the room / Floating like an island in a sea of gloom.* Is that corny? Is it hackneyed? A battered ornament? Did I make it up, or did I read it somewhere? Does this happen to Real Artists? PRACTISE THREE HOURS DAILY. What happened to the list. *List of songs to do.* STAND BY YOUR MAN. Hyuk. That'll ginger up the feminists. DIAMONDS ARE A GIRL'S BEST FRIEND. Steady on. That's going too far. Next thing'll be foot-binding. 'In my profession I have learned that women can bear more pain than men.' 'Are you a doctor, sir?' 'No. A shoe repairer.' Hyuk hyuk.

He underlined THONGS.

On the colour television, high up on a shelf, two blurs were singing.

Hey Paul, I wanna marry yew

Hey hey Paula, I wanna marry yew tew

A man at the next table called out to the barman. 'Mate! Hey mate! Turn it up.' He tried to catch Madigan's eye. Madigan nodded.

'Swallows Juniors,' said the man. He raised his glass to the screen. 'Look at those kids.'

The barman scrambled up and tuned the set.

Trew lurve means planneen a life for tew

Bein' tewgether the whole day threw

they harmonised, beaming. The boy had bands on his teeth.

Madigan cleared his throat. 'Don't you think they're a bit young to be singing that sort of stuff?'

'No fear!' protested the man. 'Have to start early, in show biz.' He was smiling, as if they were his own children.

'But what would they know about true love?'

The man stared at him. His smile faded. 'They're *very talented kids*,' he snapped, and turned reverently back to the screen.

Madigan was getting that bursting feeling. He seized his pen and in a flowing hand covered the rest of the page with song titles. Madigan was working.

A fine powder of rain flicked in through the open doorway of the tram; it seemed to spurt out from the bending street lights. He got off at the corner of the gardens and mooched along in the dampness, heading for the only house he knew north of the river. There it stood at the apex of the triangular park, with its protruding attic window beaming light. The big front door was shut and he bashed it with the knocker. A moment passed, then the door opened a crack. A small fair-haired boy stood there with his hand on the lock.

'Good evening!' said Madigan.

The boy stared at him.

'May I come in?'

'Ruth's not here,' said the boy, looking past him at the darkening street.

'Is anyone else home?'

'I have to go to the shop,' mumbled the boy.

'What for?'

'Scotty said I have to get a tin of peaches.'

'Haven't you got enough money?'

The boy dangled by one arm from the latch of the door. 'Sometimes,' he said in a conversational tone, 'when it's getting dark and cars come along, well it might be too dark for the driver to see a little kid crossing the road, and he might . . .'

'Would you like company?' said Madigan.

'What?'

'Will I come with you?'

'All right.'

'Haven't you got any shoes? It's raining.'

'Come on.' The boy pushed his hand into Madigan's and dragged him across the road.

While Madigan watched, the child bought the peaches and selected for himself a packet of chicken-flavoured chips, which he devoured noisily, not offering to share, on their way back to the house.

'Won't you spoil your tea?' said Madigan helplessly.

The boy up-ended the packet into his gaping mouth, crushed the paper and dropped it in the gutter, and wiped his face on his sleeve as he heaved the front door open with his shoulder.

He sprinted away down the hallway, leaving Madigan to make his own way into the house.

Scotty looked up as Wally flew into the kitchen.

'A bloke's here,' he shouted, a vein swelling in his neck. 'A great big bloke with glasses. Wanna see my drawing, Scotty?' He shoved the tin of peaches and a sheet of computer print-out under her nose. 'Guess who it's of.'

'I don't know,' said Scotty, not really looking. 'Is it Tom the Cabin Boy?'

Wally clicked his tongue. 'Does Tom the Cabin Boy,' he said with heavy sarcasm, 'have a red cape with a big S on it?'

'Hullo Scotty!' said Madigan. He stood just inside the door, knotting his hands, with the self-consciously interested expression of a tourist entering a museum. He was dressed in neat trousers, a tie and a cheap black jacket buttoned up to the neck. His large face looked benevolent, slightly puzzled, as innocent as a farmer's. 'Nasty damp weather, isn't it!' His manners seemed anachronistic, as if culled from a courtesy manual. Laurel put her finger between the pages of her book and gazed at him from behind.

'Are you looking for someone?' said Scotty, who was shifting sausages round under the griller with a pair of springy tongs.

'Oh, just a bit of human contact,' he said. He looked wildly at Scotty standing there in Ruth's apron, a meaner, musclier Myra, and suddenly his eyes filled with tears of self-pity and home-sickness. 'It's so cold down here!' he said in a strangled voice.

'No it's not!' Scotty laughed. 'It's hardly even the end of summer!'

'I can't stand it,' he said. He took off his glasses and wiped his eyes with a neatly folded handkerchief.

'*Is he crying?*' hissed Laurel in a piercing whisper.

Madigan took no notice, but polished his glasses busily and resettled them in their ungainly position against his eyelids. A dark flush had spread from his cheeks down his neck and inside his collar.

'Want a gin and tonic?' said Scotty. 'Get the morale up a bit?'

At the thread of kindness in her dry voice he sucked in his breath and rolled his fishy eyes in a parody of self-control. Through the pinkish blur of his steamed-up glasses he saw the intent faces of the children. He could hear the cracking of ice, unscrewing of lids, ripple of liquids, a fizz.

'Here. A little mood improver,' said Scotty, and shoved a cold glass into his hand. It was too late to ask for hot Milo, but for a second he despised her for not having offered it. He grabbed the glass and guzzled at it.

Laurel, overcome with interest and the desire to draw attention to herself, shoved past Wally and took centre stage in the kitchen. She gave two affected, feathery coughs and threw her chubby limbs into a pose: one arm bent, hand at the waist, the other arm curved up to shoulder height with its wrist sharply bent and fingers pointing downwards at the floor.

'Do I look like a teapot?' she cried shrilly.

Dinner was well finished and the children long since sent to play before Madigan had ruminated his way through his plateful. Scotty fidgeted over the empty china.

'Is there any reason why you eat so slowly?' she said.

He shrugged, carefully removed a morsel of gristle from

between his back teeth and laid it on the edge of his plate. 'There's a name for it,' he said. 'Fletcherism.'

'*Fletcherism?*' She laughed. 'Is this serious?'

'Some bloke named Fletcher reckoned you should chew each mouthful a hundred times. Actually, he said for a quarter of an hour, but I found that rendered me unfit for human company.'

'You mean you tried it?'

'For a while.' He placed his knife and fork alongside each other on his place and sat back.

Scotty studied him in the remaining daylight. 'You're not . . . sick, or anything, are you?' she said.

'Homesick.' He tried for a laugh, but could only produce a dismal cackle.

Scotty was not used to being dumbly asked for comfort. Criticism was more in her line. What would Ruth have done? Ruth knew all about misery and sympathy and hot-water bottles and snacks served up on wooden trays.

'We could make a fire,' she said at last.

'Does the chimney work?'

'Of course it works! What do you think we do in winter?'

'How would I know,' he said drearily.

'Oh come on,' said Scotty, her short patience beginning to fray. 'Bear it like the bullocks.'

An anxious voice rang out from the front of the house. 'Sco – tty!'

'Ye – es! I'm out here!'

Not loud enough.

'Sco – tty!'

She got up and went over to the kitchen door and saw Laurel

and Wally coming towards her along the dim hall. They were oddly quiet, moving hesitantly and very close together. Then Laurel saw Scotty and gave an exaggerated sigh, hand on heart, knees miming failure. 'Oh, thank God!' she cried with a shaky laugh.

'Did you think I'd gone out?' said Scotty, putting her hand on Laurel's shoulder.

'We came downstairs, and the kitchen light was off, and I thought –'

'We haven't even turned the lights on yet!' said Scotty. 'We were just talking. I wouldn't go out and leave you!'

The children looked up at her silently; even Wally was solemn with relief.

'Come on. I'll get you two into bed,' said Scotty. Over her shoulder she said to Madigan, 'How about you chop some kindling while I get this organised?'

She disappeared into the hallway.

Madigan kicked himself for not having confessed immediately that he had never chopped wood in his life. She would come back from the bedroom all bright and ready to start burning things and he'd be standing there like a shag on a rock, no wood cut, and she'd pause for a second as women do and turn on a slightly different smile and pick up the axe and do it all herself with him trailing along behind like a tin tied to her ankle. Everything always moved too fast for him. What a rotten town. It wasn't even autumn yet. He'd have to buy an electric blanket. Maybe they had second-hand ones down the Brotherhood. Surely a second-hand one couldn't be *safe*. How many days might a bloke lie out there in his hovel before someone missed him and came looking for him and discovered his charred remains?

When Scotty came back she took one look at him and marched straight through the kitchen and out to the shed. He heard a dozen solid, rhythmical blows and back she came with an armful of split kindling, which she dumped neatly on the hearth at the end of the long room. Raindrops had made shiny streaks in her black hair.

'I'll do it,' she said, tossing him a neutral look. 'Last person here from up north spent hours breaking the kindling up into icy-pole sticks. Queensland people don't know how to make fires.'

Off the hook. 'Don't they?' he said. 'I'll have to think about that.' He was struggling with a wave of a smooth, insidious comfort that rinsed away his confidence. 'Blokes these days,' he said in a murmur. 'Competent young women like you . . . it can be rather a humbling experience.'

'Don't get *too* abject.' She skilfully constructed a fire and put a match to it. It took, and she squatted in front of it watching the flames run along dry sticks. 'I haven't lost the knack,' she said, and gave a little closed-mouth laugh.

'I like you, Scotty,' he said, surprising himself, for he had at that moment felt the first twinge of rebellion.

She gave him a quick, suspicious look over her shoulder, but he was smiling at her quite openly, standing there with his feet close together and his hands by his sides like a tin soldier.

The room had darkened, and in the steadily gaining light of the fire, yellow and pink in the cave of blackened bricks, the table and chairs behind them grew larger and loomed more mysteriously.

'I once lived with this woman up in Queensland,' said Madigan in a rush. 'She was sort of – hubba hubba. She wore dresses made out of hundreds of coloured scarves, and those hippy oils that make you smell like a sweet biscuit, and sandals with high heels, and her hair went right down her back, and what a voice! She used to drive me wild. I should have had a baby with her.'

'A *baby*? What's that got to do with it?'

'Isn't that what people do?' said Madigan, still standing behind her.

'It might have been once, I suppose.'

'Oh, the world hasn't changed all that much, has it?' He gave a hearty laugh. 'You, for example. You could marry some nice bloke and have a family.'

'Come off it,' she said. 'Anyway, I've had my tubes tied.'

Madigan winced.

'Want to see my scar?' She stood up, pulled out her shirt and undid the top of her jeans to show him an inch of belly.

He forced himself to cast a glance, then turned away towards the fire. It was burning merrily. He gulped. There was a pause. Scotty tucked her shirt back into her jeans and squatted down.

'Didn't leave much of a mark, did it.' His voice was colourless, but his eyes blinked violently, pressing their lashes, bending them against the glass.

'Didn't hurt, either,' said Scotty. 'Know what? Just as I went under the anaesthetic, I could hear the radio in the operating theatre. It was Simon and Garfunkel, and they were singing *Cecilia, you're breaking my heart / You're shaking my confidence daily*.' She laughed, and sang a verse. '*Makin' love in the afternoon / With Cecilia up in my bedroom / I got up to wash my face / When I come back to bed / Someone's taken my place.*'

Madigan looked at her with a twisted smile. 'Are you trying to tell me something?' he said with difficulty.

'No.' Her smile faded. 'What do you mean?'

'It doesn't matter. I just thought . . .'

They stared into the fire.

'I suppose you've had an abortion too, have you.' His voice was as conversational as Wally's had been at the front door.

'Two, actually. Why?'

'I must be old-fashioned, or something. I can't get used to it.'

'You a Catholic, are you?'

'I can make up my own mind, thanks very much.'

'I had a religious conversion when I was twenty-two,' she said. 'Baptised, confirmed the lot. It only lasted two weeks. I was an Anglican.' She laughed.

'That woman I was telling you about,' he said. 'She had very compelling eyes. Her eyes were empty of everything but compulsion.'

He moved forward and leaned his arms against the mantelpiece, so that she could not see his face. Something in the angle of his leg and foot was childlike to her: Paddle shoes, free milk at playtime.

'What'll we talk about now?' she said.

'Do you think I could stay the night?' he said in a muffled voice.

They lay on their backs.

'The wind's getting up,' she said. 'Listen to it thumping in the chimney.'

He said nothing, but stared at the plaster garlands of the ceiling through his ugly spectacles, hands under his head.

'Aren't you going to take your glasses off?'

'Not yet.'

'Are you sleepy?'

'No.'

'I don't even know your first name,' said Scotty.

'I avoid using it. It makes me sound like a potato.'

'What is it?'

'Leo. Don't tell anyone.'

'What's wrong with that? It's Irish.'

'Go to the top of the class.'

'Wasn't there a Pope Leo?'

'Half a dozen, probably,' he said, discreetly slipping his glasses on to the floor under the bed.

'Well. Do you like your *last* name?'

'You'll try anything, won't you,' he said.

'Just want to keep things rolling along,' said Scotty. She reached out one arm and switched off the lamp. 'We don't have to fuck, if that's what's bothering you.'

He flinched. 'I thought that's what you people over here meant by inviting a bloke to stay the night.'

'It was your idea, not mine. What do you think we are, monsters? Let's go to sleep.'

He started to toss himself round in the bed, turning first his back to her and then his face with an unreadable expression on it: an angry, laughing, cynical grimace. 'I should go to sleep,' he mumbled. 'I should go home.'

'Well, go ahead! If you want to!'

'No no *no!* It's too far. I haven't got enough money for a taxi.'

'Stop thrashing round, will you? You've pulled the blankets right out at the bottom with your great feet.'

'Oh, what am I doing here?' he cried suddenly. 'I'm never

going to cut the mustard over this side of the river. I go crazy at home because no one takes anything seriously except dope, and then I come over here like a humble pilgrim, cap in hand, and I get taken so seriously I nearly die, of panic, or boredom. I try to remain aloof, suspicious, sceptical and yet trusting – isn't that how it's done?' His eyes were bulging.

'How *what's* done?' said Scotty, with an incredulous laugh.

He rounded on her. 'Well, make a joke, if you don't want me to get serious!'

'Sorry!' she said. 'I thought it *was* a joke!'

'You lot think everything's a joke.'

'*I* don't.'

'Well, don't poke fun at a bloke.'

It was like watching a war through a telescope: she could see skirmishes, wild rushes of movement to and fro, but was unable to tell whether there was a tactical intelligence in command, or whether all was lost and the armies were taking flight.

'The gulf between being awake and being asleep is *infinitesimal,*' he shouted, half mad with wakefulness, 'but it's *unbridgeable!*'

'What do you *want*?'

'I want to have fallen into a deep sleep five minutes ago!'

'Do you want me to tickle your back?' she said helplessly.

'I'll accept anything, at the moment.' He turned his broad, pink back to her, and she pulled up his ratty singlet and began to tickle him with her fingernails, making artistic patterns and swirls and not staying in the same place too long.

He flashed her a peculiar, almost malevolent smile over his shoulder. 'If you were a fightin' woman,' he said, 'you'd have thrown me out by now! You'd have said, "What sort of a place do you think this *is* we're running?" '

'Oh shut up, smartypants,' she said, furious. 'Sleep or don't sleep. I don't care.'

There was a short silence. Then he laughed quietly, and said, 'Good on you, Scotty. Sweet dreams.'

They fell asleep at last, back to back on the hard low bed.

The kids were playing pleasantly in the kitchen. Scotty brushed Wally's hair, his fly-away white straw, and clipped Laurel's toe-nails, and they sat in a row in the morning sun outside the back door. Laurel got out her finger-knitting and toiled away at it, breathing heavily through her nose.

'Look, Scotty,' she said. 'I can finger-knit. But I can't make it turn round and go the other way.'

A small brisk breeze ran round the garden. Wally stumbled about on his stilts in the damp grass, singing and laughing to himself. Red leaves on top of the gum tree skittered and sparkled in the wind.

'Do you think it's going to be warm today?' said Scotty.

'Turn on the radio and find out,' said Wally sensibly.

'I feel rather happy,' said Scotty. 'It's a bit like the olden days, don't you think?'

'We weren't born in the olden days,' said Laurel, smiling at Scotty and pushing her glasses up her nose with the back of her wrist. 'So we don't know. Do we.'

Scotty crept back into her room and stood at the table. When she turned round she saw that Madigan was awake, lying on his back watching her with his eyes half-closed. Without his spectacles, the whole area of skin round his eyes looked tender and defenceless; his lips were dark red, his pale cheeks blurred with a shimmer of new whisker.

'You look funny,' he said, 'standing there in that position.'

'Funny?'

'Yes. You sort of pull your mouth down and it gives you a double chin.'

'Thanks a lot.'

'Was I really unbearable last night?'

'No more than you are this morning.'

'What've I said?'

'I love being told I've got a double chin and look funny.'

'You're tough enough to take the truth, aren't you?'

'I *know* the truth already,' she said, 'about the way I look.'

'Sometimes you look real pretty. And other times your face is . . . kind of . . . lumpy.'

'I *know* all this! You don't have to tell me! I don't think I'm beautiful!'

'I'm not either,' he said. 'I know I'm just a clod who can play the mouth organ.'

'I *like* the way you look.'

He pulled a frog-face and laughed. 'Cut it out, Scotty. You make me feel like a matinee idol.'

'How did we get on to this subject, anyway?' she said.

'I was just watching you. I like you, Scotty. Come here.'

She took two steps towards the bed and he flung himself at her knees and tumbled her down beside him. She fell stiffly. 'Come on,' he said. 'Put your head on my shoulder. That's right. Don't take too much notice of me. I'm in shock, a lot of the time. Come on, leave your head there. People ought to be able to be nice to each other sometimes. Not crying, are you?'

'I don't know,' she said. 'There's some funny liquid coming out my eyes.'

He felt her face with his fingertips. 'I think it's tears, Scotty.'

She started to laugh in weak, silly fits, and he kept holding her head gently between his neck and shoulder.

'Ruth's going to leave, I think,' she said, 'and she'll take Laurel with her.'

'Isn't the boy hers too?'

'Yes. But Laurel's been *mine*.'

'Oh. I get it.'

'I thought you didn't understand new-fangled ideas.'

'I know what it is to like a *kid*, for Christ's sake.'

The sun was slanting through the faded pink curtains, making the wooden floor bright.

'Want me to read you a story?' he said.

'All right.'

He picked up a book from beside the bed and looked at its cover. It was one of Laurel's. '*The Juniper Tree*,' he announced in a state school 'interesting' voice. 'Let's read a page each. I'll start. *It was a long time ago now, as much as two thousand years maybe, that there was a rich man and he had a wife and she was beautiful and good, and they loved each other very much but they had no children . . .*'

When it was her turn she feared to offend with her unpopular tone of voice, but he suddenly seized her head in both hands and kissed her violently on the mouth. 'What a nice voice you've got!' he said. 'I've never really heard it before.'

'It's a teacher's voice,' she said.

'I love it,' he said casually. 'My turn. *She began to hate the little boy and would push him around from one corner to the other and push him here and pinch him there so that the poor child was always in a fright. When he came home from school there was no quiet place where he could be.*'

'This is a bit close to the bone,' said Scotty.

'It's only a simple story,' he said, looking up and marking his place with one finger.

'That's what's so terrible about it,' said Scotty. 'It's so ordinary and familiar.' She tried to wipe the tears away secretly with the corner of the sheet.

'Bear up, Scotty!'

'Aren't I allowed to cry at a sad story?'

'Of course you are.' He read on to the end, singing the little song each time – '*Tweet twee what a pretty bird am I!*' – in his cracked, true voice, glancing at her to see how she was taking it. Scotty wept away soundlessly, head between his elbow and his side, holding the sheet up to her eyes.

When the story was finished he put down the book and they lay there quietly in the bed. In the next room someone had begun to play the piano, hesitantly and with many a mistake. Madigan shifted so that his head was on her breast and she held it in her arms.

———

Ruth set off with her long, swagman's stride that Saturday morning, through the network of streets and lanes to Dennis's place. A heavy string bag stuffed with clothes and food was slung over her shoulder. Her head, borne well forward on her bowed neck, cut the air with a patient expression, her eyes half squinted against the breeze of her progress. She was thinking sketchily, in a mild, scattered panic, that she would soon have to start looking for another place to live.

She remembered the night she and Scotty had ridden their bikes to the empty house Scotty had found. They had pulled loose one of the louvres of the bathroom window and crammed themselves through the gap, breathless with stifled giggling and the intruder's voluptuous desire to shit. The torch's custardy ring of light wavered before them in the pitch-dark rooms, fleas swarmed and attacked their shins.

'What do you reckon?' said Scotty, standing the torch on the cement floor so that their ankles were bathed in its beam.

Ruth hesitated. 'I dunno. Without the others . . . two's not enough, is it?'

'I think I might know a bloke,' said Scotty.

Three had not been enough. Still, in the yard, sometimes a weird spasm occurred in Ruth's nervous system which almost passed for emotion. Her spade bit and spat. Weeds gave up their grip with a rending sound. Her mop steamed gently in morning sunlight; her arms reached up with pegs and sopping cloth. Moons speckled the concrete under the nectarine tree, and bounced off the brick wall of the shed, bright as day. The sighs and protests that weather wrung from the house were to Ruth like the familiar creak of knee or wrist. She would have to drag herself out, gather herself together once more, draw the children round her like a warm but prickling blanket, and take the leap, start it all again, make what she could of bare rooms and a back yard full of dry clods.

A red car flew past Ruth where she trudged. She glanced into it and saw, like a frozen scene from a play, a Greek man driving, intent at once on the road and on his wife who was telling a story with upflung hand and merry, moving lips. A child leaned over between them from the back seat, like his father listening eagerly, rapt, mouth trembling, ready to burst into laughter. They performed their happy moment for her and were gone. She stood on the corner waiting for the lights to change.

She came in the back way and found Dennis in bed at midday in his stuffy room, unconscious, though he swore later that he had merely been asleep. He was curled up on his side, his mouth agape so that the pillow was soaked with saliva in a wide ring under his cheek. The gas fire was on full blast, the window nailed shut, the blankets sodden with sweat. Ruth stepped forward in alarm to make sure he was still actually breathing. She turned the heater down to a hiss and opened the front door to let in a stream of sunny air. Still he did not move. She stood staring down at him, saw his blond hair all damp and sticking to his skull, his eyes tightly closed, his thick lashes, much darker than his hair, gummed together in spikes on the grey circles under his eyes. She went out into the daylight and bought a bag of oranges at the shop. When she got back he had not stirred. His boots lay where he had wrenched them off, one standing upright, the other crumpled over and drooping at the ankle. The sight of them provoked an irritable tenderness in her: she put her hand on his forehead and he rolled over suddenly on to his back. His eyes popped open and he stared blindly at her.

'G'day.'

'You're not looking *after* yourself properly!' she said angrily. 'You're *sick!*'

His greyish-blue eyes contracted; he looked puzzled. 'Mouth's all dry,' he mumbled.

She got out her pocket knife, cut up an orange into eighths and served it to him on the folded paper bag. He did not notice that she gave him three oranges in this manner, but went on greedily sucking the slices and dropping the peels among the screwed-up tissues beside the bed. He announced his draconian cure in a voice she hardly recognised. 'I'm gunna sweat it outa me system,' he grunted.

'We better forget about the Prom, then,' said Ruth.

He did not answer, but flopped back on to the pillow and closed his eyes. Roughly she pushed his head to one side and flipped the pillow over.

She stayed with him all day, as he burned away in the bed, sometimes laughing childishly to himself or champing his jaws as if chewing. Once he half sat up and saw her sitting there and let out what sounded like a sob. 'Oh, hullo sweetheart!' he said, and dozed off again. Towards late afternoon he was sleeping more gently, and his temperature had dropped.

She cleaned up his dismal kitchen, emptied food out of its packets into airtight jars and lined them up in the wire-fronted meat-safe which served him as a cupboard. At ten o'clock she went into the bathroom and cleaned her teeth, brushing noisily with the water running. She turned off the tap and the silence it left was filled with the quiet sound of rain.

When she woke at six in the morning, his skin felt cool and dry. She put one arm carefully round his back and lay there in the dim tingling of hope, the optimism of simply existing, that comes sometimes to the wakeful one in a house where others are sleeping. She heard the wind cradling the house, moving endlessly in the concrete spaces of his yard.

In the afternoon the sky was clear and the air had stilled. Dennis would not stay in bed, though his face was shadowy with thinness.

They came into the Botanic Gardens at the top corner where the big eucalypts stand becalmed, their bark wrinkled at the junction of trunk and branch like human skin after winter. On the northern horizon, beyond the city, there gathered mighty palaces of cloud, pale Italian pink and of complex, fat design.

No, Dennis would not do it.

'What's wrong with the way things are now?' he said, sliding out his chin and twisting his head about as if he were wearing a tight collar.

'You don't look after yourself,' said Ruth.

'Oh, yesterday!' He clicked his tongue. 'That was nothing. That was different.'

'I dunno,' said Ruth. 'Sometimes people need –'

'I don't wanna get married!'

'I didn't mean that!' she cried. 'I never meant married! You *know* that's not what I meant!'

'Well,' he said sullenly. 'I don't wanna *live* with anyone, either. With a woman, I mean.'

'Why not.' Her voice was already dull with defeat, but she slogged on.

'You know what happens to couples! What do you bloody

women talk about in these groups, anyway!'

'There hasn't *been* a group for two years,' said Ruth.

'Find another woman to live with, why don't you, if you don't like the set-up you're in now.' He threw up one hand and glanced after it, as if hoping for a materialisation. 'Find one with kids — you'd get the full sympathy syndrome.'

'I don't want to,' said Ruth. 'I want to live with *you.*'

'I can't.'

'But *why?*'

He punched one fist into the other palm and said in exasperation, 'Time. Time, mostly.'

'What do you mean, time.'

'I haven't *got* any. I go to work, I go to meetings.' He turned his face away, almost laughing with embarrassment.

'We'd have *more* time, if we lived in the same house,' she said, flogging the hopeless argument.

'Look, Ru. If you wanted more than what you're already gettin', you'd have to ask me to give up *politics.*' He threw down his trump card with a defiant flourish, watching her out of the tail of his eye.

Ruth's head came up, as he had foreseen. 'Oh, I'd never do *that,*' she said, chastened.

They sat opposite each other at a weathered timber table under creepers thronged with green and yellowing leaves, a tray of Devonshire tea between them. Ruth was almost crying, fumbling for her tobacco.

'I mean — you see blokes,' said Dennis, frowning and grinning and forcing the spoon again and again into the sugar bowl, 'blokes who walk round as if they've got a sack of cement on their shoulders, and the woman's sittin' there full of resentment, and he's wishin' he could –'

'That's not what I *meant*,' said Ruth again, in misery. 'I meant – it'd be *collective*. Not like a couple. We'd have separate rooms –'

'Nah, Ru. It's not on, mate. Giss a scone.'

She shoved the plate towards him and they ate, a caricature of the couples around them, unable to look at each other. She felt stuffed with food, and ate to comfort herself, though she could hardly swallow. A wasp dived repeatedly into the jam dish, then fled sideways. They eyed it, nervous of its sting. 'Shit! Oh, shit!' said Dennis, swatting, a small blob of whipped cream on the end of his nose.

They walked round the lake, wading through oceans of dead leaves. The gardens were as busy as Bourke Street: whole Jewish families, parties of nuns and old people from institutions moved along the curving paths, gesturing graciously and casting their eyes to left and right like courtly dancers. There was no hope for the human race. Everything would end in greyness.

'Oh, come on, Ru. Cheer up!' said Dennis, dropping an arm across her shoulders.

'People always say that to me,' she said bitterly, in a low voice.

'No they don't. Come on,' he insisted. He hugged her shoulders till they cracked, then gave her a hard thump between the shoulder blades. 'I'm with you all the way,' he said, and put his hands back in his pockets.

'Why don't you come round more then.'

He could hardly hear her. 'What?'

'I said, *Come round more!*' she yelled at him. 'You reckon you're on my side, but you're never there, except to sleep.'

He writhed his shoulders. 'I don't like it at your place,' he said. 'I don't feel comfortable there. Scotty puts me off.'

'She puts me off, too,' said Ruth. 'I *hate* her.' She looked almost noble with wretchedness. 'She's always tellin' me what to do.'

'Kick her out then.'

'I'd rather go myself. I've got *some* pride.'

'I'll help you, soon as you get a place,' he said, safe enough now to be generous.

'Thanks,' said Ruth dully.

She saw a dead sparrow lying half covered in leaves at the corner of a garden bed, and gave it a kick with the toe of her shoe. The little corpse flipped up oddly, its wings stiffly spread, and dived back head-first into the thick, papery carpet. She glanced crookedly at Dennis, as guilty as if she had killed the bird herself, but he had witnessed the display of sadism with a half laugh of respect, even of comradeliness. She began to talk in a rush.

'The kids used to always have funerals for dead animals,' she said. 'Laurel used to make little crosses for the graves, 'n' everything. Then when the budgies started keelin' over from old age, first they had mass graves, then the kids got sick of it, 'n' the last one that died, Wal just chucked it in the bushes.'

Dennis laughed out loud in relief. 'That's the spirit. Good on you,' he said, as if admiring a skilful performance.

Ruth laughed without mirth. 'Next thing you'll be sayin' "Well done", like Scotty does,' she said. 'Talkin' like a teacher.' She tightened her lips and mimicked Scotty: *'Well done!'*

She took another breath, but before she could speak again he had veered off the path and wandered down to the edge of the lake. He crouched there above the burnished surface of the water, looking for fish perhaps, and she stood watching him from behind, her arms wrapped round herself. In that moment she saw him separate from herself, forgetful of her, about to emerge whole into the outside world. She fell back weakly into love with his past, with the things he knew which she did not. She loved him and would appropriate for her own son the accoutrements of this idealised working-class boyhood: bare laminex tables, sagging single beds with heads made of curved iron, cheap tartan slippers, slug guns, grey tube-like shorts, playgrounds ringing with harsh cries and encircled by peppercorns and cyclone wire. The tears shrivelled in her chest: the temper of her blood was already adjusted.

Scotty knew, when Wally stuck out his tongue at her at the bottom of the stairs, that Ruth must be back. There was new resolution in the air, in Ruth's firm step and grim, purposeful expression; at dinner time people kept their eyes on their plates, embarrassed at the possibility of conversation. Only Wally seemed relaxed and oblivious of tension.

'Hey Lol,' he said, shoving a handful of rice into his mouth. 'You know that kid Sharon that I fucked?'

'You?' Laurel blushed. 'You never fucked anyone! You're too little.'

'I – did!' shouted Wally. His cheeks were greasy with food. 'Down the creek! Me 'n' her –'

'That'll do,' cut in Ruth. 'Eat your dinner. Here, Wal. Use a fork.' She pushed one into his fist. Wally looked up with his squinting grin.

'Wanna know somethink?' His smile became secretive. 'We might be movin' out. An' if we do, it'll be because of *someone*.' He ran his triumphant eyes round the assembled household. Horrified, they stared at him. Wally glowed and blossomed. 'Someone at *this table*,' he said. 'Someone *fat*, with sorta black *hair*.' His eyes came to rest on Scotty; he raised one rice-smeared hand and pointed at her. 'It's *you*, Scotty! 'Cause you treat us like *shit*!'

Wally and Scotty stared at each other. Alex and Ruth dropped their eyes, excruciated lest someone laugh.

'An' Alex, too!' shouted Wally, angry now as he felt the transitoriness of his moment of power. ''Cause *he* made us *eat cod*!'

Laurel cried out in indignation. 'You never told me, Ruth!'

'I was gunna, mate,' she said wearily.

'Won't we have a meeting?' said Alex.

There was a pause.

'I don't think we need to have a meeting,' said Ruth, staring with eyes of glass at the wall beside Alex's head. 'There's nothin' to say. Only a few loose ends to tie up.'

'You mean — it's all settled?' said Alex.

'It's time to get out,' said Ruth. 'I wish I'd gone last year.'

There was a run of movement round the table. Laurel turned to Ruth again and said, shocked and excited, 'We'll have to find a really good house, won't we, Ruth! What sort of house will we find?'

'Oh, nothin' special, matey,' said Ruth with a sharp sigh. 'Just s'long's it's a roof over our heads.'

With one accord Ruth and Scotty got up to clear the plates. They skirted each other widely in the confined space, their faces stiff with shame and hatred. People ate their desserts in haste, standing up in different parts of the room.

Ruth led the children into the lounge and turned on the television. It flickered at them where they sat in tight formation on the couch, Ruth in the middle with an arm around each child. On the screen a jet took off in California with a stuntman rigged up and strapped erect to its top.

'That's Spiderman,' said Laurel. She stuck her thumb in her mouth.

'No it's not,' said Wally. 'That's the Human Fly.'

The man's face must have been hideously stretched with the pressure of the air.

'Ruth,' said Wally.

'What, mate.'

'You know Jimmy. Well when's he comin' back? 'Cause I miss him *so much*.'

She squeezed him harder against her side, feeling the springy give of his little rib-cage.

'We should be hearin' from him any day now,' she said.

'Yeah, but *when*.' He was quite loose against her.

'I told you, Wal. Any day.'

Laurel took her thumb out. 'Ruth,' she said. 'What does the Human Fly do when he's finished?'

'Collects his pay cheque and goes home, I suppose,' said Ruth.

In the kitchen Scotty and Alex washed and dried the dishes, without speaking. Scotty passed the lounge room door on her way to the stairs, and glanced in. Laurel's head was the only one to turn. She looked straight at Scotty, and moved her left hand, on the arm of the couch, in a furtive salute.

~T~

Over the river, Scotty walked straight into the sepulchral house, past the foot of the stairs and towards the kitchen, from which conversation could be heard. She paused outside the door.

'I think we should allow for each other's idiosyncrasies,' said a man's voice, slightly raised.

'Each other's what?' said a woman.

'Do you mean laziness, Tony?' said another woman.

'There's no need to get *personal*,' said the man.

'How can you talk about idiosyncrasies and not be personal?' said the second woman.

'I think you're being a bit sharp with me,' said Tony, sounding wounded.

Scotty let herself be seen in the doorway. It was a dim room whose window was half-obscured by ivy, and no one had turned on the light, though some activity seemed to be in progress. A tall man who had rubber-banded his hair into a tight little club at the back of his neck was crossing the room holding in his fist a bunch of what looked like flowers: he passed Scotty and she saw that they were cooked sausages. Madigan was not present. The sausage-eater was drowning his food in tomato sauce and paid her no attention, but one of the women looked up at her and smiled.

'I was looking for Madigan,' said Scotty.

'He's out in his room, I think,' said Myra. 'Like a cup of tea?'

'No thank you,' said Scotty. 'I don't drink tea.'

'Don't you?' said Myra pleasantly. 'What do you do all day, then?'

Scotty would not admit Myra's gentle joke. She stood by the fridge with her hands plunged into the pockets of her zipper jacket, her eyes travelling warily round the room, her dark face cold with shyness, ready to judge.

'Which is his room?' she said.

'Out the back, past the dunny, and keep going,' said Myra.

The shed was shut. She knocked.

'What.'

She opened the door and slid in. He was lying under an eiderdown with a book open on his chest. He stared at her. The small area of room which was not bed had a temporary look, clogged with things half-unpacked from boxes, as if he had just arrived or were contemplating leaving. There did not appear to be any source of light, or air.

'You'll go blind,' said Scotty, 'trying to read in that light.'

'I'm hiding in here,' he said.

'Have you got your *pyjamas* on? At seven o'clock at night?'

'None of your business.'

'What are you hiding from?'

'Oh, the women want us to wash up more, and do the shopping.'

She grabbed the corner of the eiderdown and whisked it off him. 'Get inside then, bludger.' He was revealed on his back, fully dressed, with his hands up holding the book in front of his chin.

'What *is* this?' he cried in a rage, not moving. 'The rape of the

Sabine women? You come bursting in here while a bloke's trying to have a quiet read – is nothing sacred?'

'Oh bugger it,' she said, turning away from the bed with a gesture of disgust. 'I've got enough house problems without sticking my nose into yours.'

'You're so rude!'

'Am I? Sorry.' She sat down on a stool. 'I feel terrible. I don't know what to do with myself. I just hopped on the bus and came over. Want to come out for a coffee, or something? I promise I'll be nice. Not manful.'

'Give me a minute to think about it.'

'I'll pay, even.'

'Let me *think*, will you?'

'Entertain me, for God's sake! I'll be crazy in ten minutes. Go on – I helped you, the other night.'

'You call that help?' he scoffed. 'I'll never forgive you for that night. I felt – contemptuous.'

'*What?*'

'You were pathetic. You were so forgiving you nearly made me sick. You should've kicked me out.'

'Oh I should have, should I?'

She stood at the end of his bed looking down at his heavy crumpled figure, his thick mousy hair and resentful expression, and suddenly hurled herself on him, sending the book flying. She straddled him, grabbed a handful of his shirt front and wrenched at it violently. There was a satisfying sound of ripping cloth, and buttons peppered the wall.

'Hey!' he roared, electrified. 'I *liked* that shirt!'

'Stiff shit.' She pinned his shoulders to the bed and pounded him against the mattress till his teeth rattled, but he recovered his wits and got her leg in a lock: she fought hard, but the best she could do was to keep the upper half of him immobilised, and by now they were weak with laughter and effort.

'You know what you are, Scotty?' he gasped. 'You're a star-fucker.'

'Who, me? You flea-bitten mutt.' She could only dig her fingers into his shoulders, dead-locked as they were.

'Why didn't you kick me out?'

'Because you looked as if you wanted to stay.'

'I was bored!'

'Bored! Bored, were you? Well, fuck you! If you were bored, why didn't you say so, and go elsewhere?'

He looked abashed, and slid his eyes sideways. 'I was shy.'

'Oi was shoi,' she mimicked him. 'Why don't you just work out what you want to do, and then do it?'

'I thought I had – but suddenly I found you tickling my back.'

'I didn't hear any complaints at the time.'

'How could I complain? It was like sleeping with the district nurse!'

She let go and so did he, and she stood up, still panting, and tucked her shirt in at the waist.

'Come on,' she said. 'Let's go and have a coffee.'

'I haven't got much money,' he said automatically.

'I've got plenty. Come on.'

'Don't rush me, Scotty! You're so precipitate.' He got off the bed and scrounged under it for his shoes, which he pulled on and began to lace up in a complicated fashion.

She stood by the door waiting.

'Actually,' said Madigan, as he finished tying a bow in the first shoelace and turned his attention to the other, 'I can't really go out for a coffee. There's something I have to do.'

'What?'

'Sing.'

'Tonight?'

'Yes. In this old folkie club up the top of Collins Street. It's the sort of joint where earnest young chaps play those guitars that don't make any noise.'

'Why didn't you say so before?' she said impatiently.

'Well, it's like this,' he said, settling into a leisurely exposition. 'The pay's a bit piddling, but it's a foot in the door, as it were. I've got a couple of things planned – few jokes, few songs – bee-yodle-ay-i-hew!' he warbled in his sweet, sharp voice. 'I am a professional, after all.'

He stood up slowly and combed his hair down with both hands. 'It's not very gentlemanly, is it,' he added politely, 'keeping you hanging on like this.'

Scotty pointed the toe of one foot and described a figure of eight on the lino, her hands out of sight inside her jacket. 'Well, I suppose I ought to push off, then,' she said.

'You couldn't give us a lift into town, could you?' said Madigan, glancing around him on the floor.

She looked up at him with narrowed eyes. 'I told you,' she said in a blank voice. 'I came on the bus.'

'Oh. Never mind, then. I'll jump on the tram myself. Better get a move on,' he said, unconvincingly.

He buttoned his black corduroy jacket right up to the neck to cover his torn shirt and stood at the foot of the bed, as if on parade.

Scotty gave a short laugh. 'You look like a Jew at a funeral.'

'You wouldn't want to come with me, I suppose,' he said, not looking at her.

They got off the tram at the Town Hall and walked up Collins Street in the fresh dark. Leaves were coming down here, too: big twisted ones that crackled underfoot on the square pavement blocks, or drifted crabwise with a loud scraping sound.

In the window of an expensive shop, Scotty noticed a diaphanous flowery dress.

'Look,' she said, pointing. 'If I were that kind of person, that's the sort of dress I'd love to wear.'

'You're not, though, are you,' he said with a gusty laugh. 'Imagine you! With your big fat body and crabby face.'

She walked on quickly. He caught up with her on the steps of the Alexandra Club, where she sat between the polished brass handrails, her face expressionless. He took hold of her hand.

'Hey Scotty,' he said gently. 'Do you want me to live with you?'

'No!' she cried, trying to jerk her hand away.

He kept his grip on it, and gave it a little shake. 'What aristocratic fingers you have, Scotty,' he said.

'We don't even know each other,' said Scotty.

'But isn't that why people live together? So they *can* know each other?'

'How should I know?'

'I thought you people knew all about this kind of thing.'

'I find you extremely . . . disturbing,' she said.

'Oh! Well . . . I'll have to think about that,' he said. He dropped her hand and mooned away towards the top of the street. 'You have a decent job, of course. And I'm just the king of the dole bludgers.'

'You play for money, don't you? I thought you said you were a professional.'

'I *know*,' he snapped. 'I know, I know, I know.'

She shrugged and stood up from the cold step, plucking at the seat of her pants.

He dawdled more than usual, at the end, and when they left the building and he stood back for her at the door it was as if she were dragging him behind her. A cool wind raced up Collins Street.

'I loved the music,' she said awkwardly. 'I loved it in there. I was really surprised. The songs were beautiful. You've got a beautiful voice.'

'Don't flatter me!' he yelled, almost choking.

'I'm not! I liked the music!'

'They're only period pieces! I thought you were supposed to be intelligent! Can't you *see* that?'

'I just wanted to say I was happy in there!'

'OK! OK! I'm glad you were happy!' He jerked his big head away from her.

'What are we going to do now?' said Scotty.

'I wish you had a car,' he said. 'I feel like being waited on hand and foot.'

'Well I haven't. We'll have to get the tram, or walk.'

He stopped in his tracks and turned on her so suddenly that his shoulder jarred her chin and her teeth clashed. 'I'd like to be brutally frank with you, Scotty,' he said.

'What?'

'I think you're wasting your time with me.'

She stared at him.

'I'm a cold fish sometimes,' he said. 'Specially after a gig.'

'What are you trying to say?'

Again that run of expressions passed across his face, like the shuffling of not-quite identical cards: malevolence, dislike, a sarcastic smile. 'You want to take me home with you, don't you?' he said.

'I suppose so. Don't you want to come?'

'Why did you come to this gig, Scotty?'

'To hear you sing! You invited me!'

'Yes – but I can't be responsible, see what I mean? It's work, for me. Work first, women second. I can't be responsible for you having a good time.'

'I don't know what you're talking about,' said Scotty. 'And I think that kind of priority system is absolutely pathetic.'

They faced each other under the trees. The foliage shifted about restlessly, veiling and revealing the street lamp. Stubbornly he pressed on.

'When you go to those rock gigs, like the one I met you at – what do you go for?'

'What are you *talking* about?'

He shuffled his feet impatiently and turned his face into the wind: it flattened his hair and he looked smaller, as if standing inside a casing of garments too large for him. 'Look – before I talked to you, that night you and Alex drove me home, I was standing at the bar in that awful dump, and there was a girl next to me, pretty, but you could hardly see her face, it was so caked with make-up. One of the blokes in Alex's band walks up to the bar – that thin tall bloke with hair slicked back and trousers hitting the shoe just right, you know? And she turns and says to him in this dead voice, "Do you come here often?" And the bloke goes, "That's not a very original approach." And she keeps staring at him and says, "What?" I mean, Scotty, do you get it? She'd never even heard the joke. Oh Jesus!' he groaned, gnashing his teeth and butting his shoulder against the wall. 'They were like two corpses. I can't stand it.'

'What's all this got to do with *me?*'

'You go to those gigs, don't you? Looking for someone to go home with?'

'Where are you *getting* all this stuff from? I've never picked up a bloke in my life!' She was facing him, four-square.

He looked shocked, then nonplussed; he spun round, clapped his hands together like a master of ceremonies, and suddenly looked uncannily suave.

'Sex,' he declared, 'is a nuisance.'

'But it makes you feel good.'

'So does a Choo-Choo Bar.'

'Not *that* good.'

Way down at the bottom of the street appeared the headlights and illuminated number of a tram. 'Listen,' she said. 'If you're about to have a fit of the vapours, I'm going.'

He seized her arm. *'I don't want you to go.'*

'Lay off, will you?' She fought free and took two steps back. 'You make me feel crazy. I don't understand what you want from me.'

'Sometimes,' he said, turning humble, 'I think what I'm looking for is a surrogate mother — someone to cuddle me and tell me there's no such thing as duty — nothing I have to do.'

'You won't get that from me!' The rails were singing shrilly two blocks away. 'I thought you'd been around,' she said, talking quickly and feeling for her money. 'I didn't think you were one of those junior woodchucks. You told me you were a professional. I thought you'd been *around*.'

'I'm just a babe in the woods, compared to you!'

The sign on the tram was visible now. It was the right one. It swayed up the hill, cord lashing in the wind, the driver black in his cabin.

'You don't feel comfortable with me, do you,' he insisted. 'I wish you did. I wish I could make you feel comfortable.'

'Are you kidding?' She was stepping out on to the road with the coins in her hand. 'One minute you're talking about living together, the next you're telling me I'm a band moll.'

She was halfway across the road to the tramline, flagging the driver down as if afraid she was invisible.

'Why'd you do it, Scotty?' he cried wildly. 'All that stuff? Your tubes, or whatever you call 'em?'

'Do *what*?' Her incredulous face flashed at him over her shoulder. 'What are you crying for?'

His words were drowned in the screeching of the tram's arrival. Scotty was up the step in one bound and into a seat before it had properly stopped. The conductor grinned at her and dinged the bell so that the tram lurched away again without a pause and went keeling round the corner. Madigan stood there between the silvery tracks staring after her: she hung her head out the open doorway and waved, but she was already too far away for him to see her face. She could have been anyone. And probably was. He clenched his teeth and let out a subdued

shriek, rolling his oyster eyes to heaven and punching downwards from the waist with both fists. Then he turned rapidly
aside, crossed back to the footpath, and sloped off towards
Swanston Street. By the time he had passed Georges he was
singing to himself.

Ruth came home from the movies at midnight. She opened the
front door, then went back to the car and carried the sleeping
children in to their beds, one at a time. She put out her hand to
the knob of her own door, and noticed the folded sheet of paper
half in the room and half out, on the floor. She bent down and
picked it up.

It was one of Scotty's self-portraits: a stumpy figure in baggy
pants, a blue and white striped jumper and tiny black sunglasses. The figure was wearing a penitent expression and
holding a white flag. Out of its mouth came a balloon containing
the words *Let's bury the hatchet*.

Ruth heaved a slow, quivering sigh, stepped into her room,
and shut the door. The note aroused in her such a wave of
loathing that she thought she was going to be sick: she slouched
to the fireplace and leaned her forehead against the cold bricks.
After a moment she sat down on the bed and pulled her diary out
from under the mattress.

Scotty, lying awake in the dark, her ears sharpened by a kind
of hope, heard Ruth unfold the note and sigh.

In the morning Ruth was already in the yard when Scotty
came out to make her breakfast.

'Hey Ruth,' she called into the yard where Ruth was upending the compost bucket into the enclosure she had built with planks. 'Want me to make you a cup of camomile tea?'

'Yes please,' said Ruth, without looking up.

Scotty fiddled with the latch of the wire door. 'How do you make it?' This was as close as Scotty would ever come to appeasement.

Ruth did not give an inch. She turned round in a slow movement, holding the green plastic bucket in her arms, and stared narrowly at Scotty. 'You've made it before.'

Scotty stood still. Then she shrugged, let the wire door slam loosely shut, and went to the sink where she began to fill a yellow saucepan with water.

Ruth came into the kitchen from outside.

'Did you get my note?' said Scotty.

Ruth raised her eyes. Her mouth was a bitter line.

'Do you really think,' she said slowly and deliberately, 'that a little note with a smart drawing is gunna make any difference at all, at this stage?'

Scotty withdrew, stiff-backed.

'I've felt your hatchet too many times to drop mine for a *funny drawing*,' said Ruth.

Scotty pushed past her and out the screen door into the yard. She began to unpeg dry sheets from the line, slinging them over her shoulder. Somewhere inside the house a bell was ringing in a sharp, double rhythm. The pegs dropped into the grass and disappeared. The bell stopped. She elbowed her way in through the door and met Ruth in the middle of the room. Sun laid its bland stripes across the scarred red concrete floor.

'That was Jimmy,' said Ruth in a queer, faint voice. 'He's

comin' back. They let him out. He asked me when he could take —'

'Oh Ruth.'

For one beat of time there might have been comfort offered, accepted, a quick flooding over the barricades: but Ruth stepped back instead of forward, folding her arms and narrowing her eyes. The air sang in the room.

'Ruth,' said Scotty in a trembling voice. 'I'm finding life very difficult at the moment. Can't we try to be a bit more pleasant to each other, just till you go?'

Ruth fixed her with a terrible white stare. 'Sometimes the simplest things are the hardest to do.'

'But if we could just make an effort —'

'I don't *feel* like being particularly pleasant to you, Scotty,' said Ruth between her teeth.

Scotty swallowed. 'Maybe we could try to be civil to each other.'

'I'm being *bloody* civil to you! You know what I hate about you, Scotty? You've never really been up against it. All your life you've just taken what you need. Everything all falls into place for you. You don't even know what trouble is, or grief.'

Scotty lashed back. 'So now there's a Richter scale of suffering, is there? They'll have to extend it right up as far as martyrdom and sainthood in your case, won't they.'

Ruth's teeth cut her breath. 'You fuckin' cold bitch,' she whispered.

'Christ, Ruth, you make me feel —'

What was this?

They were on opposite sides of the room, the two women,

footsoles spreading on stone, backs against walls. Sheets floated like flags or slowly falling banners, a chair sprawled on its side, a plate struck a window-frame and smashed brilliantly, ears roared like oceans, sweat popped out in diamond chips. There was a loud noise. It was a voice screeching, 'Old! Old! Old!'

There fell a silence. Chooks crooned and clucked drowsily, tapped their silly beaks against the tin fence. A fly laboured.

So this was why people in real life screamed and broke things and grew violent: because the mind let go, and afterwards, your body was as loose and fine as a sleeper's, a dancer's, a satisfied lover's. You were empty, all your molecules were harmoniously re-aligned. You were skinned, liberated, wise. You were out of reach.

A mouth formed words. 'Now we can leave each other alone.'

'I can accept that,' said another, low, a thousand miles away.

Postcards from Surfers

'ONE NIGHT I DREAMED THAT I DID NOT LOVE, AND
THAT NIGHT, RELEASED FROM ALL BONDS, I LAY AS
THOUGH IN A KIND OF SOOTHING DEATH.'
Colette

We are driving north from Coolangatta airport. Beside the road the ocean heaves and heaves into waves which do not break. The swells are dotted with boardriders in black wet-suits, grim as sharks.

'Look at those idiots,' says my father.

'They must be freezing,' says my mother.

'But what about the principle of the wet-suit?' I say. 'Isn't there a thin layer of water between your skin and the suit, and your body heat . . .'

'Could be,' says my father.

The road takes a sudden swing round a rocky outcrop. Miles ahead of us, blurred in the milky air, I see a dream city: its cream, its silver, its turquoise towers thrust in a cluster from a distant spit.

'What — is that Brisbane?'

'No,' says my mother. 'That's Surfers.'

My father's car has a built-in computer. If he exceeds the speed limit, the dashboard emits a discreet but insistent pinging. Lights flash, and the pressure of his right foot lessens. He controls the windows from a panel between the two front seats. We cruise past a Valiant parked by the highway with a FOR SALE sign propped in its back window.

'Look at that,' says my mother. 'A WA number-plate. Probably thrashed it across the Nullarbor and now they reckon they'll flog it.'

'Pro'ly stolen,' says my father. 'See the sticker? ALL YOU VIRGINS, THANKS FOR NOTHING. You can just see what sort of a pin'ead he'd be. Brain the size of a pea.'

Close up, many of the turquoise towers are not yet sold. 'Every conceivable feature,' the signs say. They have names like Capricornia, Biarritz, The Breakers, Acapulco, Rio.

I had a Brazilian friend when I lived in Paris. He showed me a postcard, once, of Rio where he was born and brought up. The card bore an aerial shot of a splendid, curved tropical beach, fringed with palms, its sand pure as snow.

'Why don't you live in Brazil,' I said, 'if it's as beautiful as this?'

'Because,' said my friend, 'right behind that beach there is a huge military base.'

In my turn I showed him a postcard of my country. It was a reproduction of that Streeton painting called *The Land of the Golden Fleece* which in my homesickness I kept standing on the heater in my bedroom. He studied it carefully. At last he turned his currant-coloured eyes to me and said, '*Les arbres sont rouges?*' Are the trees red?

Several years later, six months ago, I was rummaging through a box of old postcards in a junk shop in Rathdowne Street. Among the photos of damp cottages in Galway, of Raj hotels crumbling in bicycle-thronged Colombo, of glassy Canadian lakes flawed by the wake of a single canoe, I found two cards that I bought for a dollar each. One was a picture of downtown Rio, in black and white. The other, crudely tinted, showed Geelong, the town where I was born. The photographer must have stood on the high grassy bank that overlooks the Eastern Beach. He lined up his shot through the never-flowing fountain with its quartet of concrete wading birds (storks? cranes? I never asked my father: they have long orange beaks and each bird holds one leg bent, as if about to take a step); through the fountain and out over the curving wooden promenade, from which we dived all summer, unsupervised, into the flat water; and across the bay to the You Yangs, the double-humped, low, volcanic cones, the only disturbance in the great basalt plains that lie between Geelong and Melbourne. These two cards in the same box! And I find them! Imagine! '*Cher Rubens,*' I wrote. '*Je t'envoie ces deux cartes postales, de nos deux villes natales . . .*'

Auntie Lorna has gone for a walk on the beach. My mother unlocks the door and slides open the flywire screen. She goes out into the bright air to tell her friend of my arrival. The ocean is right in front of the unit, only a hundred and fifty yards away. How can people be so sure of the boundary between land and sea that they have the confidence to build houses on it? The white doorsteps of the ocean travel and travel.

'Twelve o'clock,' says my father.

'Getting on for lunchtime,' I say.

'Getting towards it. Specially with that nice cold corned beef sitting there, and fresh brown bread. Think I'll have to try some of that choko relish. Ever eaten a choko?'

'I wouldn't know a choko if I fell over it.'

'Nor would I.'

He selects a serrated knife from the magnetised holder on the kitchen wall and quickly and skilfully, at the bench, makes himself a thick sandwich. He works with powerful concentration: when the meat flaps off the slice of bread, he rounds it up with a large, dramatic scooping movement and a sympathetic grimace of the lower lip. He picks up the sandwich in two hands, raises it to his mouth and takes a large bite. While he chews he breathes heavily through his nose.

'Want to make yourself something?' he says with his mouth full.

I stand up. He pushes the loaf of bread towards me with the back of his hand. He puts the other half of his sandwich on a green bread and butter plate and carries it to the table. He sits with his elbows on the pine wood, his knees wide apart, his belly relaxing on to his thighs, his high-arched, long-boned feet planted on the tiled floor. He eats, and gazes out to sea. The noise of his eating fills the room.

My mother and Auntie Lorna come up from the beach. I stand inside the wall of glass and watch them stop at the tap to hose the sand off their feet before they cross the grass to the door. They are two old women: they have to keep one hand on the tap in order to balance on the left foot and wash the right. I see that they are two old women, and yet they are neither young nor old. They are my mother and Auntie Lorna, two institutions. They slide back the wire door, smiling.

'Don't tramp sand everywhere,' says my father from the table.

They take no notice. Auntie Lorna kisses me, and holds me at arms' length with her head on one side. My mother prepares food and we eat, looking out at the water.

'You've missed the coronary brigade,' says my father. 'They get out on the beach about nine in the morning. You can pick 'em. They swing their arms up really high when they walk.' He laughs, looking down.

'Do you go for a walk every day too?' I ask.

'Six point six kilometres,' says my father.

'Got a pedometer, have you?'

'I just nutted it out,' says my father. 'We walk as far as a big white building, down that way, then we turn round and come back. Six point six altogether, there and back.'

'I might come with you.'

'You can if you like,' he says. He picks up his plate and carries it to the sink. 'We go after breakfast. You've missed today's.'

He goes to the couch and opens the newspaper on the low coffee table. He reads with his glasses down his nose and his hands loosely linked between his spread knees. The women wash up.

'Is there a shop nearby?' I ask my mother. 'I have to get some tampons.'

'Caught short, are you?' she says. 'I think they sell them at the shopping centre, along Sunbrite Avenue there near the bowling club. Want me to come with you?'

'I can find it.'

'I never could use those things,' says my mother, lowering her voice and glancing across the room at my father. 'Hazel told me about a terrible thing that happened to her. For days she kept noticing this revolting smell that was . . . emanating from her. She washed and washed, and couldn't get rid of it. Finally she was about to go to the doctor, but first she got down and had a look with the mirror. She saw this bit of thread and pulled it. The thing was *green*. She must've forgotten to take it out – it'd been there for days and days and *days*.'

We laugh with the tea towels up to our mouths. My father, on the other side of the room, looks up from the paper with the bent smile of someone not sure what the others are laughing at. I am always surprised when my mother comes out with a word like 'emanating'. At home I have a book called *An Outline of English Verse* which my mother used in her matriculation year. In the margins of *The Rape of the Lock* she has made notations: 'bathos; reminiscent of Virgil; parody of Homer'. Her handwriting in these pencilled jottings, made forty-five years ago, is exactly as it is today: this makes me suspect, when I am not with her, that she is a closet intellectual.

Once or twice, on my way from the unit to the shopping centre, I think to see roses along a fence and run to look, but I find them to be some scentless, fleshy flower. I fall back. Beside a patch of yellow grass, pretty trees in a row are bearing and dropping white blossom-like flowers, but they look wrong to me, I do not recognise them: the blossoms too large, the branches too flat. I am dizzy from the flight. In Melbourne it is still winter, everything is bare.

I buy the tampons and look for the postcards. There they are, displayed in a tall revolving rack. There is a great deal of blue. Closer, I find colour photos of white beaches, duneless, palmless, on which half-naked people lie on their backs with their knees raised. The frequency of this posture, at random through the crowd, makes me feel like laughing. Most of the cards have GREETINGS FROM THE GOLD COAST or BROADBEACH or SURFERS PARADISE embossed in gold in one corner: I search for pictures without words. Another card, in several slightly differing versions, shows a graceful, big-breasted young girl lying in a seductive pose against some rocks: she is wearing a bikini and her whole head is covered by one of those latex masks that are sold in trick shops, the ones you pull on as a bandit pulls on a stocking. The mask represents the hideous, raddled, grinning face of an old woman, a witch. I stare at this photo for a long time. Is it simple, or does it hide some more mysterious signs and symbols?

I buy twelve GREETINGS FROM cards with views, some aerial, some from the ground. They cost twenty-five cents each.

'Want the envelopes?' says the girl. She is dressed in a flowered garment which is drawn up between her thighs like a nappy.

'Yes please.' The envelopes are so covered with coloured maps, logos and drawings of Australian fauna that there is barely room to write an address, but something about them attracts me. I buy a packet of Licorice Chews and eat them all on the way home: I stuff them in two at a time: my mouth floods with saliva. There are no rubbish bins so I put the papers in my pocket. Now that I have spent money here, now that I have rubbish to dispose of, I am no longer a stranger. In Paris there used to be signs in the streets that said, 'Le commerce, c'est la vie de la ville.' Any traveller knows this to be the truth.

The women are knitting. They murmur and murmur. What they say never requires an answer. My father sharpens a pencil stub with his pocket knife, and folds the paper into a pad one-eighth the size of a broadsheet page.

'Five down, spicy meat jelly. ASPIC. Three across, counterfeit. BOGUS! Howzat.'

'You're in good nick,' I say. 'I would've had to rack my brains for BOGUS. Why don't you do harder ones?'

'Oh, I can't do those other ones, the cryptic.'

'You have to know Shakespeare and the Bible off by heart to do those,' I say.

'Yairs. Course, if you got hold of the answer and filled it out looking at that, with a lot of practice you could come round to their way of thinking. They used to have good ones in the *Weekly Times*. But I s'pose they had so many complaints from cockies who couldn't do 'em that they had to ease off.'

I do not feel comfortable yet about writing the postcards. It would seem graceless. I flip through my mother's pattern book.

'There's some nice ones there,' she says. 'What about the one with the floppy collar?'

'Want to buy some wool?' says my father. He tosses the finished crossword on to the coffee table and stands up with a vast yawn. 'Oh – ee – oh – ooh. Come on, Miss. I'll drive you over to Pacific Fair.'

I choose the wool and count out the number of balls specified by the pattern. My father rears back to look at it: this movement struck terror into me when I was a teenager but I now recognise it as long-sightedness.

'Pure wool, is it?' he says. As soon as he touches it he will know. He fingers it, and looks at me.

'No,' I say. 'Got a bit of synthetic in it. It's what the pattern says to use.'

'Why don't you –' He stops. Once he would have tried to prevent me from buying it. His big blunt hands used to fling out the fleeces, still warm, on to the greasy table. His hands looked as if they had no feeling in them but they teased out the wool, judged it, classed it, assigned it a fineness and a destination: Italy, Switzerland, Japan. He came home with thorns embedded deep in the flesh of his palms. He stood patiently while my mother gouged away at them with a needle. He drove away at shearing time in a yellow car with running boards, up to the big sheds in the country; we rode on the running boards as far as the corner of our street, then skipped home. He went to the Melbourne Show for work, not pleasure, and once he brought me home a plastic trumpet. 'Fordie,' he called me, and took me to the wharves and said, 'See that rope? It's not a rope. It's a hawser.' 'Hawser,' I repeated, wanting him to think I was a serious person. We walked along Strachan Avenue, Manifold Heights, hand in hand. 'Listen,' he said. 'Listen to the wind in the wires.' I must have been very little then, for the wires were so high I can't remember seeing them.

He turns away from the fluffy pink balls and waits with his hands in his pockets for me to pay.

'What do you do all day, up here?' I say on the way home.

'Oh . . . play bowls. Follow the real estate. I ring up the firms that advertise these flash units and I ask 'em questions. I let 'em lower and lower their price. See how low they'll go. How many more discounts they can dream up.' He drives like a farmer in a ute, leaning forward with his arms curved round the wheel, always about to squint up through the windscreen at the sky, checking the weather.

'Don't they ask your name?'

'Yep.'

'What do you call yourself?'

'Oh, Jackson or anything.' He flicks a glance at me. We begin to laugh, looking away from each other.

'It's bloody crook up here,' he says. 'Jerry-built. Sad. "Every conceivable luxury"! They can't get rid of it. They're desperate. Come on. We'll go up and you can have a look.'

The lift in Biarritz is lined with mushroom-coloured carpet. We brace our backs against its wall and it rushes us upwards. The salesman in the display unit has a moustache, several gold bracelets, a beige suit, and a clipboard against his chest. He is engaged with an elderly couple and we are able to slip past him into the living room.

'Did you see that peanut?' hisses my father.

'A gilded youth,' I say. ' "Their eyes are dull, their heads are flat, they have no brains at all." '

He looks impressed, as if he thinks I have made it up on the spot. '*The Man from Ironbark*,' I add.

'I only remember *The Geebung Polo Club*,' he says. He mimes leaning off a horse and swinging a heavy implement. We snort with laughter. Just inside the living room door stand five Ionic pillars in a half-moon curve. Beyond them, through the glass, are views of a river and some mountains. The river winds in a plain, the mountains are sudden, lumpy and crooked.

'From the other side you can see the sea,' says my father.

'Would you live up here?'

'Not on your life. Not with those flaming pillars.'

From the bedroom window he points out another high-rise building closer to the sea. Its name is Chelsea. It is battle-ship grey with a red trim. Its windows face away from the ocean. It is tall and narrow, of mean proportions, almost prison-like. 'I wouldn't mind living in that one,' he says. I look at it in silence. He has unerringly chosen the ugliest one. It is so ugly that I can find nothing to say.

It is Saturday afternoon. My father is waiting for the Victorian football to start on TV. He rereads the paper.

'Look at this,' he says. 'Mum, remember that seminar we went to about investment in diamonds?'

'Up here?' I say. 'A *seminar*?'

'S'posed to be an investment that would double its value in six days. We went along one afternoon. They were obviously con-men. Ooh, setting up a big con, you could tell. They had sherry and sandwiches.'

'That's all we went for, actually,' says my mother.

'What sort of people went?' I ask.

'Oh . . . people like ourselves,' says my father.

'Do you think anybody bought any?'

'Sure. Some idiots. Anyway, look at this in today's *Age*. "The Diamond Dreamtime. World diamond market plummets." Haw haw haw.'

He turns on the TV in time for the bounce. I cast on stitches as instructed by the pattern and begin to knit. My mother and Auntie Lorna, well advanced in complicated garments for my sister's teenage children, conduct their monologues which cross, coincide and run parallel. My father mumbles advice to the footballers and emits bursts of contemptuous laughter. 'Bloody idiot,' he says.

I go to the room I am to share with Auntie Lorna and come back with the packet of postcards. When I get out my pen and the stamps and set myself up at the table my father looks up and shouts to me over the roar of the crowd, 'Given up on the knitting?'

'No. Just knocking off a few postcards. People expect a post-card when you go to Queensland.'

'Have to keep up your correspondence, Father,' says my mother.

'I'll knit later,' I say.

'How much have you done?' asks my father.

'This much.' I separate thumb and forefinger.

'Dear Philip,' I write. I make my writing as thin and small as I can: the back of the postcard, not the front, is the art form. 'Look where I am. A big red setter wet from the surf shambles up the side way of the unit, looking lost and anxious as setters always do. My parents send it packing with curses in an inarticulate tongue. Go orn, get orf, gorn!'

'Dear Philip. THE IDENTIFICATION OF THE BIRDS AND FISHES. *My father*: "Look at those albatross. They must have eyes that can see for a hundred miles. As soon as one dives, they come from every-where. Look at 'em dive! Bang! Down they go." *Me*: "What sort of fish would they be diving for?" *My father*: "Whiting. They only eat whiting." *Me*: "They do not!" *My father*: "How the hell would *I* know what sort of fish they are." '

'Dear Philip. My father says they are albatross, but my mother (in the bathroom, later) remarks to me that albatross have shorter, more hunched necks.'

'Dear Philip. I share a room with Auntie Lorna. She also is writing postcards and has just asked me how to spell TOO. I like her very much and *she likes me*. "I'll keep the stickybeaks in the Woomelang post office guessing," she says. "I won't put my name on the back of the envelope."'

'Dear Philip. OUTSIDE THE POST OFFICE. My father, Auntie Lorna and I wait in the car for my mother to go in and pick up the mail from the locked box. *My father*: "Gawd, amazing, isn't it, what people do. See that sign there, ENTER, with the arrow pointing upwards? What sort of a thing is that? Is it a joke, or just some no-hoper foolin' around? That woman's been in the phone box for half an hour, I bet. How'd you be, outside the public phone waiting for some silly coot to finish yackin' on about everything under the sun, while you had something important to say. That happened to us, once, up at —" My mother opens the door and gets in. "Three letters," she says. "All for me."'

Sometimes my little story overflows the available space and I have to run over on to a second postcard. This means I must find a smaller, secondary tale, or some disconnected remark, to fill up card number two.

'*Me*: (opening cupboard) "Hey! Scrabble! We can have a game of Scrabble after tea!" *My father*: (with a scornful laugh) "I can't wait."'

'Dear Philip. I know you won't write back. I don't even know whether you are still at this address.'

'Dear Philip. One Saturday morning I went to Coles and bought a scarf. It cost four and sixpence and I was happy with my purchase. He whisked it out of my hand and looked at the label. "Made in China. Is it real silk? Let's test it." He flicked on his cigarette lighter. We all screamed and my mother said, "Don't *bite*! He's only teasing you." '

'Dear Philip. Once, when I was fourteen, I gave cheek to him at the dinner table. He hit me across the head with his open hand. There was silence. My little brother gave a high, hysterical giggle and I laughed too, in shock. He hit me again. After the washing up I was sent for. He was sitting in an armchair, looking down. "The reason why we don't get on any more," he said, "is because we're so much alike." This idea filled me with such revulsion that I turned my swollen face away. It was swollen from crying, not from the blows, whose force had been more symbolic than physical.'

'Dear Philip. Years later he read my mail. He found the contraceptive pills. He drove up to Melbourne and found me and made me come home. He told me I was letting men use my body. He told me I ought to see a psychiatrist. I was in the front seat and my mother was in the back. I thought, "If I open the door and jump out, I won't have to listen to this any more." My mother tried to stick up for me. He shouted at her. "It's your fault," he said. "You were too soft on her." '

'Dear Philip. I know you've heard all this before. I also know it's no worse than anyone else's story.'

'Dear Philip. And again years later he asked me a personal question. He was driving, I was in the suicide seat. "What went wrong," he said, "between you and Philip?" Again I turned my face away. "I don't want to talk about it." I said. There was silence. He never asked again. And years after *that*, in a café in Paris on my way to work, far enough away from him to be able to, I thought of that question and began to cry. Dear Philip. I forgive you for everything.'

Late in the afternoon my mother and Auntie Lorna and I walk along the beach to Surfers. The tide is out: our bare feet scarcely mark the firm sand. Their two voices run on, one high, one low. If I speak they pretend to listen, just as I feign attention to their endless, looping discourses: these are our courtesies: this is love. Everything is spoken, nothing is said. On the way back I point out to them the smoky orange clouds that are massing far out to sea, low over the horizon. Obedient, they stop and face the water. We stand in a row, Auntie Lorna in a pretty frock with sandals dangling from her finger, my mother and I with our trousers rolled up. Once I asked my Brazilian friend a stupid question. He was listening to a conversation between me and a Frenchman about our countries' electoral systems. He was not speaking and, thinking to include him, I said, 'And how do people vote *chez toi*, Rubens?' He looked at me with a small smile. 'We don't have elections,' he said. Where's Rio from here? 'Look at those clouds!' I say. 'You'd think there was another city out there, wouldn't you, burning.'

Just at dark the air takes on the colour and dampness of the sub-tropics. I walk out the screen door and stand my gin on a fence post. I lean on the fence and look at the ocean. Soon the moon will thrust itself over the line. If I did a painting of a horizon, I think, I would make it look like a row of rocking, inverted Vs, because that's what I see when I look at it. The flatness of a horizon is intellectual. A cork pops on the first-floor balcony behind me. I glance up. In the half dark two men with moustaches are smiling down at me.

'Drinking champagne tonight?' I say.

'Wonderful sound, isn't it,' says the one holding the bottle.

I turn back to the moonless horizon. Last year I went camp-ing on the Murray River. I bought the cards at Tocumwal. I had to write fast for the light was dropping and spooky noises were coming from the trees. 'Dear Dad,' I wrote. 'I am up on the Murray, sitting by the camp fire. It's nearly dark now but earlier it was beautiful, when the sun was going down and the dew was rising.' Two weeks later, at home, I received a letter from him written in his hard, rapid, slanting hand, each word ending in a sharp upward flick. The letter itself concerned a small financial matter, and consisted of two sentences on half a sheet of quarto, but on the back of the envelope he had dashed off a personal message: 'P.S. Dew does not rise. It *forms*.'

The moon does rise, as fat as an orange, out of the sea straight in front of the unit. A child upstairs sees it too and utters long werewolf howls. My mother makes a meal and we eat it. 'Going to help Mum with the dishes, are you, Miss?' says my father from his armchair. My shoulders stiffen. I am, I do. I lie on the couch and read an old *Woman's Day*. Princess Caroline of Monaco wears a black dress and a wide white hat. The knitting needles make their mild clicking. Auntie Lorna and my father come from the same town, Hopetoun in the Mallee, and when the news is over they begin again.

'I always remember the cars of people,' says my father. 'There was an old four-cylinder Dodge, belonging to Whatsisname. It had —'

'Would that have been one of the O'Lachlans?' says Auntie Lorna.

'Jim O'Lachlan. It had a great big exhaust pipe coming out the back. And I remember stuffing a potato up it.'

'A *potato?*' I say.

'The bloke was a councillor,' says my father. 'He came out of the Council chambers and got into the Dodge and started her up. He only got fifty yards up the street when BA—BANG! This damn thing shot out the back — I reckon it's still going!' He closes his lips and drops his head back against the couch to hold in his laughter.

I walk past Biarritz, where globes of light float among shrubbery, and the odd balcony on the half-empty tower holds rich people out into the creamy air. A barefoot man steps out of the take-away food shop with a hamburger in his hand. He leans against the wall to unwrap it, and sees me hesitating at the slot of the letterbox, holding up the postcards and reading them over and over in the weak light from the public phone. 'Too late to change it now,' he calls. I look up. He grins and nods and takes his first bite of the hamburger. Beside the letterbox stands a deep rubbish bin with a swing lid. I punch open the bin and drop the postcards in.

All night I sleep safely in my bed. The waves roar and hiss, and slam like doors. Auntie Lorna snores, but when I tug at the corner of her blanket she sighs and turns over and breathes more quietly. In the morning the rising sun hits the front windows and floods the place with a light so intense that the white curtains can hardly net it. Everything is pink and golden. In the sink a cockroach lurks. I try to swill it down the drain with a cup of water but it resists strongly. The air is bright, is milky with spray. My father is already up: while the kettle boils he stands out on the edge of the grass, the edge of his property, looking at the sea.

The dark, the light

We heard he was back. We heard he was staying in a swanky hotel. We heard she was American. We washed our hair. We wore what we thought was appropriate. We waited for him to declare himself. We waited for him to call.

No calls came. We discussed his probable whereabouts, the meaning of his silence, the possibilities of his future.

We thought we saw him getting into a taxi outside the Rialto, outside the Windsor, outside the Regent, outside the Wentworth, outside the Stock Exchange, outside the Diorama. Was it him? What was he wearing? What did he have on? A tweed jacket, black shoes. Even in summer? His idea of this town is cold. He's been away. He's lost the feel of it. He's been in Europe. He's been in America. He's been in the tropics. He's left. He's gone. He doesn't live here any more. He's only visiting. He's only passing through. Was his face white? His shirt was white. His hair was longer. Did you see her? She wasn't there. He was on his own.

We saw them in a club. We saw her. She was blond. They were both blond. They were together. They were dressed in white, in cream, in gold, in thousands of dollars' worth of linen and leather. They sat at a table with their backs to the wall. The wall was dark. They were light. Their hair and their garments shone. They knew things we did not know, they owned things we had never heard of. They were from somewhere else. They were not from here. They were from further north, from the sunny place, the blue and yellow place, the sparkling place, the water place. They were from the capital. More than one of us had to be led away weeping. He's gone. He won't live here again. He has left us behind. He has gone away and left us in the cold. The music stopped and they got up and left and the door closed. We stood in our dark club in our dark clothes.

Invitations came, but not many. Hardly any. Very few. Did you get one? Neither did I. Maybe the mail . . . a strike . . . a bottleneck at the exchange . . . There were very few. Only three or four. Will you go? Of course not. It wouldn't be right. It would hurt, it would be wrong, I couldn't do it, I wouldn't be able to live with myself, I would lose friends, I wouldn't be seen dead, if you don't I won't either, it's a moral issue, I couldn't possibly.

What happened up there? Did you go? Did you hear? What was it like? Tell us what happened. It was summer, he was early, she was late, she made an entrance, the bells were ringing, the organ thundered, his hair lay in stiff sculpted curls, she was all in cream, her hair was up, she was choked with pearls, his family was there, the church was packed, he gave her his arm, they stood sides touching. The minister threw back his head and shouted *Come into their hearts Lord Jesus!* The guests were embarrassed, they fluffed their bobs, they brushed their shoulders, they read the brass plaques, it was religious, it was low church, it was not what we thought, we imagined something else, it was not his style, it was a bit much, it was over the top, it was a church after all and what did you expect, the guests were clever, they knew better, they were modern, they sat in the pews and sneered.

And afterwards? Outside? The trees were covered in leaves and threaded with coloured lights, it was night in the garden, the air was warm, the night was tender, French at least we thought, we thought French, we held out our glasses, the waiters twirled among us, the bottles were napkinned, it was local, we had hoped for better, we drank it anyway, we became more grateful, the families stood in line, they shook our hands, they welcomed us, we were ashamed of our ingratitude. We saw him standing alone for a moment under a tree, we stepped quickly towards him to show him we had come, we had come a very long way, we had come to show him we had come, to deliver the compliments, to bring the greetings of the other place, we stepped up, we reached out, our fingers touched his elbow and she came swooping all creamy with pearls, he spun on one heel, his hands opened, he showed us his palms, he smiled, he melted, he was no longer there, he was gone, the trees were covered in leaves, their branches were threaded with coloured lights, our clothes were stiff, our clothes were dark, our clothes came from the other place, and we too came from the other place, we put down our glasses, we turned away, we turned to go back to the other place, we turned and went back to the other place, we went without bitterness, humbly we went away.

In Paris

The apartment was on the fourth floor. The building had no lift. On his day off the man lay on the mattress that served as a sofa and read, slowly and carefully, all the newspapers of his city. The tall windows were open on to the balcony. Every twenty minutes a bus swerved in to the stop down below, and the curtain puffed past his face. At two o'clock the woman came into the living room with her boots on.

'I feel like going for a walk,' she said.

'Bon. D'accord,' said the man.

'Want to come with me?'

'Tu vas où?'

'Up to Sacré Coeur and back. Not far.'

'Ouf,' said the man. 'All those steps.' He put one paper down and unfolded the next.

'Oh, come on,' said the woman. 'Won't you come? I'm bored.'

'I don't want to go down into the street,' said the man. 'I have to go down there every day. I get sick of it. Today I feel like staying home.'

The woman pulled a dead leaf off the pot plant. 'Just for an hour?' she said.

'Too many tourists,' said the man. 'You go. I'll have a little sleep. Anyway it's going to rain.'

Late in the afternoon the man went into the kitchen and opened the refrigerator. He looked inside it, then shut it again. He walked across the squeaking parquet to the bedroom. The woman was lying on her stomach reading a book by the light of a shaded lamp. Her wet boots stood in the corner by the window.

'There's nothing to eat,' said the man. 'No one went to the market.'

The woman looked up. 'What about the fish?'

'Yes, the fish is there.'

'We can eat the fish, then.'

'There's nothing to have with it.'

The woman marked her place with one finger.

'What happened to the brussels sprouts?' she said. 'Did the others eat them last night?'

'No.'

'Well, let's have fish and brussels sprouts.'

Before she had finished the sentence the man was shaking his head.

'Why not?'

'Fish and green vegetables are never eaten together.'

'What?'

'They are not eaten together.'

The woman closed the book. 'People have salad with fish. That's green.'

'Salad is different. Salad is a separate course. It is not served on the same plate.'

'Can you explain to me,' said the woman, 'the reason why fish and green vegetables must not be eaten together?'

The man looked at his hand against the white wall. 'It is not done,' he said. 'They do not complement each other. Fish and potatoes, yes. Frites. Pommes de terre au four. But not green vegetables.'

'It's getting on for dinner time,' said the woman. She turned on her back and clasped her hands behind her head. 'The others will be back soon.'

'I don't know what to do,' said the man. He moved his feet closer together and pushed his hands into his pockets.

'If I were you,' said the woman. 'If I were you and it was my turn to cook, and if there was nothing to eat except fish and green vegetables, do you know what I'd do? I'd cook fish and green vegetables. That's what I'd do.'

'Ecoute,' said the man. 'There are always good chemical and aesthetic reasons behind customs.'

'Yes, but what *are* they.'

'I'm sure if we looked it up in the *Larousse Gastronomique* it would be explained.'

The woman got off the low bed and went to the window in her socks and T-shirt. She looked out.

'I'm hungry,' she said. 'Where I come from, we just eat what's there.'

'And it is not a secret,' said the man, 'that where you come from the food is barbaric.'

The woman kept her back to the room. 'My mother cooked nice food. We had nice meals.'

'Chops,' said the man. 'Hamburgers. I heard you telling my mother. "La bouffe est dégueulasse," you said. That's what you said.'

'I said "était". It was. It used to be. But it's not any more. It's not now.'

The man took a set of keys out of his pocket and began to flip them in and out of his palm.

'Aren't there any onions?' said the woman, still looking out the window.

'No. Not even onions.'

'I don't see,' said the woman, 'that you've got any choice. What choice have you got? Unless you cook the fish by itself, or just the sprouts.'

'There would not be enough for everybody.'

The woman turned round from the grey window. 'Why don't you go out into the kitchen and cook it up. Cook what's there. Just cook it up and see what happens. And if the others don't like it they can take their custom elsewhere.'

The man took a deep breath. He put the keys back in his pocket. He scratched his head until his hair stood up in a crest. 'J'ai mal fait mon marché,' he said. 'I should have planned better. We should have —'

'For God's sake,' said the woman. She leaned against the closed window. 'What's the matter with you? It's only food.'

The man put his bare foot on the edge of the mattress and bounced it once, twice.

'Tu vois?' he said. 'Tu vois comment tu es? "Only food." No French person would ever, ever say "It's only food".'

'But it *is* only food,' said the woman. 'In the final analysis that's what it *is*. It's to keep us alive. It's to stop us from feeling hungry for a couple of hours so we can get our minds off our stomachs and go about our business. And all the rest is only decoration.'

'Oh là là,' said the man. 'Tu es —'

He flattened his hair with one hand, and let his hand fall to his side. Then he turned and walked back into the kitchen. He opened the refrigerator. The fish lay on its side on a white plate. He opened the cupboard under the window. The brussels sprouts, cupped in their shed outer leaves, sat on a paper bag on the bottom shelf. The man stood in the middle of the room and looked from one open door to the other, and back again.

Little Helen's Sunday afternoon

Late on a winter Sunday afternoon, Little Helen stood behind her mother on the verandah of Noah's house. Her mother raised her finger to the buzzer but the door opened from the inside and Noah's father came hurrying out.

'Bad luck, girls,' he said. He was pulling on his jacket. 'Just got a call from Northern General. Some kid's cut his finger off.'

'His whole finger?' said Little Helen. 'Right off?'

'I hope someone slung it in the icebox,' said Little Helen's mother. 'What a time to make you work.'

'*Unpaid* work,' said Noah's mother. 'Will I save you some soup, Jim?'

'Let's see,' said Noah's father. 'Four thirty. I'll have to do a graft. Five thirty, six, six thirty. Yeah. Save me some.'

As he talked he walked, and was already in the car. The drive was full of coloured leaves.

Little Helen's mother and Noah's were sisters and liked to shriek a lot when visiting.

'Little Helen!' said Noah's mother. 'Jump up! Let me have a hold of you!'

Little Helen stepped out from behind her mother, bent her knees, raised her arms and sprang. Noah's mother caught her, but staggered and gave a cry. 'Ark! You used to be such a fairy little thing. Last time you were here you sat on my knee and do you know what you said? You said, "I *love* being small!"'

Little Helen went red and dropped her eyes. She saw her own foot, in its large, strapped blue shoe, swinging awkwardly near her aunt's hip.

'Come on, Meg,' said Little Helen's mother. 'Let's pop into the bedroom. I've got some business to conduct. It's in this bag.'

Noah's mother unclasped her hands under Little Helen's bottom and let her slide to the ground.

'Another hair shirt, is it,' she said to Little Helen's mother. 'I suppose I'll be left holding the baby.'

'What are you going to call it if it's a boy?' said Little Helen.

The women looked at each other. Their cheeks puffed out and their lips went tight. They went into the bedroom and closed the door without answering her question. Little Helen could hear them screeching and crashing round in front of the mirror. She knew that it was not a hair shirt at all, but a pair of shoes her mother had paid a lot of money for and worn once then discovered they were too big, and which she hoped that Noah's mother would buy from her. Little Helen brushed the back of her tartan skirt down flat and stood in the hallway. She saw her own feet parallel. She thought of a waitress. It was a long time ago, in the dining room of the Bull and Mouth Hotel in Stawell. The wait-ress was quite old and she stood patiently, holding her order pad and pencil, while Little Helen's father took a long time to make up his mind what to have. Little Helen, who always had roast lamb, tried to stop looking at the waitress's feet, but could not. There was nothing special about the feet. But the neatness of their position, two inches apart and perfectly parallel on the carpet's green and orange flowers, caused Little Helen to experience a painful sadness. She decided to have chicken instead.

'Chicken's pretty risky,' said her father.

'I want chicken, though,' said Little Helen.

She got chicken. It was all right but rather dry. She ate more of it than she wanted.

'How's the chicken?' said her father.

'A bit risky,' said Little Helen.

Her father laughed so much that everyone at the other tables turned to stare.

Little Helen knew she was clever but she noticed that words did not always bear the same simple, serious meaning that they had at school when she copied them into her exercise book. On her spelling list she had the word 'capacious' to put into a sentence. 'The elephant is a capacious beast,' she wrote. Her mother's mouth trembled when Little Helen showed her the twenty finished sentences, in best writing and ruled off. She explained why 'capacious' was not quite right. Her polite kind-ness and her trembling mouth made Little Helen blush until tears filled her eyes.

Little Helen stood outside her aunt's bedroom and waited for something to happen. Time became elastic, and sagged. She hated visiting. She had to be dragged away from her wooden table, her full set of Derwents, her different inks and textas, her special paper-cutting scissors, her rulers and sharpeners and rubbers. The teacher never gave her enough homework. She could have worked all weekend.

She did not like the feeling of other people's houses. There was nothing to do. Pieces of furniture stood sparsely in chilly rooms. The long stretches of skirting board were empty of meaning, and the kitchen smells were mournful, as if the saucepans on the stove contained nothing but grey bones boiling for a soup.

The bedroom door opened and Little Helen's mother poked her head out. She had been laughing. Her face was pink and she was wearing nothing but a bra and pants and a black hat like a box with a bit of net hanging over her eyes.

'We're having dress-ups,' she said. 'Want to come in and play?'

Little Helen was embarrassed and shook her head. They didn't know how to play properly. They were much too tall and had real bosoms, and they talked all the time about how much they had paid for the clothes and where they would go to wear them, instead of being serious and thoughtful about what the clothes meant in the game.

'Oh, don't be so unsociable!' said her mother. 'Go and see Noah.'

'He won't want to see me,' said Little Helen. 'Anyway I don't know where he is.'

'He's out the back,' shouted his mother from inside the bedroom. 'Probably making something. Some white elephant or other.'

They started to laugh again, and Little Helen's mother went back into the bedroom and slammed the door.

Little Helen plodded down the hall and entered the kitchen. The lunch dishes were all over the sink. Between the stacked plates she found quite a lot of tinned sweet corn, crusted with cold butter. She put her mouth down to the china and sucked up the scrapings. Her palate took on a coating of grease. She moved over to the pantry cupboard and helped herself to five Marie biscuits, some peeled almonds, four squares of cooking chocolate and a handful of crystallised ginger. Eating fast and furtively, bolting the food inside the big dark cupboard, she started to get that rude and secret feeling of wanting to do a shit. She crossed her legs and squeezed her bum shut, and went on guzzling. A little salvo of farts escaped into her pants and if something funny had occurred to her at that moment she would not have been able to hang on; but she kept her mind on that poor boy who had cut his finger off, and gradually she felt the lump go back up inside her for later.

If she ate any more she would spoil her tea. She hitched up her skirt, wiped her palms on her pants, and set out across the kitchen towards the wide glass door.

Noah's yard was long and sloped steeply down to the back fence. The trees had no leaves, and from the porch steps Little Helen could see for miles and miles, as far as the centre of the city. She paused to stare at the tiny bunch of skyscrapers, like a city in a film, and at the long curved bridge beyond them with its chain of lights already flicking on. The afternoon was nearly over. It was not raining now. Water lay in puddles on the sky-blue plastic cover of the swimming pool. The branches of bare bushes were a glossy black, like a licked pencil lead.

Little Helen's feet sank into the spongy grass. Her shoes looked very large and blue on the greenness. The grass was so green that it made her feel sick. The sky was low. An unnatural light leaked out of the clouds, and the chords the light played were in the same dull, complicated key as the grass-sickness. The air did not move. It was cold. Her legs felt white and thin under the pleated skirt.

Grass grew right up to the shed door, which was shut. Noah must be in there. She stood outside it and paid attention. There was a noise like somebody using sandpaper on a piece of wood, but softer; like two people using sandpaper, two rhythms not quite hitting the same beat. Someone laughed.

Little Helen saw a red plastic bucket half under the shed. She pulled it out and turned it upside down. Its bottom was cracked and it was almost too weak to hold her, but by keeping her shoes on the very outside of its rim she could balance on it and get her head up to the window. Rags had been hooked across it on the inside, and only one small corner was uncovered. She put her eye to it. It was even darker inside. In there the night had already begun. How could he see what he was doing?

She shifted her left foot on the bucket and missed the rim. The toe of her shoe pierced the split base. Her fingers lost their hold on the windowsill. A fierce sharpness scraped through her sock and raked its claws up her shin. She swivelled sideways with a grunt, lurched against the shed wall, and stumbled out on to the lawn. Shocked and gasping, she found herself still upright, but with the red bucket clamped round her left leg just below the knee.

In the upper part of the sky, above the bunch of skyscrapers, the clouds split like rotten cloth and let a flat blade of light through. It leaned between sky and earth, a crooked pillar. Little Helen took a breath. She clenched her fists. She opened her mouth and bellowed.

'Noah!'

There was a silence, then a harsh scrabbling inside the shed.

'Come out!' bawled Little Helen. 'Come out and see me! It's not fair! I'm tired of waiting!'

Her shin was stinging very hard, as if her mother had already pressed on to the broken skin the Listerine-soaked cotton wool. Her invisible left sock felt wet. Little Helen thought, 'I could easily be crying.' The shed door was wrenched open and a huge boy with red hair and skin like boiled custard burst through. He was croaking.

'You were spying! Who said you could spy on me?'

Something strange had happened to Noah, and not only to his voice. The whole shape of his head had changed. He didn't look like a boy any more. He looked like a dog, or a fish. His eyes were like slits, and had moved higher up his face and outwards into his temples.

'Look, Noah,' whispered Little Helen. She was not sure whether she meant the drunken pillar of light or the bucket on her leg. He took three steps towards her and grabbed her by the arm. She jerked her face away from the smell of him: not just sweaty but raw, like steak.

'If you tell what you saw,' he choked. Red patches flared low on his speckled cheeks.

'It was dark,' said Little Helen. She could feel blood running down into her cotton sock. 'I couldn't even see in. I couldn't see anything. I only heard the noise. I promise.'

He dragged her towards the shed door. The grass squelched under his thick-soled jogging shoes. She had to stagger with her legs apart because of the bucket, but he did not notice it, and pushed her up the step. Another boy was standing just inside. Their great bodies, panting and stinking, filled the shed.

'Don't bring her in here, you fuckwit!' said the other boy. His shoelaces were undone and he was doing up his trousers. 'I'm going home.'

The shed smelt of cigarettes. They must have smoked a whole packet. They would get lung cancer. They would get into really bad trouble. The other boy bent to tie his lace and Little Helen saw that there was a third person in the shed. A girl was sitting on a sleeping bag that was spread out on the floor. She was pulling on her boots. As she scrambled to her feet she spotted Little Helen's bucket. She stopped on all fours in dog position and looked up into Little Helen's face. Her eyes were caked with black stuff and her hair was stiff, like burnt grass. She laughed; Little Helen could see all her back teeth.

'Ha!' said the girl. 'Now you know what happens to people who snoop. Come on, Justin. Let's go.'

She stood up and buckled her belt. The two of them barged out the door. Little Helen heard their feet thumping on the grass and then crunching on the gravel drive.

'I know what *you've* been doing,' said Little Helen. The butts were everywhere. Some had lipstick on the yellow end.

'Shut your face,' said Noah. In the grey light from the open door his head with its short orange hair and flat temples was as smooth and savage as a bull terrier's. He gave a high snigger. 'You look stupid with that bucket on your leg.'

The moment for crying was long gone. She would have had to fake it, though she knew she had the right. 'It hurts,' said Little Helen. 'I can feel blood still coming out. It hurts quite a lot, actually. It might be serious.'

'You want to know about blood?' said Noah. His small, high, dog's eyes began to glow, as if a weak torch battery had flicked on inside his head. 'I'll show you what can happen to people.'

'I think I'd better speak to my mother,' said Little Helen. 'I need to ask her about something very important.'

'First I'll show you something,' said Noah.

'I can't walk,' said Little Helen. She folded her arms and stood square, with her knees apart to accommodate the bucket, but he scooped her off the ground in one round movement and ran out of the shed and across the garden.

From her sideways and horizontal position Little Helen saw the grassy world bounce and swing. She kept her left leg stuck out straight so the bucket would not be interfered with. His big hip and thigh worked under her waist like a horse's. He took the back steps in a couple of bounds. At the top he swung her across his front while he fumbled with the glass door, and in its broad pane she saw reflected her own white underpants, twisted half off her bottom, and down in its lower corner, half-obscured by the image of her faithful bucket, the bunch of skyscrapers flaming with light. She writhed to cover her pants and his hard fingers gripped her tighter. He forged through the kitchen, along the passage and into a small dim room that smelt of leather and Finepoint pens with their caps off.

Dumped, she staggered for the door, but he got past her and kicked it shut.

'Mum!' said Little Helen, without conviction.

'Look,' said Noah. He kept one foot against the door and reached behind her to a large, low, wooden cupboard that stood on legs against one wall. He slid open its front panel and switched on a light inside it.

It was not a cupboard. It was a box. It was deep, and it was full of pictures, tiny square ones, suspended in space, arranged in neat horizontal rows and lit gently from behind so that they glowed in many colours, jewel-like, but mostly yellow, brown and red. The magical idea, the bright orderliness of it, took Little Helen's breath away. She limped forward, smiling, favouring her bucketed leg. Noah left the door and crouched beside her. He must have forgiven her: he was panting from his run, from his haste to bring her to this wonder.

The pictures were slides. They seemed to be of children's faces. But there was something unusual about them. Were they children in face paint? Were they dressed in Costumes of Other Lands, or at a Hat Competition? Were they disguised as angels, or fairies? Little Helen tried to kneel, but her bucket bothered her. She spread her legs wide and bent them, and opened her arms to keep her balance. In this Balinese posture she lowered herself to contemplate the mystery.

The children were horrible. Their heads were bloodied. Their hair had been torn out by the roots, their scalps were raw and crisscrossed with black railway lines. Their lips were blue and swollen and bulged outwards, barely contained by stitches. Their eyes had burst like pickled onions, their foreheads were stove in, their chins were crushed to pink pulp. One baby, too new to sit up, had a huge purple furry thing growing from its temple to its chin. Another had two dark holes instead of a nose and its top lip was not there at all.

But the worst thing was that not a single one of them was crying. The ones whose eyes still worked looked straight at Little Helen with a patient, sober gaze. They were not surprised that these terrible things had happened to them, that their mothers had turned away at the wrong moment, that the war had come, that men with guns and knives had got into the house and found them. Little Helen's hackles went lumpy and her stomach rose into her throat. She shut her eyes and tried to straighten up, but Noah put his hand down hard on her shoulder and croaked, 'See that kid there? A power line fell on him. His brain woulda blown right out of his skull.'

Little Helen squirmed out from under his hand and crawled away. He did not follow her, but watched her drag her bucket to the door and stand up and reach the high handle. She got her good foot out into the hall and looked back. He was crouching before the picture box. The soft white light from inside it polished his furry hair. Little Helen saw that he could not stop looking at the pictures. He turned to her.

'See?' he said. 'See what can happen to little kids?'

She nodded.

'Don't you like it?' The dim torch battery went on behind his eyes. He was smiling. 'You don't, do you. Piss weak. Look at this equipment. Best that money can buy.'

'What —' She cleared her throat. 'Did they all die?'

'Die? Course they didn't die. My dad sewed 'em up. But they were very sick. And afterwards they were always ugly. For the rest of their lives.'

Little Helen let go the door handle and slid out into the hall-way. Her palms were sticky and the backs of her hands had shrunk and gone hard, but she was not going to be sick. She stumped away down the passage towards the front of the house. The bucket made a soft clunk with every second step.

Her mother and Noah's were sitting quietly on the edge of the big double bed. They were dressed in their ordinary clothes and sat with their hands folded in their laps as if waiting for some-thing. Little Helen clumped into the doorway and stopped. They looked up. She saw their two white faces, round and flat as dinner plates, shining above their dark dresses in what remained of the light.

La chance existe

I am the kind of person who always gets stopped at Customs. Julie says it's because I can't keep my eyes still. 'You look as if you're constantly checking the whereabouts of the exits,' she said. She'll never really trust me again, I suppose. It shits me but I can't blame her. I love her, that's all, and I feel like serving her.

When we got to Boulogne we had to hang around for three hours waiting for the ferry because of a strike on the other side. I would have sat in a café and read *Le Monde*, but Julie wanted to walk round and look at things, seeing she'd only been in France a couple of days. Her French was hopeless and she was too proud to try. When I met her plane at Orly she was already agitated about not being able to understand. We went straight to a bar in the airport and she insisted on ordering. The waiter, tricked by her good accent, made a friendly remark which seemed to require an answer: her face went rigid with panic and she turned away. The waiter shrugged and went back behind the counter. She hit the table with her fist and groaned between clenched teeth. 'It's pathetic! I should be able to! I'm not stupid!'

'For Christ's sake, woman,' I said. 'You've only been in the country fifteen minutes. What do you *want* from yourself?'

Boulogne was dismal, as I had predicted. I kept telling her we should go south, down to Italy where she'd never been, but she had to go to London, she said, to meet this bloke she'd fallen in love with just before she left Australia. He was coming after her, she was dying to see him again. She fell in love with this guy, who was a musician, because at a gig she found him between sets sitting by himself in a sort of booth thing reading a book called *The Meaning of Meaning*. She told me he was extremely thin. It sounded like a disaster to me. Love will not survive a channel crossing, I pointed out, let alone the thirty-six hours from Melbourne to London. But I was so glad to be with her again, and she wasn't listening.

We walked, in our Paris boulevard shoes, over the lumpy cobbles of Boulogne. We found a huge archway which led on to a beaten dirt track that curved round the outside of the old city, at the foot of its high walls. Julie was excited. 'It's old! It must have been trying to be impregnable!' The track was narrow. 'Single file, Indian style,' she chanted, charging ahead of me.

It was eleven o'clock on a weekday morning in July, and there was no one about. A nippy breeze came up off the channel. The water was grey and disturbed, a sea of shivers.

We tramped along merrily for twenty minutes, round the shoulder of the hill the old city stood on, turning back now and then to look at the view. The track became narrower.

'Let's go back,' I said. 'You can't see the sea round this side. It stinks.'

'Not yet. Look. What are those caravans down there?'

'I dunno. Gipsies or something. Come on, Julie.'

She pressed on. The track was hardly a track at all: it was brambly, and was obviously about to run out against a wing of a castle about a hundred yards ahead. I was ten steps behind her when she gave a sharp cry of disgust and stopped dead. I caught up with her. There was a terrible smell, of shit and things rotting. At her feet was the mangled corpse of a large bird: it looked as if it had been torn to bits. Its head was a yard away from its neck, half its beak had been wrenched off, and there were dirty feathers everywhere, stuck in the spiky bushes, fluttering in the seawind. The shit was human. Its shapes were man-made; it was meat-eater's shit, foul.

We looked at each other. The murder was fresh. In the crisp breeze the feathers on the creature's breast riffled and subsided like an expensive haircut. It was very quiet up there.

'Someone's looking at us from one of those caravans,' said Julie without moving her lips. 'This is their shitting place. It's their fucking dunny. They must be laughing at us.' She gave a high-pitched giggle, pushed past me, and ploughed away through the prickly bushes, back the way we'd come.

Back amongst houses, we stood at the top of an alley in the depths of which two little boys were engaged in a complicated, urgent game with a ball and a piece of rope. One dropped his end in annoyance and walked away. The other, who had glasses and a fringe and a white face, sang out after him, in a voice clear enough for even Julie to understand.

'*La chance exis — te!*'

'What a sophisticated remark,' said Julie.

On the boat, when it finally turned up, we didn't even have the money for a drink. The sky and the sea were grey. The line between them tilted this way and that.

'Will it be rough?' said Julie. 'What if I spew?'

'You won't spew. We'll walk around and talk to each other. I'll keep your mind off your stomach.'

My glasses are the kind that are supposed to adapt automatically to the intensity of the light, but they failed to go clear again when we went down into the inside part of the ship. Cheap rubbish. The downstairs part was badly lit. I hate going back to England. I hate being able to understand everything that's going on around me. I miss that feeling of your senses having to strain an inch beyond your skin that you get in places where people aren't speaking your language.

Julie darted down the stairs and grabbed a couple of seats. We got out books and kicked our bags under the little table. On the wall near us was the multi-lingual sign warning passengers about the danger of rabies and the fines you get. Julie knelt up on her seat and read it with interest.

'Rabies. What's that in French. *La rage*. Ha. You don't have to be a dog to die of *that*.'

Julie is suspicious, and full of disgust. When she laughs you see that one of her back teeth is missing on the left side. If she chooses you she loves you fiercely, lashes you if you fail yourself. A faint air of contempt hangs about her even when she's in good spirits. She says she's never going home. Everyone always says that when they first get here.

She flung herself round into the seat. 'I saw Lou just before I left Melbourne,' she said. 'I told him I'd be seeing you. He laughed. He said, "*That* fuckin' little poofter!"' She glanced sideways.

'News travels fast.' I knew that's what Lou would have said. It made me tired. He could do the dope and the bum cheques on his own now. I took a breath and went in at the deep end.

'When I first got here,' I said, 'I knew I was going to have to do something. That's what I came for. I used to walk around Paris all night, looking for men and running away from them. For example. One night I was in the metro. It was packed and I was standing up holding on to one of those vertical chrome poles. A boy got on at Clignancourt. He squeezed through the crowd to the pole.

'He wasn't looking at me, but I could feel him – I might've been imagining it, but warmth passed between us. I was burning all down one side. My heart was thumping. His hand on the pole was so close to my mouth I could have kissed it. The train was swaying, all the people were swaying, and I edged my hand up the pole till it was almost touching his. I felt sick, I wanted to touch him so much. I could smell his skin. I thought I was going to pass out. Then at the next stop he calmly let go of the pole and pushed through the crowd and got off.'

Julie put her feet up on the low table between us and folded her arms round her legs and laid her head sideways on her knees. She was having trouble controlling her mouth. 'What's your favourite name of a metro station?' she said.

'What? I don't know. Trocadéro.'

'Mine's Château d'Eau.'

'Ever been up on top of that station? You'd hate it. It's not safe for women.'

'Remember that time you shat on my green Lois Lane jacket?'

'It was an accident! I had diarrhoea!'

'You were so busy looking at yourself in the mirror you didn't know you were standing on my clothes.'

'The dry cleaner got it off! Why do you have to remind me?'

'"It's dog mess," you said to the lady at the dry cleaner. Dog *mess*.' She gave a snort of laughter.

'It came off, anyway.' I opened the newspaper and rattled it.

'Being homosexual must mean something,' she said. 'What happens? Is everything possible?'

'How do you mean?' Was she going to ask me what we did? I'd tell her. I'd tell her anything.

'I mean, if both of you have the same equipment does that mean it's more equal? Do people fall into habits of fucking or being fucked? Or does everyone do everything?'

'It's not really all that different,' I said, feeling shy but trying to be helpful. 'Not when you're in a relationship, anyway.'

'Oh.' She looked disappointed, and stared out the porthole at the grey sky and the grey water. Her cardigan sleeves were pushed up to her elbows and I could see the mist of blond hairs that fogged her skin. Her legs were downy like that, too. We can wear each other's clothes. She's the same height as me, with slightly more cowboy-like hips: light passes between the tops of her thighs.

'I never want to fuck with anyone unless it puts me in danger,' she said suddenly. 'I don't mean physical. I mean unless there's a chance they'll make me sad.'

'Break your heart.'

'I'll never get married. Or even live with anyone again, probably.'

'What about shithead? The bass player? Isn't that why we're making this fucking trip?'

'Are you afraid of getting old?' she said in a peculiar voice.

'My hair's starting to recede.' I pulled it back off my forehead to show her.

'Oh, bullshit. What are you, twenty-five? Look at your little round forehead. A pretty little globe.'

'And I'm getting hairs on my back,' I said, 'like my father.' I didn't mention that I twist round in front of the bathroom mirror with the tweezers in my hand.

'Can't we afford one drink and share it?' she said.

'No. We have to get the bus to Rowena's.'

'Last week,' she said, her head still on her knees, 'I was in the Louvre. I was upstairs, heading along one of the main galleries. I saw this young bloke sitting on a bench with a little pack on his back. He was about your age, English I'd say. He looked tired, and lonely, and he gave me a look. I wanted to go and sit next to him and say, "Will we go and have a cup of coffee? Or talk to each other?" But I was too . . . I kept walking and went down the steps to the room where all those Rubens paintings are, of Louis Whichever-it-was and Marie de Medici. I stayed in there for ten minutes walking round, and I hated the paintings, they made me feel like spewing – all those pursed-up little mouths smirking. I went back up the steps and the boy was gone.'

The boat heaved on towards Folkestone.

'Why is it so hard to talk about sex?' she said, almost in tears. 'Every time you think you're close to saying what you mean, your mind just veers away from it, and you say something that's not quite the point.'

What would they know here about summer? The wind was sharp. People in the queue had blue lips. I was stopped before we got anywhere near Customs, this time by a smart bastard in plain clothes who was cruising up and down the bedraggled line of tourists with passports in their hands.

'His *jacket*,' muttered Julie. It was orange and black houndstooth. 'My God. What's happened to this country?'

'Don't get me started on that subject.' I stood still and proffered my bag. Some look must appear on my face in their presence, or maybe it's the smell of fear they say dogs can pick up. He was nasty in that bored way; idle malice. No point getting hot under the collar. While he rooted through our bags, and Julie stood with her arms folded and her chin up and her eyes far away over his garish shoulder, he asked her an impertinent question.

'How long've you known this feller?'

'I beg your pardon?'

'I said, how long've you known this feller you're travelling with?'

You can't take that tone to a woman these days. 'What's that got to do with you?' said Julie.

He stopped rummaging and looked up at her, with one of her shirts in his hand. God, she still had that old pink thing with the mended collar. He narrowed his eyes and let his slot of a mouth drop open half an inch. Here's a go, he was thinking. I kicked her ankle. She reached out, took the pink shirt and said, folding it as skilfully as a salesgirl in Georges, 'Six years or so. Nice jacket. Is that Harris?'

He wasn't quite stupid enough to answer. He shoved the pink shirt back in among the other garments and walked away. Our bags stood unzipped, sprouting private objects.

On the train to London I read and she stared at people. At Leicester Square we ran down the stairs into the tube. I caught the eye of a good-looking boy who was coming up. I turned to look back at him as he passed and she slashed me across the face with her raincoat. The zip got me near the eye.

'What did you –' I yelled.

She was laughing furiously. 'You should have seen the look on your face.'

'What look?'

'Like *this*.' She pulled a face: mouth half-open, eyes rolling up and to one side, like a dim-witted whore.

In the basement room we were supposed to keep the wooden shutters closed because Rowena said there was a prowler who stood up on the windowsill. But the room was dim and stuffy. I took off my clothes, then slid the window up and shoved open the top half of the slatted shutter. Julie whipped off her dress and stared at me.

'You still look like a little goat,' she said. 'Pan, up on his hind legs.'

I got under the sheet. 'Come on. Let's go to sleep.'

'I'm all speeded up. I'm looking for something to read.'

'Well, don't rustle the pages all night.' I turned on my side and closed my eyes. When she got into the bed she hardly weighed it down at all.

'Talk to me,' she said behind me.

I flipped over on to my back and saw she was lying there with her hands under her head. 'What'll I say?'

'Do you get just as miserable as you used to when you were straight?'

'Are you kidding?'

She shifted so that the sides of our legs touched lightly, all the way down. 'Come on. Talk.'

'Maybe more miserable,' I said. 'It's all real now. Before, I was in a dream for years, even when I was with you. Everything was blurred and messy. Now I know exactly what I want, and I also know I'll never get it.'

'Oh hell.'

'What?'

'What *do* you want?'

'Everything. I want to love some man forever and at the same time I want to fuck everyone I see. Some days I could fuck trees. Lamp posts! Dogs! The air!'

She whistled a little tune, and laughed.

'In the Tuileries,' I said, 'there is a powdery white dust.'

'What else?'

'It's a cruising place at night. Not that part with the rows of trees: they lock that. The part between the gates and the Maillol statues. I love it.'

'Why?'

'It's like a dance. It's mysterious. People move together and apart, no one speaks, everyone's faceless. It's terrifically exciting, and graceful. The point of it is nothing to do with *who*.'

Her face was quite calm, her eyes raised to the ceiling. Turning my head I could see pale freckles, a gold sleeper, a series of tiny parallel cracks in her lower lip. The skin of her leg felt very much alive to me, almost humming with life.

'Once,' she said, 'I was coming down that narrow winding staircase in one of the towers of Notre Dame. Two American blokes were coming down behind me, and I heard one of them say, "Hey! This is *steep*! My depth perception is shot already!"'

We rolled towards each other and into each other's arms. I pushed myself against her belly, pushed my face into her neck and she took me in her arms, in her legs. I cooled myself on her. Her limbs were as strong as mine. Her face hung over me and blurred in the dim room. I could smell her open flesh, she smelled like metal, salty. I swam into her and we fucked, so slow I could have fainted. She turned over and lay on her back on me; I was in her from behind and had my hand on her cunt from above as if it were my own, my arm holding her.

And then under the hum and murmur of breathing I heard the soft thump of the man's foot against the closed lower half of the shutter. Fingers gripped the edge and a head floated in silhouette, fuzzy against the glimmer of the garden. My skin opened to welcome him.

The life of art

My friend and I went walking the dog in the cemetery. It was a Melbourne autumn: mild breezes, soft air, gentle sun. The dog trotted in front of us between the graves. I had a pair of scissors in my pocket in case we came across a rose bush on a forgotten tomb.

'I don't like roses,' said my friend. 'I despise them for having thorns.'

The dog entered a patch of ivy and posed there. We pranced past the Elvis Presley memorial.

'What would you like to have written on your grave,' said my friend, 'as a tribute?'

I thought for a long time. Then I said, '*Owner of two hundred pairs of boots.*'

When we had recovered, my friend pointed out a head-stone which said, *She lived only for others.* 'Poor thing,' said my friend. 'On *my* grave I want you to write, *She lived only for herself.*'

We went stumbling along the overgrown paths.

~

My friend and I had known each other for twenty years, but we had never lived in the same house. She came back from Europe at the perfect moment to take over a room in the house I rented. It became empty because the man — but that's another story.

~

My friend has certain beliefs which I have always secretly categorised as *batty*. Sometimes I have thought, 'My friend is what used to be called "a dizzy dame".' My friend believes in reincarnation: not that this in itself is unacceptable to me. Sometimes she would write me long letters from wherever she was in the world, letters in her lovely, graceful, sweeping hand, full of tales from one or other of her previous lives, tales to explain her psychological make-up and behaviour in her present incarnation. My eye would fly along the lines, sped by embarrassment.

~

My friend is a painter.

~

When I first met my friend she was engaged. She was wearing an antique sapphire ring and Italian boots. Next time I saw her, in Myers, her hand was bare. I never asked. We were students then. We went dancing in a club in South Yarra. The boys in the band were students too. We fancied them, but at twenty-two we felt ourselves to be older women, already fading, almost predatory. We read *The Roman Spring of Mrs Stone*. This was in 1965; before feminism.

My friend came off the plane with her suitcase. 'Have you ever noticed,' she said, 'how Australian men, even in their forties, dress like small boys? They wear shorts and thongs and little stripy T-shirts.'

A cat was asleep under a bush in our back yard each morning when we opened the door. We took him in. My friend and I fought over whose lap he would lie in while we watched TV.

My friend is tone deaf. But she once sang *Blue Moon*, verses and chorus, in a talking, tuneless voice in the back of the car going up the Punt Road hill and down again and over the river, travelling north; and she did not care.

My friend lived as a student in a house near the university. Her bed was right under the window in the front room downstairs. One afternoon her father came to visit. He tapped on the door. When no one answered he looked through the window. What he saw caused him to stagger back into the fence. It was a kind of heart attack, my friend said.

―⁀―

My friend went walking in the afternoons near our house. She came out of lanes behind armfuls of greenery. She found vases in my dusty cupboards. The arrangements she made with the leaves were stylish and generous-handed.

―⁀―

Before either of us married, I went to my friend's house to help her paint the bathroom. The paint was orange, and so was the cotton dress I was wearing. She laughed because all she could see of me when I stood in the bathroom were my limbs and my head. Later, when it got dark, we sat at her kitchen table and she rolled a joint. It was the first dope I had ever seen or smoked. I was afraid that a detective might look through the kitchen window. I could not understand why my friend did not pull the curtain across. We walked up to Genevieve in the warm night and ate two bowls of spaghetti. It seemed to me that I could feel every strand.

―⁀―

My friend's father died when she was in a distant country.

'So now,' she said to me, 'I know what grief is.'

'What is it?' I said.

'Sometimes,' said my friend, 'it is what you expect. And sometimes it is nothing more than bad temper.'

When my friend's father died, his affairs were not in order and he had no money.

⌐⌐

My friend was the first person I ever saw break the taboo against wearing striped and floral patterns together. She stood on the steps of the Shrine of Remembrance and held a black umbrella over her head. This was in the 1960s.

⌐⌐

My friend came back from Europe and found a job. On the days when she was not painting theatre sets for money she went to her cold and dirty studio in the city and painted for the other thing, whatever that is. She wore cheap shoes and pinned her hair into a roll on her neck.

⌐⌐

My friend babysat, as a student, for a well-known woman in her forties who worked at night.

'What is she like?' I said.

'She took me upstairs,' said my friend, 'and showed me her

bedroom. It was full of flowers. We stood at the door looking in. She said, "Sex is not a problem for me." '

⌐⌐

When the person . . . the man whose room my friend had taken came to dinner, my friend and he would talk for hours after everyone else had left the table about different modes of perception and understanding. My friend spoke slowly, in long, convoluted sentences and mixed metaphors, and often laughed. The man, a scientist, spoke in a light, rapid voice, but he sat still. They seemed to listen to each other.

'I don't mean a god in the Christian sense,' said my friend.

'It is egotism,' said the man, 'that makes people want their lives to have meaning beyond themselves.'

⌐⌐

My friend and I worked one summer in the men's underwear department of a big store in Footscray. We wore our little cotton dresses, our blue sandals. We were happy there, selling, wrapping, running up and down the ladder, dinging the register, going to the park for lunch with the boys from the shop. *I* was happy. The youngest boy looked at us and sighed and said, 'I don't know which one of youse I love the most.' One day my friend was serving a thin-faced woman at the specials box. There was a cry. I looked up. My friend was dashing for the door. She was sobbing. We all stood still, in attitudes of drama. The woman spread her hands. She spoke to the frozen shop at large.

'I never said a thing,' she said. 'It's got nothing to do with *me*.'

I left my customer and ran after my friend. She was halfway down the street, looking in a shop window. She had stopped crying. She began to tell me about . . . but it doesn't matter now. This was in the 1960s; before feminism.

—T—

My friend came home from her studio some nights in a calm bliss. 'What we need in work,' she said, 'are those moments of abandon, when the real stuff runs down our arm without obstruction.'

—T—

My friend cut lemons into chunks and dropped them into the water jug when there was no money for wine.

—T—

My friend came out of the surgery. I ran to take her arm but she pushed past me and bent over the gutter. I gave her my hanky. Through the open sides of the tram the summer wind blew freely. We stood up and held on to the leather straps. 'I can't sit down,' said my friend. 'He put a great bolt of gauze up me.' This was in the 1960s; before feminism. The tram rolled past the deep gardens. My friend was smiling.

—T—

My friend and her husband came to visit me and my husband. We heard their car and looked out the upstairs window. We could hear his voice haranguing her, and hers raised in sobs and wails. I ran down to open the door. They were standing on the mat, looking ordinary. We went to Royal Park and flew a kite that her husband had made. The nickname he had for her was one he had picked up from her father. They both loved her, of course. This was in the 1960s.

—ᛊ—

My friend was lonely.

—ᛊ—

My friend sold some of her paintings. I went to look at them in her studio before they were taken away. The smell of the oil paint was a shock to me: a smell I would have thought of as masculine. This was in the 1980s; after feminism. The paintings were big. I did not 'understand' them; but then again perhaps I did, for they made me feel like fainting, her weird plants and creatures streaming back towards a source of irresistible yellow light.

—ᛊ—

'When happiness comes,' said my friend, 'it's so thick and smooth and uneventful, it's like nothing at all.'

—ᛊ—

My friend picked up a fresh chicken at the market. 'Oh,' she said. 'Feel this.' I took it from her. Its flesh was pimpled and tender, and moved on its bones like the flesh of a very young baby.

⌐

I went into my friend's room while she was out. On the wall was stuck a sheet of paper on which she had written: 'Henry James to a friend in trouble: "throw yourself on the *alternative* life . . . which is what I mean by the life of art, and which religiously invoked and handsomely understood, je vous le garantis, never fails the sincere invoker – sees him through everything, and reveals to him the secrets of and for doing so." '

⌐

I was sick. My friend served me pretty snacks at sensitive intervals. I sat up on my pillows and strummed softly the five chords I had learnt on my ukulele. My friend sat on the edge of a chair, with her bony hands folded round a cup, and talked. She uttered great streams of words. Her gaze skimmed my shoulder and vanished into the clouds outside the window. She was like a machine made to talk on and on forever. She talked about how much money she would have to spend on paint and stretchers, about the lightness, the optimism, the femaleness of her work, about what she was going to paint next, about how much tougher and more violent her pictures would have to be in order to attract proper attention from critics, about what the men in her field were doing now, about how she must find this out before she began her next lot of pictures.

'Listen,' I said. 'You don't have to think about any of that. Your work is *terrific.*'

'My work is terrific,' said my friend on a high note, 'but *I'm not.*' Her mouth fell down her chin and opened. She began to sob. 'I'm forty,' said my friend, 'and I've got *no money.*'

I played the chords G, A and C.

'I'm lonely,' said my friend. Tears were running down her cheeks. Her mouth was too low in her face. 'I want a man.'

'You could have one,' I said.

'I don't want just any man,' said my friend. 'And I don't want a boy. I want a man who's not going to think my ideas are crazy. I want a man who'll see the part of me that no one ever sees. I want a man who'll look after me and love me. I want a grown-up.'

I thought, If I could play better, I could turn what she has just said into a song.

'Women like us,' I said to my friend, 'don't have men like that. Why should *you* expect to find a man like that?'

'Why shouldn't I?' said my friend.

'Because men won't do those things for women like us. We've done something to ourselves so that men won't do it. Well – there are men who will. But we despise them.'

My friend stopped crying.

I played the ukulele. My friend drank from the cup.

All those bloody young Catholics

Watto! Me old darling. Where have you been. Haven't seen you since . . . Let me buy you a drink. Who's your mate? Jan. Goodday Jan. What'll it be, girls? Gin and tonic, yeah. Lemon squash. Fuckin' – well, if that's what you. Hey mate. Mate. Reluctant barmen round here. Mate. Over here. A gin and bloody nonsense, a scotch and water for myself, and a – Jesus Mary and Joseph – *lemon squash*. I know. I asked her but that's what she wanted. Well and how's the world been treating you Watto me old mate. No, not a blue. I was down the Yarra last week in the heat, dived in and hit a snag. Gerry? Still in Perth. I saw him not so long ago, still a young pup, still a young man, a young Apollo, a mere slip of a lad. I went over to Perth. I always wanted to go over. I've been everywhere of course in Australia, hate to hear those young shits telling me about overseas, what's wrong with here? anyway what? yeah well

I've got this mate who's the secretary of the bloody Waterside Workers, right? I says to him, think I'll slip over to Perth. He says, Why don't you go on a boat? I says, What? How much? Don't shit me, he says. For you – nothin'. Was I seasick? On the Bight? No fear. Can't be seasick when you're as drunk as. Can't be the two at the same time. All those seamen drunk, playin' cards, tellin' lies – great trip, I tell you, great trip. Course I got off at the other end had a bit of trouble, once you're back on dry land the booze makes itself felt, but anyway there I was. Yeah yeah, I'm gettin' to Gerry. Blokes on the boat asked me where I was goin', I says, Don't worry, I've got this mate, he works at the university – I didn't tell 'em he was a bloody senior – what is it? senior lecturer? Reader. Anyway first bloke I run into was this other mate, Jimmy Clancy, you'd remember him I suppose, wouldn't like him, bi-i-ig strong bloke, black beard, the lot, always after the women, well he hasn't changed, still running after 'em, I told him off, I lectured him for an hour. Anyway it was great to see him again. He used to hang round with Laurie Driscoll, Barney O'Brien, Vincent Carroll, Paddy Sheehan, *you* know. Paddy Sheehan? Pad hasn't had a drink in – ooh, must be eight years. He was hittin' it before, though. Tell you about Pad. I was in Sydney not so long ago, went up for the fight, well, on the way home I went through Canberra and I tell you it was shockin'. Yeah I said *shockin'*. Ended up in a sort of home for derelicts – the Home for Homeless Men! Well, I come to out there, I had plenty of money see, it was the fight, the time Fammo beat Whatsisname up Sydney, I had tons of money, tons of it, I says to this Christian bloke out there – he wasn't one of those rotten Christians, he was one of the ones with heart –

I says to him, Listen mate, I don't want to stay here, I've got plenty of money, just get me out of here – I've got this mate Paddy Sheehan who's a government secretary or something, so the bloke comes out to pick me up in a bloody chauffeur-driven car, bloke in front with a peaked cap and that, Paddy with his little white freckly face sitting up in the back in his glory – he really laid it on for me. So I says goodbye to the Christian bloke, I says Here, have some of this and I give him some money. How much? Oh I dunno, I had handfuls of it, it was stickin' out of me pockets, I just passed him a handful of notes and away I went in the big black car. All right all right, I'm gettin' to Gerry. Perth wasn't I. Yeah well we sat and we talked of the times that are gone, with all the good people of Perth looking on. Ha ha! Course we did. He's still a boy, full of charm, like a son to me. He was a young tough buck then, love, all handsome and soft, wet behind the ears, and Watto here done the dirty on him, didn't you Watto! Yes you did, you broke his heart, and he was only a boy, yes sweetheart – what was your name again? Watto here she hates me to tell this story, yes she does! He was only a child, straight out of a priestery – no, must have been a monkery because he said he had to wear sandals – course he'd never fucked in his life! Didn't know what to do with his prick! And Watto here goes through him like a packet of salts! Makes mincemeat out of him! Poor bloke never knew what hit him. Drove us all crazy with his bloody guitar playing. She told him didn't you Watto that she didn't want no bloody husband but he wouldn't listen, he was besotted, drawin' her pictures, readin' her the poems of W. B. Yeats, playin' his flamin' guitar – they used to fuck all day and all night, I swear to you love – no shutup Watto!

it's true isn't it! I dunno what the other young Catholics in the house thought was goin' on in there – but one day I gets this lettuce and I opens their door a crack and I shoves the lettuce through and I yells out, If you fuck like rabbits you better eat like 'em too! He he! Look at her blush! Ah Watto weren't they great times. Drinkin' and singin' and fightin' over politics. I remember a party at Mary Maloney's place when Laurie Driscoll spewed in the back yard and passed out – next morning at home he wakes up without his false teeth – he had to call poor Mary and get her to go out in the garden and poke around and see if he hadn't left his teeth behind as well as the contents of his guts. Oh, all those bloody young Catholics – 'cept for Gerry, who was corrupted by Watto here – don't get me wrong Wats! you done him a favour – they were all as pure as the driven snow – dyin' of lust but hangin' on like grim death for marriage, ha ha! They thought they were a fire-eatin' mob in those days but they're all good family men now. Course, *I* was never allowed to bring no women home, bloody Barney he tells me, Don't you dare bring those hooers of yours back here, you old dero – I had to sneak them round the lane and into me loft out the back. And finally Watto here gives young Gerald the khyber, he moons tragically for weeks till we're all half crazy – and then he met Christine. *Byoodiful*. Wasn't she Watto. *Byoodiful* . . . ah . . . she's still me best mate. Gerry was that keen to impress her the first time he got her to come back to our place, he says to me, Now you stay away, I don't want no foul language, she's a lovely girl. So I stays away and that night I come back real late from the Waiters' Club with this sheila and we're up in the loft and in the morning I didn't know how I was goin' to get her out of there! They were all down in the yard doin' their bloody exercises, Barney and Dell and Derum — so in despair I pushes her out the door of the loft and she misses the ladder and falls down into the yard and breaks both her flamin' legs. Lucky Barney was a final year medical student. Oh Christine was beautiful though — I'll never forget the night you and her brought Gerry back here, Watto, he was that drunk, he'd been found wallowing with his guitar in the flowerbeds outside that girls' dormitory joint you two lived in — youse were draggin' him along between you and he was singin' and laughin' and bein' sick — and then you went off, Watto, and left the poor young girl stranded with this disgusting drunk on her hands! Laugh! Aaahhhhh. Course much later she goes off with Chappo. I remember the night she disappeared. And years after *that* she took off with that show pony McWatsisname, McLaughlin. Didn't you know that? Yeah, she went off with him — course, she's livin' with someone else now. Oh, a beautiful girl. Gorgeous. They fought over her, you know. They fought in the pub, and bloody McLaughlin had a fuckin' aristotle behind his back while poor Chappo had his fists up honourable like this — I got the bottle off McLaughlin. At least if you blue you should do it proper. Cut it out, I says, look you don't have to fight over cunt! If I was to fight over every sheila I'd ever fucked there'd be fights from here to bloody Darwin! Why do they have to fight over them? Those bloody young Catholics. Gerry. All right all right. And fighting over women! You don't have to *fight* for it! Look if I can't get a fuck there's a thousand bloody massage parlors between here and Sydney, I can go into any one of them and get myself a fuck, without having to *fight* for it. I never put the hard word on you, did I Watto, in all those years? Well, Gerry.

Yeah, he was in great form, lovely boy, always felt like a father to him, I taught him everything he knew, I brought him up you might say. Oh, he's been over London and all over the place but he's back over the west now, just the same as ever. Aaaah Watto I've been in love with you for twenty years. Go on. It must be that long. Look at her – turns away and giggles. Well, fifteen then. You're looking in great shape. Gerry. Yeah, yeah . . . he was a lovely boy. Don't I remember some story about you and him in Perth once? Something about a phone box in the middle of the night? Oh. Right. I'll stop there. Not a word more. You're lookin' in great shape Watto. Your tits are still little though aren't they. How's the baby, my girlfriend? How old is she now? *Nine.* Jeesus Christ. She still goin' to marry me? I seen her come in here lookin' for your old man one time, he was drinkin' in here with some of the old crowd, she comes in the door there and looks round and spots him. Comes straight up to him and says, Come home! And bugger me if he doesn't down his drink and get up and follow her out the door as meek as a lamb. *Pleeez* sell no more drink to my father / It makes him so strange an' so wild . . . da da dummm . . . / Oh pity the poor drunkard's child. A real little queen. Imagine the kid you and I would have had together eh Watto – one minute swingin' its little fists smashin' everything, next minute mai poetry, mai music, mai drawing! Schizo. Aaah Jesus. Have another drink. You're not going? Ah stay! I only ever see you once every five years. Give us a kiss then. I always did love ya. Ha ha! Don't thank me. Happy New Year and all the best. Ta ta.

A thousand miles from
the ocean

At Karachi they were not allowed off the plane. She went and stood at the open back door. Everything outside was dust-coloured, and shimmered. Two men in khaki uniforms squatted on the tarmac in the shadow of the plane's tail. They spoke quietly together, with eloquent gestures of the wrists and hands. Behind her, in the cool, the other passengers waited in silence.

The Lufthansa DC10 flew on up the Persian Gulf. Some people were bored and struck up conversations with neighbouring strangers. The Australian beside her opened his briefcase and showed her a plastic album. It contained photographs of the neon lighting systems he sold. He turned the pages slowly, and told her in detail about each picture. *I should never have come. I knew this before I got on the plane. Before I bought the ticket.* 'Now this one here,' said the Australian under his moustache, 'is a real goer.' His shoes were pale grey slip-ons with a heel and a very small gold buckle. She found it necessary to keep her eyes off his shoes, which were new, so while she listened she watched another young man, a German, turn and kneel in his seat, lay his arms along the head-rest, and address the person behind him. He looked as if the words he spoke were made of soft, unresisting matter, as if he were chewing air. While she waited for the lavatory she stooped and peered out through a round, distorting window the size of a hubcap. Halfway between her window and the long straight coastline a little white plane, a sheik's plane, spanked along smartly in the opposite direction. If I were on that plane I would be on my way home. I am going the wrong way.

She woke in the hotel. Her watch said 8.30. It was light outside. She went to the window and saw people walking about. The jackhammer stopped. She picked up the phone.

'Excuse me,' she said. 'Is it day or night?'

The receptionist laughed. 'Night,' he said.

She hung up.

In the Hauptbahnhof across the road she bought four oranges, and walked away with them hanging from her hand in a white plastic bag. I will be all right: I can buy. Ich kann kaufen. I should not be here. I can hardly pronounce his name. I am making a very expensive mistake.

In her room she began to dial a number.

On the way up the stairs he kept his hand on the back of her head. He laughed quietly, as if at a private joke.

'I am so tired,' he said. 'I must rest for one hour.'

'I'll read,' she said.

He threw himself face down, straight-legged, fully dressed, on his bed. She wandered away to the white shelves in the hallway. There were hundreds and hundreds of books. The floor was of blond wood laid in a herringbone pattern. The walls were white. The brass doorknobs were polished. The windows were covered with unbleached calico curtains. She took down *Dubliners* and sat at the kitchen table. She sat still. She heard his breathing slow down.

The coffee pot, the strainer, the bread knife still had price stickers on them. In the shelves there were no plates, but several small, odd objects: a green mug with yellow flowers and no handle, a white egg cup with a blue pattern. The kitchen windows opened on to a balcony which was stuffed with empty cardboard cartons stacked inside each other. Beyond the balcony, in someone else's yard, stood a large and leafy tree.

She sat at the table for an hour. Every now and then she turned a page. The sun, which had been shining, went behind a cloud. It did not appear to be any more one season than another.

He came to the kitchen doorway. 'I wish I could have gone to sleep,' he said.

'You were asleep,' she said. 'I heard you breathing.'

Without looking at her he said rapidly, 'I went very deep inside myself.'

She stood up.

'Do you want to see my bicycle?' he said. 'That is mine. Down there.'

'The black one?'

'Ja.'

He stopped the car at a bend in the road. It seemed to be evening but the air was full of light. Flies hovered round the cows' faces. These are the first living creatures, except pigeons and humans, I have seen since I left home.

Frogs creaked. Darkness swam down. They walked. They walked into a wood. While they were passing through it, night came. The paths were wet. Dots of light flickered, went out, rekindled. Under the heavy trees a deer, hip-deep in grass, moved silently away.

They came out of the wood and walked along a road. The road ran beside a body of water. The road was lined with huge trees that touched far overhead. Wind off the water hissed through the trees. Behind them stood high, closed villas with shuttered windows and decorated wooden balconies.

'Beautiful. Beautiful,' he said.

Shutup. On the dark water a pleasure boat passed. Its rails were strung with fairy lights. Broken phrases of music bounced across the cold ripples. Couples danced with their whole fronts touching, out on the deck.

'Is that . . . the ocean?' she said.

He looked at her, and laughed. 'But we are a souzand *miles* from the ocean!'

They walked by the lake.

'Have you ever had a boat?' she said.

'A boat?'

'Yes.'

'A paddle boat, yes. My father used to take me out in his paddle boat.'

'Do you mean a canoe?' she said. 'A kayak?'

'Something. I hated it. Because my father was a very good . . . paddler. And he was trying to make me . . .'

'Tough?'

'Not tough. I was very small and I hated everything. I hated living with my family. I hated my brothers and sisters. He was only trying to make me like something. But I was so small, and sitting in front of this great, strong giant made me feel like a dwarf. And out on the sea – on the lake – he would say "Which way is Peking? Which way is New York?" And I would be so nervous that I couldn't even think. I would guess. And he would say "No!" and hit me, bang, on the head with the paddle.'

There was only one bed. It was narrow. It was his. He sat in the kitchen drinking with his friend. The friend said to her, 'Two main things have changed in this country over the past twenty years. The upbringing of children has become less authoritarian. And there is less militarism.' After midnight, while the two men talked to each other in the kitchen, she undressed and lay on the inside edge of the narrow mattress. At the hotel the sheet on my bed was firmly drawn, and the doona was folded like a wafer at the foot: I paid for comfort, and I got it. She slept till he came to bed, and then it was work all night to keep her back from touching his. Tomorrow I will feel better. Tomorrow I will be less the beaten dog. I will laugh, and be ordinary. His snoring was as loud as the jackhammer. The window was closed tight. Why did he sing to me, at the end of the summer on the other side of the world? Why did he hold me as I was falling asleep and sing me the song about the moon rising? I bled on the sheets and he laughed because the maid was angry. We stood on the cliff edge above an ocean of trees and he borrowed my nail clippers. As he clipped, the tiny sound expanded and rang in the clean air. 'Pik, pik, pik,' he said. Why did he make those phone calls? Why did he cry on the phone in the middle of the night?

He grumbled all the time. He laughed, to pretend it was a joke, but grumbling was his way of talking. Everything was *aw*-ful. His life was *aw*-ful.

'I'm sorry to keep laughing,' she said. 'Why don't you – no.'

'What? What?'

'I keep wanting to make useful suggestions. I know that's annoying.'

'No! No! Zey are good!'

'Why don't you have a massage every week?'

'Who? But who?'

'Why don't you do less of the same work?'

He laughed. 'Zat would be a very bad compromise.'

'You could live on less money, couldn't you?'

He looked distracted. 'But I have to pay for zis *apartment*.'

He went to work and the heavy door closed behind him. She tipped her coffee down the sink. The plughole was blocked by a frill of fried egg white.

She washed herself. She looked at the mirror and away again. She found the key and went down to the courtyard for the bike. An aproned woman on another balcony watched her unchain it, and did not respond to a hand raised in greeting.

The sky was clouded. The seat was high and when she wobbled across an intersection a smoothly pedalling blonde called out, 'Vorsicht!' She stopped and bought a cake of soap and an exercise book with square-ruled pages. She laboured over a map and found her way to a gallery. She passed between its tremendous pillars. It is my duty to look at something. I must drag my ignorance round on my back like a wet coat. He will ask me what I have seen and I must answer. Is there something the matter with me? The paintings look as vulgar as swap-cards, the objects in them as if made of plaster. *Grotte auf Malta 1806*: waves like boiled cauliflower. A heaven full of tumbling pink flabby things. Here is the famous Tintoretto: *Vulkan Uberrascht Venus und Mars.* Venus has buds for breasts; a little dog hides under the table. 'The Nazis,' said a Frenchwoman behind her, 'got hold of that Tintoretto and never gave it back.' A small boy lay flat on his stomach on the floor, doing a pencil drawing of an ancient sculpture. His breathing was audible. His pencil made trenches in the paper. His father sat on a bench behind him, waiting and smiling.

In the lavatory she found her pants were black with blood.

The apartment was still empty. It was hard to guess the season or the time of day.

In his apartment there was no broom. There was no iron.

A narrow cupboard full of clothes: the belted raincoat, the Italian jumpers, the dozens of shirts still wrapped from the laundry, each one sporting its little cardboard bow-tie.

A Beethoven violin sonata on the turntable.

Under the bed, a copy of *Don Quixote* and a thermometer.

Through the double-glazed windows passed no sound.

Perhaps he has run away, left town, to get away from me and my unwelcome visit.

On the kitchen wall, a sepia poster of a child, a little girl in romantic gipsy rags, whose glance expressed a precocious sexuality. I am in the wrong country, the wrong town. When I heard the empty hiss of the international call I should have put down the phone. In the middle of his night he took the pills that no longer worked. He cried on the phone. For me, though, it was bright day. I was on the day side of the planet where I had a garden, a house, creatures to care for. I should have hung up the phone. Man muss etwas *machen*, he said, gegen diese Traurigkeit: something has to be *done* about this sadness. Shutup, Oh, shutup. Is that the ocean? But we are a souzand *miles* from the ocean!

She walked closer to the furniture. She picked things up and examined them. She went into the cupboard again and pulled a jacket towards her face, then let it drop. That's better. Already making progress.

She went towards the window where his white desk stood. There was a little typewriter on it, and loose heaps of paper, books, envelopes. She twitched the curtain away from a framed picture it was hiding. It was a photo. She took it in her hand. It was herself. A small, dark face, an anxious look. And beneath the photo, under the glass, a torn scrap of paper, non-European paper with horizontal lines instead of squares. Her own handwriting said, *I'm sorry you had to sleep in my blood, but everything else I'm happy about.* She put it back on its hook, dropped the curtain over it, and began to go through the papers.

The apartment was full of letters from women. Barbara, Brigit, Emanuele, Els. Dozens of them. On his work desk. On top of the fridge. In the bedroom. He left the women's letters, single pages of them, scattered round the apartment like little land-mines to surprise himself: under a saucer, between the pages of a book. She read them. Their tone! Dry, clever, working hard at being amusing, at being light. Pathetic. A pathetic tone. Grown women, like herself. 'Capri, c'est pas fini,' wrote one on the back of a postcard. Si, c'est fini. I have spent thousands of dollars to come here and see myself on these pieces of paper. I am now a member of an honourable company.

The telephone began to ring: long, single, European blasts. She dithered. She picked it up. It was not him. It was a young woman. They found a common language and spoke to each other.

'He has my poems,' said the young woman. She was shy, and light-voiced. 'He said that I could call him this weekend. He said we could have a drink together to discuss my poems.'

'I'll take a message.'

'My name is Jeanne. You know? In the French way of writing?'

'I'll tell him, I promise.'

The young woman laughed in her light, nervous voice. 'Thank you. You are very kind.'

Capri, c'est pas fini.

She picked up her bag and went out the door.

At the Hauptbahnhof a ragged dark-haired gipsy woman ran out of a door marked POLIZEI. Her shoes were broken, her teeth were broken. She ran with bent knees and bared teeth. She ran in a curving path across the station and out on to the street. Men looked at each other and laughed.

The train went south. South, and south. It stopped at every station. People got in and people got out. It ran along between mountains whose tops were crisp. People carried parcels and string bags, and sometimes children. They greeted each other in blurred dialects. The train crossed borders, it ran across a whole country. A grandmother ate yogurt out of a plastic jar. She raised and dipped the spoon with a mechanical gesture. She licked the white rim off her lips and swallowed humbly. The train slid through a pass beside a jade river. Tremors rose from the river's depths and shuddered on its swollen surface. After the second border she opened the window. The train passed close to buildings the colour of old flowerpots, buildings set at random angles among dense foliage, buildings whose corners were softened with age. The shutters were green; they were fixed back against the walls to make room for washing and for red geraniums. The air had colour and texture. You could touch the air. It was yellow. It was almost pink. She turned back to the compartment and it was full of the scent of sleeping children.

Did he pay?

He played guitar. You could see him if you went to dance after midnight at Hides or Bananas, horrible mandrax dives where no one could steer a straight course, where a line of supplicants for the no-cost miracle, accorded to some, waited outside the door, gazing through the slats of the trellis at his shining head. Closer in, they saw him veiled in an ethereal mist of silvery-blue light and cigarette smoke, dressed in a cast-off woman's shirt and walked-on jeans, his glasses flashing round panes of blankness as they caught the light, his blond hair matted into curls: an angel stretched tight, grimacing with white teeth and anguished smiles. In the magic lights, that's how he looked.

He was a low-lifer who read political papers, and who sometimes went home, or to what had once been home, to his fierce wife who ran their child with the dull cries of her rage and who played bass herself, bluntly thumping the heart rhythm, learning her own music to set herself free of his. They said she was rocking steady.

'To papa from child' wrote the little girl on his birthday card. She was a nuggety kid with cowlicks of blond hair, a stubborn lower lip and a foghorn voice. Her parents were engaged in their respective and mutual struggles, and imperiously she demanded the bodies and arms of other grown-ups, some of whom recoiled in fear before the urgency of her need. A performers' child, she knew she existed. She knew the words of every song that both her parents' bands played. You'd hear her crooning them in the huge rough back yard where the dope plants grew, chuckling in her husky voice at the variations she invented:

'Don't you know what love is? Don't you love your nose?'

'Call me papa!' he shouted in the kitchen.

'Papa! Papa!' she cried, thumping joyfully round him on her stumpy legs. Having aroused this delight he turned away, forgot her, picked up his guitar and went to work. The child wept loudly with her nose snotting down her face: like her mother, she was accustomed to the rage of rejection and knew no restraint in its expression. In her room she made a dressing-table out of an upturned cardboard carton covered with a cloth. She lined up a brush, a comb and an old tube of lipstick upon it.

The parents had met in a car-park in a satellite town, where kids used to hang out. Everyone wondered how they'd managed to stay together that long, given his lackadaisical ways and her by now chronic anger. The women knew her rage was just, but she frightened even the feminists with her handsome, sad monkey's face and furious straight brows. It was said that once she

harangued him from the audience when he was on stage at one
of the bigger hotels. Somehow it was clear that they were tied to
each other. Both had come from another country, as children.
'When he's not around I just . . . miss him,' she said to her
friend. It cost her plenty to say this.

'Old horse-face,' he called himself once, when they ran an
unflattering photo of him in the daily paper, bent like licorice
to the microphone, weighed down by the heavy white Gibson,
spectacles hiding from the viewer all but his watchful corner-
smile. He was sickeningly thin; his legs and hips were thin past
the point of permission. In spite of guitar muscles, his finger
and thumb could meet round his upper arm. One of the
women asked him why he was doing this, in bed one morning.
'Finger-lengthening exercises,' he said, and she didn't even
laugh.

He was irresistible. His hair was silvery blond, short, not silky
but thick, and he had a habit of rubbing the back of his head and
grinning like a hick farmer, as if at his own fecklessness. He
would hold your gaze a second longer than was socially necessary, as if promising an alliance, an unusual intimacy. When he
smiled, he turned his mouth down at the corners, and when he
sang, his mouth stretched as if in agony; or was it a smile? It did
for women, whatever it was. Some people, if they had got
around to talking about it, might have said that there was something in his voice that would explain everything, if you could
only listen hard enough: maybe he had a cold; or maybe he did
what everyone wants a musician to do – cry for you, because
you have lost the knack.

Winter was a bad time in that town. Streets got longer and greyer, and it was simply not possible to manage without some sort of warmth. He was pathetic with money, and unable to organise a house for himself when his wife wouldn't have him any longer. Yes, she broke it. Not only did she give him the push: she installed another man, and told her husband that if he wasn't prepared to be there when he said he would, he could leave the child alone. He ground his teeth that day. He hadn't known he would run out of track, but he knew enough to realise he had no right to be angry. He walked around all afternoon, in and out of kitchens, unable to say what the matter was. He couldn't sit still.

After that he drifted from house to house between gigs, living on his charm: probably out of shame rather than deviousness, he never actually asked for anything. Cynics may say his technique was more refined: pride sometimes begets tenderness, against people's will. He just hung around, anyway, till someone offered, or until it eventuated with the passing of time: a meal, a place to sleep, a person to sleep with. If someone he was not interested in asked him to spend the night with her, he was too embarrassed to say no. Thus, many a woman spent a puzzled night beside him, untouched, unable to touch.

In the households he was never in the way. In fact, he was a treat to have around, with his idle wit and ironic smile, and his bony limbs and sockless ankles, and his way of laughing incredulously, as if surprised that anything could still amuse him. He was dead lazy, he did nothing but accept with grace, a quality rare enough to pave his way for a while at least. If any of the men resented his undisputed sway, his exemption from the domestic criticism to which they themselves were subjected, their carpings were heard impatiently by the women, or dismissed with contempt as if they were motivated only by envy. Certain women, feeling their generosity wearing thin, or reluctantly suspecting that they were being used, suppressed this heresy for fear of losing the odd gift of his company, the illusion of his friendship. Also, it was considered a privilege to have other people see him in your kitchen. He had a big reputation. He was probably the best in town.

After his late gigs he was perfect company for people who watched television all night, warmed by the blue glow and the hours of acquiescence. The machine removed from him the necessity of finding a bed. The other person would keep the fire alight all through the night, going out every few hours to the cold shed where the briquettes were kept, lugging the carton in and piling the dusty black blocks on to the flames. He would flick the channel over.

'That'll do,' she'd say, whoever she was.

'No. That's *War and Peace*. No. Let's watch *Cop Shop*. That's all right, actually. That's funny.'

It wasn't really his fault that people fell in love with him. He was so passive that anyone could project a fantasy on to him, and so constitutionally pleasant that she could well imagine it reciprocated. His passivity engulfed women. They floundered in it helplessly. Surely that downward smile meant something? It wasn't that he didn't *like* them, he merely floated, apparently without will in the matter.

It was around this time that he began to notice an unpleasant phenomenon. When he brought his face close to a woman's, to kiss, he experienced a slow run of giddiness, and her face would dwindle inexorably to the size of a head viewed down the wrong end of a telescope, or from the bottom of a well. It was disagreeable to the point of nausea.

All the while he kept turning out the songs. His bands, which always burnt out quickly on the eve of success, played music that was both violent and reasonable. His guitar flew sometimes, worked by those bony fingers. He did work, then? It could be said that he worked to give something in exchange for what he took, were this not such a hackneyed rationalisation of the vanity and selfishness of musicians; let us divest him of such honourable intent, and say rather that what he played could be accepted in payment by those who felt that something was due. He could play so that the blood moved in your veins. You could accept and move; or jack up on him. It was all the same to him, in the end.

He worked at clearing the knotty channels, at re-aligning his hands and his imagination so harmoniously that no petty surge of wilfulness could obstruct the strong, logical stream. It was hard, and most often he failed, but once in a while he touched something in himself that was pure. He believed that most people neither noticed nor cared, that the music was noise that shook them up and covered them while they did what they had come for. Afterwards he would feel emptied, dizzy with unconsumed excitement, and very lonely.

Sometimes guitar playing became just a job with long blank spaces which he plugged with dope and what he called romance, a combination which blurred his clarity and turned him soggy. In Adelaide he met a girl who came to hear the band and took him home, not before he had kept her waiting an hour and a half in the band room while he exchanged professional wise-cracks with the other musicians. In the light that came in stripes through her venetian blinds she revealed that she loved to kiss. He didn't want to, he couldn't. 'Don't maul me,' he said. She was too young and too nice to be offended. She even thought he liked her. Any woman was better than three-to-a-room motel nights with the band. He was always longing for something.

A woman came to the motel with some sticks for the band. She had red henna'd hair, a silver tooth earring, a leopard skin sash, black vinyl pants. She only stayed a minute, to deliver. When she left, he was filled with loss. He smoked and read all night.

When the winter tour was over, he came south again. He called the girl he thought had been in love with him before he went away.

'I don't want to see you,' she said. 'Have a nice band, or something.'

She hung up. At his next gig he saw this girl in the company of his wife. They stood well back, just in front of the silent, motionless row of men with glasses in their hands. They did not dance, or talk to each other, or make a move to approach him between sets, but it was obvious that they were at ease in each other's company. He couldn't help seeking out their two heads as he played. Late in the night, he turned aside for a second to flick his lead clear of an obstruction, and when he looked back, the women were gone.

When he got to the house the front was dark, but he could see light coming from the kitchen at the back. He knocked. Someone walked quickly up the corridor to the door and opened it.

It was not his wife, but the girl. He made as if to enter, but she fronted her body into the doorway and said in a friendly voice, 'Look – why don't you just piss off? You only make people miserable. It's easier if you stay away.'

The kitchen door at the other end of the hall became a yellow oblong standing on end with a cut-out of his wife's head, sideways, pasted on to it halfway down.

'Who is it?' she called out. He heard the faint clip of the old accent.

'No one,' shouted the girl over her shoulder, and shut the door quietly in his face. He heard her run back down the corridor on her spiky heels. He thought she was laughing. Moll.

That night he dreamed: as the train moved off from the siding, he seized the handrail and swung himself up on to the step. Maliciously it gathered speed: the metal thing hated him and was working to shake him off. He hung on to the greasy rail and tried to force the van door open, but the train had plunged into a mine, and was turning on sickening angles so that he could not get his balance. There was roaring and screeching all around, and a dank smell. Desperately he clung, half off the step, his passport pressed between his palm and the handrail.

The train heeled recklessly on to the opposite track and as he fought for balance the passport whisked away and was gone, somewhere out in the darkness. Beneath the step he saw the metal slats of a bridge flash by, and oily water a long way down. He threw back his head and stretched open his mouth, but his lungs cracked before he could utter a sound.

The band folded. He might get used to it, but he would never learn to like the loosened chest and stomach muscles, the vague desolation, the absence where there ought to have been the nightly chance to match himself against his own disorder and the apathy of white faces. He got a job, on the strength of his name and what he knew about music, doing a breakfast show on FM radio. You could hear him every morning, supposed to start at seven thirty on the knocker, but often you'd roll over at twenty to and flick on the transistor and hear nothing but the low buzz of no one there. Lie back long enough and you'd hear the click, the hum and at last his voice, breathless but not flustered.

'Morning, listeners. Bit late starting. Sorry. Here's the Flaming Groovies.'

He had nowhere much to sleep, now, so different women knew the stories behind these late starts. Shooting smack, which he had once enjoyed, only made him spew. One night when nothing turned up he slept on the orange vinyl couch at the studio. The traffic noise woke him, and at seven thirty he put on a record, and chewed up a dried-out chocolate eclair and some Throaties. He thought he was going to vomit on air.

With the radio money, dearly earned by someone with his ingrained habit of daylight sleeping, he took a room in a house beside a suburban railway station. There was nothing in the room. He bought a mattress at the Brotherhood, and borrowed a blanket. He shed his few clothes and lay there with his face over the edge of the mattress, almost touching the lino. In the corner stood his Gibson in its rigid case. He dozed, and dreamed that the drummer from his old band took him aside and played him a record of something he called 'revolutionary music', music the likes of which he had never heard in his life, before the sweetness and ferocity of which his own voice died, his instrument went dumb, his fingers turned stiff and gummy. He woke up weeping, and could not remember why.

The girl who kissed arrived from Adelaide one Saturday morning, unheralded. She invaded the room with her niceness and her cleanliness and the expectation that they would share things. That night he stayed away, lounged in kitchens, drifted till dawn, and finally lent himself to a woman with dyed blond hair and a turn of phrase that made him laugh. When he went back the next night, the kisser had gone.

There were no curtains in the room, and the window was huge. He watched the street and the station platform for hours at a time, leaning lightly against the glass. People never looked up, which was just as well, for he was only perving. At five thirty every morning a thunderous diesel express went by and woke him. It was already light: summer was coming. He supposed that there were questions which might be considered, and answered. He didn't try to find out. He just hung on.

Civilisation and its
discontents

Philip came. I went to his hotel: I couldn't get there fast enough. He stepped up to me when I came through the door, and took hold of me.

'Hullo,' he said, 'my dear.'

People here don't talk like that. My hair was still damp.

'Did you drive?' he said.

'No. I came on the bus.'

'The *bus*?'

'There's never anywhere to park in the city.'

'You've had your hair cut. You look like a boy.'

'I know. I do it on purpose. I dress like a boy and I have my hair cut like a boy. I want to *be* a boy. So I can have a homosexual affair with *you*.'

He laughed. 'Good girl!' he said. At these words I was so flooded with well-being that I could hardly get my breath. 'If you were a boy some of the time and a girl the rest,' he said, 'I'd be luckier. Because I could have both.'

'No,' I said. 'I'd be luckier. Because I could *be* both.'

I scrambled out of my clothes.

'You're so thin,' he said.

'I don't eat. I'm sick.'

'Sick? Are you?' He put his two hands on my shoulders and looked into my eyes like a doctor.

'Sick with love.'

'Your eyes are healthy. Lustrous. Are mine?'

His room was on the top floor. Opposite, past some roofs and a deep street, was the old-fashioned tower of the building in which a dentist I used to go to had his rooms. That dentist was so gentle with the drill that I never needed an injection. I used to breathe slowly, as I had been taught at yoga: the pain was brief. I didn't flinch. But he made his pile and moved to Queensland.

The building had a flagpole. Philip and I stood at the window with no clothes on and looked out. The tinted glass made the cloud masses more detailed, richer, more spectacular than they were.

'Look at those,' I said. 'Real boilers. Coming in from some-where.'

'Just passing through,' said Philip. He was looking at the building with the tower. 'I love the Australian flag,' he said. 'Every time I see it I get a shiver.'

'I'm like that about the map.' Once I worked in a convent school in East London. I used to go to the library at lunchtime, when the nuns were locked away in their dining room being read to, and take down the atlas and gaze at the page with Australia on it: I loved its upper points, its vast inlets, its fat sides, the might of it, the mass from whose south-eastern corner my small life had sprung. I used to crouch between the stacks and rest the heavy book on the edge of the shelf: I could hardly support its weight. I looked at the map and my eyes filled with tears.

'Did I tell you she's talking about coming back to me?' said Philip.

'Do you want her to?'

'Of course I do.'

I sat down on the bed.

'We'll have to start behaving like adults,' he said. 'Any idea how it's done?'

'Well,' I said, 'it must be a matter of transformation. We have to turn what's happening now into something else.'

'You sound experienced.'

'I am.'

'What can we turn it into?'

'Brother and sister? A lifelong friendship?'

'Oh,' he said, 'I don't know anything about that. Can't people just go on having a secret affair?'

'I don't like lying.'

'You don't have to. I'm the liar.'

'What makes you so sure she won't find out? People always know. She'll take one look at you and know. That's what wives are for.'

'We'll see.'

'How can you stand it?' I said. 'It's dishonourable. How can you lie to someone and still love her?'

'Forced to. Forced by love to be a hypocrite.'

I thought for a second he was joking.

'We could drop it now,' I said.

'What are you *saying*?'

'I don't mean it.'

Not yet. The sheets in those hotels are silky, but crisp. How do they get them like that? A lot of starch, and ironing, things no housewife in her right mind could be bothered doing. The bed was wide enough for another two people to have lain in it, and still none of us would have had to touch sides. I don't usually go to bed in the daylight. And as if the daylight were not enough, the room was full of lamps. I started to switch them off, one after another, and thinking of the phrase 'full of lamps' I remembered something my husband said to me, long after we split up, about a Shakespearean medley he had seen performed by doddering remnants of a famous British company that was touring Australia. 'The stage,' he said, 'was covered in *thrones*,' and his knees bent with laughter. He was the only man I have ever known who would rejoice with you over the petty triumphs of the day. I got under the sheet. I couldn't help laughing to myself, but it was too complicated to explain why.

Philip had a way of holding me, when we lay down: he made small rocking movements, so small that I sometimes wondered if I were imagining them, if the comfort of being held were translating itself into an imaginary cradling.

'I've never told anyone I loved them, before,' said Philip.

'Don't be silly,' I said.

'You don't know anything about me.'

'At your age?' I said. 'A married man? You've never loved any-one before?'

'I've never *said* it before.'

'No wonder she went away,' I said. 'Men are really done over, aren't they. At an early age.'

'Why do you want to fuck like a boy, then?'

'Just for play.'

'Is it allowed?' he said.

'Who by?' I said. I was trying to be smart; but seriously, who says we can't? Isn't that why women and men make love? To bend the bars a little, just for a little; to let the bars dissolve? Philip pinched me. He took hold of the points of my breasts, between forefingers and thumbs. I could see his teeth. He pinched hard. It hurt. I liked it. And he bit me. He *bit* me. When I got home I looked in the mirror and my shoulders and arms were covered in small round bruises.

I went to his house, in the town where he lived. I told him I would be passing through on my way south, and he invited me, and I went, though I had plenty of friends I could have stayed with in that city.

There was a scandal in the papers as I passed through the airport that evening, about a woman who had made a contract to have a baby for a childless couple. The baby was born, she changed her mind, she would not give it up. Everyone was talking about her story.

I felt terrible at his house, for all I loved him, with his wife's forgotten dressing-gown hanging behind the door like a witness. I couldn't fall asleep properly. I 'lay broad waking' all night long, and the house was pierced by noises, as if its walls were too flimsy to protect it from the street: a woman's shoes striking the pavement, a gate clicking, a key sliding into a lock, stairs breathing in and out. It never gets truly dark in cities. Once I rolled over and looked at him. His face was sleeping, serene, smiling on the pillow next to mine like a cherub on a cloud.

He woke with a bright face. 'I feel unblemished,' he said, 'when I've been with you.' This is why I loved him, of course: because he talked like that, using words and phrases that most people wouldn't think of saying. 'When I'm with you,' he'd say, 'I feel happy and free.'

He made the breakfast and we read the papers in the garden.

'She should've stuck to her word,' he said.

'Poor thing,' I said. 'How can anyone give a baby away?'

'But she promised. What about the couple? They must be dying to have a kid.'

'Are you?'

'Yes,' he said, and looked at me with the defiant expression of someone expecting to be crossed. 'Yes. I am.'

The coffee was very strong. It was bad for me in the mornings. It made my heart beat too fast.

'I think in an ideal world everyone would have children,' I said. 'That's how people learn to love. Kids suck love out of your bones.'

'I suppose you think that only mothers know how to love.'

'No. I don't think that.'

'Still,' he said. 'She signed a contract. She *signed*. She made a promise.'

'Philip,' I said, 'have you ever smelled a baby's head?'

The phone started to ring inside the house, in the room I didn't go into because of the big painting of her that was hanging over the stereo. Thinking that he loved me, though I understood and believed I had accepted the futurelessness of it, I amused myself by secretly calling it The Room in Which the First Wife Raved, or Bluebeard's Bloody Chamber: it repelled me with an invisible force, though I stood at times outside its open door and saw its pleasantness, its calm, its white walls and wooden floor on which lay a bent pattern of sunlight like a child's drawing of a window.

He ran inside to answer the phone. He was away for quite a while. I thought about practising: how it is possible to learn with one person how to love, and then to apply the lesson learnt to somebody else: someone teaches you to sing, and then you wait for a part in the right opera. It was warm in the garden. I dozed in my chair. I had a small dream, one of those shockingly vivid dreams that occur when one sleeps at an unaccustomed time of day, or when one ought to be doing something other than sleeping. I dreamed that I was squatting naked with my vagina close to the ground, in the posture we are told primitive women adopt for childbearing ('They just squat down in the fields, drop the baby, and go on working'). But someone was operating on me, using sharp medical instruments on my cunt. Bloody flesh was issuing from it in clumps and clots. I could watch it, and see it, as if it were somebody else's cunt, while at the same time experiencing it being done to me. It was not painful. It didn't hurt at all.

I woke up as he came down the steps smiling. He crouched down in front of me, between my knees, and spoke right into my face.

'You want me to behave like a married man, and have kids, don't you?'

'*Want* you to?'

'I mean you think I should. You think everyone should, you said.'

'Sure — if that's what you want. Why?'

'Well, on the phone just now I went a bit further towards it.'

'You mean you *lined* it *up*?'

'Not exactly — but that's the direction I'm going in.'

I looked down at him. His forearms were resting across my knees and he was crouching lightly on the balls of his feet. He was smiling at me, smiling right into my eyes. He was waiting for me to say, *Good boy!*

'Say something reassuring,' he said. 'Say something close, before I go.'

I took a breath, but already he was not listening. He was ready to work. Philip loved his work. He took on more than he could comfortably handle. Every evening he came home with his pockets sprouting contracts. He never wasted anything: I'd hear him whistling in the car, a tiny phrase, a little run of notes climbing and falling as we drove across the bridges, and then next morning from the room with the synthesiser in it would issue the same phrase but bigger, fuller, linked with other ideas, becoming a song: and a couple of months after that I'd hear it through the open doors of every café, record shop and idling car in town. 'Know what I used to dream?' he said to me once. 'I used to dream that when I pulled up at the lights I'd look into the cars on either side of me and in front and behind, and everyone would be singing along with the radio, and they'd all be singing the same song. Even if the windows were wound up we'd read each other's lips, and everyone would laugh, and wave.'

I made my own long distance call. 'I'll be home tonight, Matty,' I said.

His voice was full of sleep. 'They rang up from the shop,' he said. 'I told them you were sick. Have you seen that man yet?'

'Yes. I'm on my way. Get rid of the pizza boxes.'

'I need money, Mum.'

'When I get there.'

Philip took me to the airport. I was afraid someone would see us, someone he knew. For me it didn't matter. Nothing was secret, I had no one to hide anything from, and I would have been proud to be seen with him. But for him I was worried. I worried enough for both of us. I kept my head down. He laughed. He would not let me go. He tried to make me lift my chin; he gave it soft butts with his forehead. My cheeks were red.

'I'm always getting on planes with tears in my eyes,' I said.

'They'll be getting to know you,' he said. 'Are you too shy to kiss me properly?'

I bolted past the check-in desk. I looked back and he was watching me, still laughing, standing by himself on the shining floor.

On the plane I was careful with myself. I concentrated on the ingenuity of the food tray, its ability to remain undisturbed by the alterations in position of the seatback to which it was attached. I called for a scotch and drank it. My mistake was to look inside a book of poems, the only reading matter I had on me. They were poems so charged with sex and death and long-ing that it was indecent to read them in public: I was afraid that their power might leak out and scandalise the onlookers. Even as I slammed the book shut I saw '*I want to know, once more, / how it feels / to be peeled and eaten whole, time after time.'* I kept the book turned away from two men who were sitting between me and the window. They were drinking German beer and talking in a European language of which I did not recognise a single word. One of them turned his head and caught my eye. I expected him to look away hastily, for I felt myself to be ugly and stiff with sadness; but his face opened into a dazzling smile.

My son was waiting for the plane. He had come out on the airport bus. He saw how pleased I was, and looked down with an embarrassed smile, but he permitted me to hug him, and patted my shoulder with little rapid pats.

'Your face is different,' he said. 'All sort of emotional.'

'Why do you always pat me when you hug me?'

'Pro'ly 'cause you're nearly always in a state,' he said.

He asked me to wait while he had a quick go on the machines. His fingers swarmed on the buttons. *Death By Acne* was the title of a thriller he had invented to make me laugh: but his face in concentration lost its awkwardness and became beautiful. I leaned on the wall of the terminal and watched the people passing.

A tall young man came by. He was carrying a tiny baby in a sling against his chest. The mother walked behind, smooth-faced and long-haired, holding by the hand a fat-nappied toddler. But the man was the one in love with the baby. He walked slowly, with his arms curved round its small bulk. His head was bowed so he could gaze into its face. His whole being was adoring it.

I watched the young family go by in its peaceful procession, each one moving quietly and contentedly in place, and I heard the high-pitched death wails of the space creatures my son was murdering with his fast and delicate tapping of buttons, and suddenly

I remembered walking across the street the day after I brought him home from hospital. The birth was long and I lost my rhythm and made too much noise and they drugged me, and when it was over I felt that now I knew what the prayerbook meant when it said *the pains of death gat hold upon me*. But crossing the road that day, still sore from knives and needles, I saw a pregnant woman lumbering towards me, a woman in the final stages of waiting, putting one heavy foot in front of the other. Her face as she passed me was as calm and as full as an animal's: 'a face that had not yet received the fist'. And I envied her. I was stabbed, pierced with envy, with longing for what was about to happen to her, for what she was ignorantly about to enter. I could have cried out, Oh, let me do it again! Give me another chance! Let me meet the mighty forces again and struggle with them! Let me be rocked again, let me lie helpless in that huge cradle of pain!

'Another twenty cents down the drain,' said my son. We set out together towards the automatic doors. He was carrying my bag. I wanted to say to him, to someone, 'Listen. Listen. I am *hopelessly in love*.' But I hung on. I knew I had brought it on myself, and I hung on until the spasm passed. And then I began to recreate from memory the contents of the fridge.

A happy story

I turn forty-one. I buy the car. I drive it to the river-bank and park it under a tree. The sun is high and the grass on the river-bank is brown. It is the middle of the morning. I turn my back on the river and walk along the side of the Entertainment Centre until I find a door. I am the only person at the counter. The air inside is cool. The attendant has his feet up on a desk in the back room. He sees me, and comes out to serve me.

'Two tickets to Talking Heads,' I say.

He spins the seating plan round to face me. I look at it. I can't understand where the band will stand to play. I can't believe that the Entertainment Centre is not still full of water, is not still the Olympic Pool where, in 1956, Hungary played water polo against the USSR and people said there was blood in the water. What have they done with all the water? Pumped it out into the river that flows past two hundred yards away: let it run down to the sea.

I buy the tickets. They cost nearly twenty dollars each. I drive home the long way, in my car which is almost new.

I give the tickets to my kid. She crouches by the phone in her pointed shoes. Her friends are already going, are going to Simple Minds, are not allowed, have not got twenty dollars. It will have to be me.

'I can't *wait*,' says my kid every morning in her school uniform. The duty of going: I feel its weight. 'What will you wear?' she says.

I'm too old. I won't have the right clothes. It will start too late. The warm-up bands will be terrible. It'll hurt my ears. I'll get bored and spoil it for her. I'll get bored. I'll get bored. I'll get bored.

I sell my ticket to my sister. My daughter tries to be seemly about her exhilaration. My sister is a saxophone player. Her hair is fluffy, her arms are brown, she will bring honour upon my daughter in a public place. She owns a tube of waxed cotton ear-plugs. She arrives, perfumed, slow-moving, with gracious smiles.

We stop for petrol. My daughter gets out too, as thin as a clothes peg in narrow black garments, and I show her how to use the dip-stick. My sister sits in the car laughing. 'You look so like each other,' she says, 'specially when you're doing something together and aren't aware of being watched.'

On Punt Road the car in front of us dawdles.

'Come on, fuckhead,' says my sister.

I accelerate with a smooth surge and change lanes.

'Helen!' says my sister beside me. 'I didn't know you were such a *reckless driver!*'

'She's not,' says my daughter from the back seat. 'She's only faking.'

My regret at having sold the ticket does not begin until I turn right off Punt Road into Swan Street and see the people walking along in groups towards the Entertainment Centre. They are happy. They are going to shout, to push past the bouncers and run down the front to dance. They are dressed up wonderfully, they almost skip as they walk. Shafts of light fire out from the old Olympic Pool into the darkening air. Men in white coats are waving the cars into the parking area.

'We'll get out here,' says my sister.

They kiss me goodbye, grinning, and scamper across the road. I do a U-turn and drive back to Punt Road. I shove in the first cassette my hand falls on. It is Elisabeth Schwarzkopf: she is singing a joyful song by Strauss. I do not understand the words but the chorus goes '*Habe Dank!*' The light is weird, there is a storminess, it is not yet dark enough for headlights. I try to sing like a soprano. My voice cracks, she sings too high for me, but as I fly up the little rise beside the Richmond football ground I say out loud, 'This is it. I am finally on the far side of the line.' *Habe Dank!*

Acknowledgements

'My Hard Heart' first appeared in *The Adelaide Review*; 'The Psychological Effect of Wearing Stripes' in *The Australian*; 'What We Say' in *The Faber Book of Contemporary Australian Short Stories*, edited by Murray Bail (Faber and Faber, 1988).

'Honour' and 'Other People's Children' were first collected in *Honour & Other People's Children* (McPhee Gribble Publishers, 1980).

'Postcards from Surfers', 'The Dark, the Light', 'In Paris', 'Little Helen's Sunday Afternoon', 'La Chance Existe', 'The Life of Art', 'All Those Bloody Young Catholics', 'A Thousand Miles from the Ocean', 'Did He Pay?', 'Civilisation and its Discontents' and 'A Happy Story' were first collected in *Postcards from Surfers* (McPhee Gribble Publishers, 1985). Some of the stories from *Postcards from Surfers* previously appeared in *Australian Short Stories*, *Tabloid Story*, *Australian Express* and *Scripsi*; the author's thanks to those publications.

The poem that the narrator of 'Civilisation and its Discontents' reads on the plane is 'Come Back' by Kevin Hart, from his collection *Your Shadow*. The author gratefully acknowledges the permission of the poet and his publisher (HarperCollins Publishers) to quote the lines in question.